Awakened

Awakened

The Awakened Series: Book One

Kenneth Creech

Awakened

For information, contact:
Kenneth Creech
www.kennethcreech.com
kbcreech@me.com

Cover Art by Jesh Art Studio

Cover Design by Kenneth Creech

Publisher's Cataloging-in-Publication Data

Names: Creech, Kenneth, 1982- .
Title: Awakened / Kenneth Creech.
Description: Humble, TX : K.B. Creech 2022. | Summary: Caleb McEllis discovers he's a member of a pack of shifters called Awakened, who can change their shape beginning when they turn 18. But as the son of the current Alpha, 17-year-old Caleb is being hunted to stop him from becoming the next leader of the pack, and he has no idea who he can trust.
Identifiers: ISBN 9798986880112 (pbk.) | ISBN 9798986880105 (ebook)
Subjects: LCSH: Sexual minority youth – Fiction. | Gay college students – Fiction. | Dating (Social customs) – Fiction. | Shifter – Fiction. | Paranormal – Fiction. | California – Fiction. | BISAC: YOUNG ADULT FICTION /

Other books by Kenneth Creech:

Challenged
The Awakened Series: Book Two

**Fate, Coincidence, and Other Curse
Words**

Dedication:

To my grandparents, who taught me so much about telling stories and being myself. To my parents, who always pushed me to do better and find my next challenge. To my siblings, who helped me be a fighter, but only when it truly matters. And to Cameron, for supporting everything I do!

One

A sharp knock rattled my apartment door, jolting me from a restless sleep and a nightmare I'd been having regularly for the last month. Groggy, I swung my legs off the couch and rubbed my eyes before stumbling to the door. I pulled it open to find Sue, the apartment manager and my mom's best friend, standing there with a patient smile.

"Caleb, there you are. I came by earlier, but no answer."

"Sorry. I've been asleep most of the day, I had to work late this morning and didn't fall asleep until almost noon." My voice came out rough, my mind still catching up.

Sue tilted her head slightly, her expression unreadable. Her usual bandana covered her hair, and small sores dotted her cheeks and forehead. I assumed she was undergoing chemo, but I'd never asked.

She sighed. "Your rent was due two days ago. Do you have it?"

I raked a hand through my already-messy hair, counting the days in my head. I'd completely forgotten.

"I don't have it handy," I admitted. "But I'll bring it by tonight before work."

She studied me for a beat before nodding, the lines on her face softening. "That's fine. If I'm not home, just slip it through the mail slot."

"Will do." As if on cue, my stomach grumbled loudly. Sue chuckled as I placed a hand over my traitorous stomach.

"Sounds like you need to eat something," she said. "I'll get outta your hair. Say hi to your mom for me."

I muttered a promise as I shut the door and grabbed my keys. A quick dinner before work wouldn't hurt.

The shopping center's neon lights buzzed against the darkening sky as I parked outside my favorite hole-in-the-wall Chinese place. The couple who ran it always treated me well, and best of all, it was usually empty.

As I waited for my food, my phone vibrated. My mom's name flashed across the screen.

"Hey, Mom."

"Caleb! How are you?" Her tone was too casual.

"I'm fine. How are you and Dad?"

"Oh, the usual. Your father's holed up in his office, yelling at his computer. I think that means his presentation is going well."

I smirked. Mom's sarcasm was one thing I'd definitely inherited despite the whole not being biologically related thing.

After a few minutes of small talk, I cut to the chase. "Alright, what's up?"

She exhaled dramatically. "Can't I call my only son without an ulterior motive?"

"You could, but you don't."

"Fine," she huffed. "Sue called. She said you didn't pay your rent."

"I already talked to her about this, Mom. I'm dropping it off before work. Why did you really call?"

There was a moment of silence long enough that I looked at my phone to make sure I hadn't lost service on my cell, "I want you to come visit. I never see you, and we barely talk anymore."

My grip on my phone tightened. "We've been over this. I'm not going back there. I can't."

"You expect us to drop everything and come to San Diego?"

"If you want to see me, yes. Home is hardly the welcoming paradise you think it is, and I refuse to pretend to be straight so people will leave me alone."

We'd danced this dance too often, but at least it kept my mind off the dream I'd had earlier. I promised to call again soon and ended the conversation before it could spiral further.

As I finished my meal, a chime signaled someone else entering the restaurant, pulling me back to reality. I dumped my trash, thanked the owners, and headed home.

Back in my apartment, I caught my reflection in the mirror and paused.

My dark brown hair, once warm in tone, had deepened to near-black. My light blue eyes stood out against my pale skin, glowing almost unnaturally. I ran a hand through my messy strands, noting how little I resembled the person I used to be.

I jumped into the shower, letting the hot water work through my tension. I tried not to think about the dream, but the memory clung to me. The darkness swallowing me whole. My hands clawing at the air, desperate for something or someone.

The water ran cold before I realized I hadn't even washed yet. Cursing, I hurried through the motions. By the time I was dressed, I was running late. Again.

My boss already had it out for me. I really didn't need to give him more reason to hate me.

I grabbed my things and rushed out the door, the unease from my reflection still lingering like a shadow I couldn't shake.

I loved San Diego at night. The lights from downtown were beautiful, and the air always seemed to have a salty taste, which I found soothing. I usually drove with my windows down to feel the wind in my hair and the salt on my tongue. Tonight, the wind whipped through my car and cleared away any negative feelings lingering in my head.

As I merged onto the 163 South, my cell phone started to ring again, and I touched the button on my steering wheel to answer the phone. "Hello?"

"Hey, Bitch! How're you?"

Megan and I had been friends since high school. She was the last girl I dated and the first person I came out to when I finally realized I was gay. She was, by far, my best friend, and 'Bitch' was her favorite pet name for me.

"Hey, I'm doing all right; headed to work. How are you? What're you up to?"

"I'm doing great. Nate is supposed to come over and make me dinner. I told him I would supply dessert," she added, laughing.

"What'd you buy?"

"Who said I bought something?" she asked.

"Well, the last time you made a cake, you dropped it on the floor right after icing it, and the pie before that almost burned down your old apartment!" She and I had lived near each other back home, and we'd both decided to get away as soon as we could.

"That cake was good, and you know it, the little of it that I ate off the floor anyway. The pie was a mistake, but I only burned the inside of the oven. The apartment was completely safe…I think." We laughed again at the memory, which took my mind off being late. I could tell Nate made her happy, and even though part of me wished my love life was as plentiful as hers, I was happy for her. "And I never said dessert would be food." I could practically see her smile and eyebrow wiggle as I finally figured out where she was going with this line of thought.

I laughed loudly. "Well, you have always been good at—oh my god!" As I was changing lanes, a shadow from the side of the freeway moved out onto the road, and I was going way too fast to stop in time. I slammed on my brakes and spun the wheel to the right.

My car went off the shoulder and into the trees and bushes surrounding Balboa Park. I'd always thought the greenery was pretty, but tonight, I feared being impaled by a rogue tree branch. My tire hit something, and my stomach dropped as the back of my car flipped up and over the front. The abruptness of the movement caused my head to jerk violently to the left, smacking into the doorframe. I fought to remain conscious, but my vision began to get hazy.

I closed my eyes and shook my head, which only made my head hurt. My vehicle stopped sliding down the embankment and came to a stop, but my body felt like it was rocking back and forth. I tried to listen for the sound of people yelling or the feeling of any heat in case something had caught fire. I knew that movies and television made car crashes more extreme than they usually would be for the dramatic quality they added. But I had no idea how many of those explosions were based on reality. I hoped it was very few.

Pain radiated from my head through my shoulders and down into my chest, and something warm and wet dripped off my hair onto the car's roof. I tried to undo my seatbelt, but nothing happened. I kept pushing the button, but it must have locked up during my trip into the ditch and wouldn't release me. Then I remembered Megan was still on the phone when it happened.

"Megan? Megan, are you there?" I hoped the crash hadn't disconnected the call. "Megan! Megan, can you hear me? Call the police! Please!" There was no response, and I realized that something was broken if she wasn't there and wasn't calling me back.

I continued yelling into the darkness for another minute before giving up. I hoped she would have immediately called 911 when the line went dead, but she had no idea where I was, other than that I was on my way to work. I kept waiting for other cars to pull off the freeway to help me, but I knew they probably couldn't see me anymore. I didn't think any other vehicles had been around me as I careened off the road.

Just then, I heard movement outside the car. My windows were still down, and there was a crunch of dead leaves and footsteps. I strained my neck to see who was out in the darkness.

"Hello? Hello! Is someone out there? I need help!" I yelled as loudly as I could. The longer I hung upside down, the more blood rushed into my head making it difficult to remain conscious. "Please help me…I'm stuck in my car. I think I smelled gas earlier!"

I hadn't, but I figured no one would question the guy with the possible concussion who was bleeding from the head.

When I started yelling, the movement outside the car stopped. The crunching approached my window when I was quiet, but it was moving slower now. I started to shiver, making it nearly impossible to speak clearly or the a full breath. "Who—ever you ar—are, please help me," I begged, "or ca-call for help. I don't think I can last mu—much longer in here."

I stopped and thought about it. I had seen an enormous shadow detach itself from the darkness and move onto the road. It had been solid; I was sure about that. My headlights didn't penetrate the shape as I swerved around it. Whatever it had been, it seemed like it was now stalking me. The shivering got even worse, and my jaw had now started to clench so tightly that I wasn't sure I would be able to speak if I wanted to. I tried my last option. I punched the horn and held it down; the noise piercing the silence. I figured this was what would save me.

As I started to feel like help might find me, something jumped on my car, and after the sound of metal being ripped apart, the horn went silent. Now, I was out of options, and the full body shivering, and blood pounding in my head made it hard to focus. Tears streaked down my face as I put my arms up to relieve some of the pressure on my chest and legs and tried to take a deep breath. I kept hoping for this nightmare to end and for me to be able to wake up safely in my apartment, but deep down I knew that tonight wasn't another nightmare. Tonight it was finally reality.

Two

Suddenly, my car rocked to the left, and the sound of ripping metal continued, followed by a snarl or growl and a high-pitched yelp.

I let out the loudest scream I'd ever screamed in my life, which caused white spots to start popping in front of my eyes. There was more rustling to the right of me in the distance, but now I was sure it wasn't footsteps. I tried to see what was happening outside my car when an arm shot into the driver's side window and grabbed me. The grip was much stronger than I thought possible, and because I was still buckled into the seatbelt, my arm was nearly yanked from the socket when they tried to remove me from the car.

"Ouch! You're going to rip my arm off!" I cried.

"Trust me. If I were trying to rip your arm off, I would have," a deep voice growled from outside the car. Then a dark figure appeared next to my window, and the grip on my arm loosened as he reached for the buckle. When pushing the button didn't work, he crushed the buckle mechanism, and I fell onto the roof of my car. "Now, let's go!" he said, grabbing my arm again and dragging me from the vehicle. He reached back into my car, and I could hear my keys jingle briefly before he shoved them into his pocket. He hoisted me onto his shoulder and carried me like a sack to a black car, idling about 100 yards behind my own.

I could hear sirens faintly in the distance and the much closer sound of the freeway traffic. My head was reeling from the past few minutes, and I didn't know whether to go with him or put up a fight. Not that I could actually put up a fight. My head was pounding, and my ribs felt like a few had been dislocated. Fortunately, nothing felt broken, which was the only positive thing I had going for me at the moment. Meanwhile, he had just crushed my seatbelt buckle in his hands and possibly ripped my car's undercarriage apart. Then again, he had also saved me from the wreck, which was good.

As I thought about it, he continued to trudge through the bushes and undergrowth, seemingly unaware of my weight. At 6'2" and 175 pounds, I wasn't the biggest guy, but I certainly wasn't light.

"Will you please put me down? I hit my head when my car flipped, and I think I'm bleeding. Badly. I should walk so the bleeding can hopefully slow down." My request sounded weak, even to me.

"No. We're almost to my car; you can relax there, but I have to get you out of here. Now."

"Why? Who are you? Where are you taking me? I don't want to go to the hospital—" I began.

"I'm not taking you to the hospital. It isn't safe, and your cuts aren't that deep. I'll look at them later and clean them if needed." His voice was clipped and sounded angry.

"What do you mean it isn't safe?"

Without answering, he practically threw me into his passenger's seat and buckled me in. "Just sit there and shut up!" he yelled before slamming the door in my face. This night had gone from zero to shitty fast. And I still had no idea what was going on.

When he got in the driver's seat, I started talking almost immediately, "Listen, thanks for getting me out of the wreck and everything. I appreciate it, but I can wait for the ambulance or police to arrive alone." When that didn't prompt a response, I tried another tactic. "I was thinking that maybe I *should* go to the hospital in case of internal bleeding." I continued to ramble, but he never even glanced over at me. The shivering from earlier had returned, and I was finding it hard to speak again.

As we passed my ruined car, he rolled down his window and threw something over the roof of his car toward mine. We tore onto the freeway without pausing for oncoming traffic, which caused a blue SUV to slam on its brakes.

"All right, clearly you aren't going to let me go, but will you at least not kill us both by crashing the car?" I felt the heat crawl up my neck and face, which chased the shivers away for the moment.

"I'll take it easy, but you're right; I'm not letting you go." As he said it, I saw a bright flash of orange and heard a loud explosion behind us.

"Did you just set my car on fire?" He didn't take his eyes off the road. "I asked you if you just set my car on fire?"

"It was already totaled," he said, his voice a deep grumble.

"That—I—you—fuck you." I didn't know what was happening or what he wanted from me, and clearly, he wasn't the kind of person who valued people's things.

We sped along the 163, then took the freeway east, away from my home. I realized that this night was only just beginning, and I wondered if I would ever get to see my parents or Megan again. As bad days go, this was worse than I could have imagined. I flipped my car, which had been set on fire, and now I was being abducted by a stranger who crushed a metal buckle with his hands.

It wasn't until I thought about all the events together that I realized it was probably more than happenstance that rained all this crap on me. I cautiously looked at the man driving us deeper into the mountains surrounding San Diego as the freeway lights flew past us, illuminating his face.

He was intimidating, even without making eye contact with me or saying anything. He never checked the rearview mirrors, which either meant he was so comfortable with abducting people that he didn't need to worry. Or he was reasonably sure the police were not following us. Neither of those prospects made me feel very optimistic about my future.

"Where are you taking me?" I tried to sound calm, so he might be willing to tell me what was happening. But he only continued to drive in silence.

"Why are you doing this?" His face didn't twitch, so I gave up on trying to make him talk. I decided I would stare at him, hoping that my gaze would begin to make him uneasy, or at the very least, if I did get out of the situation, I would have a relatively clear memory of his features.

I leaned against the doorframe, crossed my arms, and focused my full attention on him. His blond hair was slicked back off his face, giving him a rugged appearance. His light brown eyes were narrowed but seemed to almost glow in the dim light streaming through his car windshield. I could tell from how he sat that he was taller than me, but it was hard to say how much taller without seeing him stand in front of me.

When he pulled me from my car, I hadn't thought to gauge his height before being hoisted onto his shoulders. Looking at the rest of his body, he seemed to work out a lot because his muscles were evident under his clothing. And his skin was nearly the opposite of mine, a dark bronze color, covered in a smattering of golden blond hairs.

Having finished my assessment, I returned to his face to begin again when his voice cut through the silence. "What?"

I jumped because I hadn't expected him to speak, "Nothing."

"Why are you staring at me?"

"You wouldn't talk to me, so I just figured I'd sit here quietly. And I'm trying to place you. Your face looks familiar." There was no way I would admit I was trying to memorize his features. I had seen plenty of TV shows where people talked about abductions. If they covered their face, you might get to walk away. An uncovered face almost always meant you wouldn't be a threat when they were through with you.

"I'm trying to figure out if I know you, and this may be just a mean practical joke." By the end of the sentence, I sounded less sure of myself, a clear indication of my lie.

"I promise you this is serious. Your life is in danger, and that isn't something I would find particularly funny." His deep voice had almost no inflection, making his threat even more terrifying.

I was stunned into silence, and my stomach dropped as tears began to well up in my eyes. "What kind of danger? What did I do? I'm literally nobody, I'm just a front desk person at a hotel.?"

"Sit there and shut up...and quit staring at me." He still hadn't taken his eyes off the freeway as we twisted our way out of East County. We left the city behind, and only small towns and desert remained. I looked down at my hands and thought about what to do next. "I can give you money. I don't have any on me, but I can get some. How much do you want?"

"I don't want your money. You can't buy your way out of this situation." It was nearly imperceptible, but it looked like he flinched and swallowed. Maybe that wasn't just an expression.

"What if I just ran away? You could say you took care of me, and I swear I'll never return to San Diego."

"Running away wouldn't save your life. It would just prolong the inevitable. And they want to take care of you themselves. I'm just supposed to bring you back."

"Who does?" I couldn't believe I was important enough to warrant everything that had happened to me. "You're making a mistake!" I yelled.

He chuckled when I said it and looked me full in the face, "I don't think so, kid. Caleb McEllis, age seventeen, 821 E. Laurel Ave. I've been watching you for a while now."

"I'm eighteen, actually." I'm not sure why I corrected that mistake, especially since it confirmed the rest. He just laughed at me again.

Anger and fear flooded my body; I could feel it, like heat dancing through my veins. My fight or flight reflex kicked in, but I didn't have enough space to fight. And a moving car going 100 miles an hour down the freeway made flight even more dangerous than fighting. Without thinking, my right fist shot out and struck him in the face, whipping his head to the side. My other fist was right behind it, but he braced for it this time, and it felt like the small bones in my hand broke from the impact.

It was how I imagined punching a skin-covered brick wall would feel. He snarled at me, and his teeth seemed sharper than they had been. Adrenaline can be a significant benefit, but it also messes with your mind, and I didn't need to start hallucinating now. I unbuckled my seatbelt, pulled hard on the lever next to the door, and forced my torso backward. I kicked the windshield as hard as I could. It cracked but didn't shatter, so much for Plan A.

As I tried to pull my legs back to kick it again, he grabbed my left leg and squeezed. The pain would have been overwhelming, but I couldn't feel anything. My hand had also stopped aching. It was useless at my side, but at least it wasn't a distraction. I used my right leg to kick toward his face, but he quickly blocked that and pushed my legs away, grabbed my shirt, and pulled me toward him. His features twisted in anger, and I prepared for the impact.

I tried to imagine what being hit in the face would feel like. I had been the victim of teasing when I was in school and had a bruised cheek for nearly a month when the varsity pitcher chucked a baseball at my face. It was like the world had exploded into pain and color simultaneously. My face swelled almost immediately, and I couldn't see right for two weeks until the swelling subsided. I expected the pain of his fist would be similar to that. He said he couldn't kill me, not that he couldn't beat me into submission.

As the force of the impact rocked through me, I was surprised that I could barely feel his fist as it smashed into my mouth. It seemed to shape itself around the contours of my lips and was more pressure than pain. But the pressure hadn't gone away after a few seconds, so I opened my eyes.

Rather than looking up the golden, hair-covered length of his forearm, I stared him in the eyes, with his mouth pressed against mine. I tried to pull away, but his hold on my shirt wasn't letting up. I was stuck in the kiss, and sure, we would die from the car careening off the road since his eyes were now closed. I stopped struggling and enjoyed my last moments on earth. If I had to go, I'd rather die kissing someone than be beaten up.

When he realized I had stopped trying to fight him, his grip relaxed, and I could pull away slowly from his body. My adrenaline had run its course, and even though I had not moved from my seat, it felt like I had run a mile. My heart pounded in my chest, and my lungs ached for oxygen. Worst of all, the numbness in my hand had been replaced by a dull ache, which was becoming increasingly hard to ignore.

"What are you doing? Are you trying to kill us? Watch the road!" I was processing the situation and trying to get a handle on what had just happened. I wanted to make sure he was driving safely again. His chuckle filled the cab of the car. "What?"

"You're telling me to drive safely after cracking the windshield and punching and kicking the driver. If anyone should be concerned about their safety in this car, it's me." He looked at me again and smiled, but with my adrenaline gone, his teeth were back to normal this time.

"Hollow words, especially from the guy taking me to the people who will kill me. I figured I would try to slow down the process. Besides, I think I broke my hand trying to punch you the second time, and you haven't even rubbed your jaw once." Mentioning my hand caused the pain to flare up again, and now, the fire in my veins was concentrated in my wounded hand.

"Taking you to the people who are going to kill you? I think your concussion is getting worse because you're a little loopy." His eyes had returned to the road, but we slowed down, making me feel safer. "Look, if you promise not to kick or punch me again, I promise not to put your life in danger tonight. Deal?"

This sounded like the best deal I was going to manage, but I still had no reason to trust him. "I don't even know your name, but you seem to know a lot about me. Why should I trust you?" I was about to continue when he took an exit off the freeway and turned toward the dark one-lane street.

"That's fair. My name is Adam Fordham. Nice to meet you officially," he turned and smirked at me, but I refused to swoon over my abductor, even if he had just kissed me. With the cracked glass in front of me, cool air was streaming in and hitting me in the face. It no longer tasted like salt but now carried the sweet taste of apple blossoms. I had heard about the apple farms outside of San Diego, but I had never been there before. I guessed my first trip would be my last and somehow doubted I had hot apple pie waiting for me wherever we were headed.

"You said you'd be in trouble if you let me escape. That they want to 'take care of me themselves.' I made a mental leap that killing would be involved…doesn't that kind of go against your 'no danger' proposal?"

His eyes narrowed and then crinkled as laughter erupted from his mouth, "You thought I meant they were going to kill you?"

"It wouldn't be the first time my life was in danger tonight!" I felt somewhat ridiculous yelling at him when he was laughing as hard as he was. I still failed to see the humor in my death. "Stop laughing!"

"I'm sorry…you're right." Tears streamed down his cheeks, glittering with moonlight before being wiped away. "I shouldn't have laughed, but you're hilarious. A lot funnier than I thought you'd be."

"I'm glad one of us can walk away from tonight on a light note." I hunched down in my seat. I'd begun to pout, and I knew it. I'd gone from scared to enraged to confused, and now I just felt foolish. This emotional roller coaster was unusual for me, and I didn't like not knowing what would happen next. "If they aren't going to kill me, what do they want with me?"

"To protect you from the people trying to kill you." His straightforward answer was both shocking and comforting. No one likes to hear that they are in danger, but somehow hearing it stated plainly made it easier for me to process.

Then I snapped out of my stupor. "What do you mean 'the people trying to kill me'? What the hell have I done?"

"It's not what you did. It's who you are that made you a target." As he spoke, he turned off the minor road onto a private, tree-lined driveway. I tried to read the house number as we passed an open gate, but the darkness swallowed them up as we left the lights of the rest of the world behind.

"I'm just a kid from the middle of nowhere. What makes me so special?" I was starting to feel that familiar tightness in my stomach that I used to get in high school when people would ask me personal questions or speak with a lisp and limp wrist around me. I wanted to disappear and lash out at the world all at once, and this internal warring was more than I could handle. "You know what, forget who I am, who are these people? These protectors who want to keep me from getting killed by God knows who?"

The car stopped, and he turned toward me before responding. "People who can explain why you will never escape the consuming darkness in your dreams." With that, he got out and walked around to my door. He opened it, reached down, and took my right hand, which had not been broken in our fight. He pulled me from the car, released my hand, and walked away.

"How do you know about those dreams? Who the hell are you people?" He ignored me, opened the front door, and then waited for me to follow him.

"Well?" I demanded.

"Among others…your birth mother." He turned on his heel and walked through the front door.

Three

My mind raced at the possibility of it…my birth mother? I had always known my parents adopted me when I was a few months old. They told me my birth parents couldn't care for me when they had me and gave me up for adoption so I could have a better life than they could have provided. I was given their phone number a few months earlier when I turned eighteen, but I never really felt the need to call. They weren't part of my life, and though my parents and I had our issues, they'd given me a good life, and I wasn't looking to replace them.

Now that I had the chance to meet my birth mother in person, I was excited. There were so many things I'd always wanted to know but would never admit. I took a deep breath and started to walk toward the door, which stood open, casting a rectangle of light on the porch.

Gravel crunched under my feet as I approached the door; my palms began sweating. I wiped them on my dress pants and stepped into the light of the foyer before closing the door behind me. Inside the Tudor-style home, I felt immediately at ease, a feeling that had been elusive for the past few hours. The house was warm and inviting, the paint on the walls had seen better days, and scuffs on the chair rail ran along the wall in the hallway. It gave the rooms a lived-in look, increasing my comfort. Lamps on side tables in the formal sitting room cast a dim yellow light around the foyer, while the brighter lights from deeper inside the home called me forward.

Without thinking, I took three steps, then paused, "Hello? It's Caleb..." I said as though I had let myself in the home for a social visit. I smacked my forehead and kept moving cautiously until I saw Adam step into the hallway and smile at me. I hadn't noticed it in the car, but he had a dimple on his left cheek that made him look more "All-American" than hit man for hire. Suddenly, even he felt safer than he had just moments before.

"Hey, we're all down here. Come meet everyone." With that, he walked back behind the bend in the wall and out of sight. I picked up the pace a little bit, and as I got closer to the rest of the house, I smelled apples and cinnamon and immediately remembered my apple pie thought from earlier. When I finally turned the corner, I looked for the homemade pie with steam rising from the vents in the crust, but found a candle flickering on the kitchen table with a picture of a slice of apple pie instead. I laughed, just as I lifted my gaze to meet the eyes of the five other people in the room.

My smile faltered, and I must have started to back away because Adam came out of the crowd and grabbed my arm lightly, leading me to the kitchen table. As we moved, the faces of the others followed our progression. They all had eager, smiling, and interested expressions, which helped me feel at least a little more at ease.

Adam pointed to the nearest person, a young woman with a short Afro, wearing a dark skirt and a dress shirt. She looked like she had come from work to the meeting and was immaculate. "This is Karen Jefferies. She helps out with any media relations we need. You've probably seen her work around town."

Karen smiled, holding her hand out, "Nice to meet you, Caleb. I look forward to hearing about you and your plans for our future."

"Karen!" This came from a Hispanic man who appeared to be in his sixties, standing on the other side of the table. His admonishment seemed to have caused physical pain in the young woman, but his anger smoothed out when he came toward me and grabbed my hand. "Caleb, it's great to see you again, son. My name is Carlos Reyes, and I have been a friend of your family for many years. We're glad to have you home with us, where you should've been all along." He smiled, but it seemed more like a baring of his teeth. "This is my wife, Rosa," he said, wrapping his arms around her waist and pulling her forward.

"Mijo!" she cried, throwing her arms around me and kissing my cheeks repeatedly. "How are you? You look so skinny! Why haven't you been eating better? You need to fill out more! I will make you something to eat. What do you like?"

"Rosa, give the boy a minute to adjust. He's just come back to us. No reason to send him running because you were too eager to get some food in his stomach." Carlos kissed his wife and lightly pulled her away from my chair. Then he gestured to a woman I hadn't been able to look away from since walking into the room. "And this is your mother, Lorelai Sakkara."

Even without being told who she was, I would have known she was my birth mother. I recognized her from the photo I had seen when I was younger. It had been a comfort to know that I looked so much like my birth parents because my adoptive parents did not look like me. Her eyes were a perfect replica of my own, suddenly wet with unshed tears.

"Hello," I smiled at her, and when she returned my smile, I walked slowly toward her.

"Caleb, welcome home." She reached out and wrapped her arms around me, holding me close and smoothing my hair, a move that seemed familiar and comforting at once. I relaxed even more and let go of the tension I hadn't realized I still held onto until that moment. I inhaled deeply and took in the scent of her graying blonde hair. She was a stranger to me, but I felt like I'd known her my whole life. "Come with me, and I will fill in the gaps you have no doubt realized exist in the story of your life and our family." She smiled and rubbed my arms as she took me in again. I winced as she grabbed my left hand, which started throbbing, but I tried to smile. "Adam, get Caleb a bag of ice for his hand, and then tell me why you damaged my son." She seemed like she was joking, but the anger in her eyes had Adam out of the room in a second.

"It was my fault. I punched him in the face, and I think I broke it." I stared down at my hand, which was now swollen and red, but saw that my fingers had been moving, so maybe it wasn't broken after all.

Carlos let out one of the loudest laughs I had ever heard, and when I looked up, everyone had a smile on their face, including Lorelai. Adam returned to the room with the ice and a towel and handed them to me.

"So he showed you who was boss early on, huh?" Carlos laughed again, and Adam smiled and rolled his eyes.

Lorelai hugged me again and then pulled out two chairs near us, sitting in one and motioning for me to do the same. The others followed her movement and pulled up their chairs. Rosa had ducked into the kitchen after talking to me and emerged with a plate stacked high with different foods, which she placed in front of me before moving to her seat next to her husband. Though it had only been a few hours since

I had eaten, I found that the smell of the food made me hungry, and without a second thought, I began to eat. The others just stared at me as I finished off my plate in what felt like record time.

"You going to lick it clean?" Karen joked.

"I thought about it, actually, but I think I'll leave a little something for later," I retorted. I was sure my face had become flushed from embarrassment, but Rosa beamed at me, pleased that I had enjoyed her cooking as much as I did. Seeing that made me feel better, and I pushed the plate away and then turned to look at my mother. Even the thought of that gave me goosebumps. Sitting across from her was going to take some getting used to.

"Now that you've eaten, let's talk. There is a lot you must know and not very much time to learn the truth and prepare yourself for what is about to happen. So, for all our sakes, please listen, and believe everything I tell you. We don't have time for anything less." She stared at me, and the lack of humor on her face told me she was very serious.

"I promise to do my best."

"We may require more than your best, but I will accept that for now." She took a deep breath, which I assumed meant she was about to launch into a lengthy story. Before she could begin, however, Carlos cut her off.

"Lorelai, perhaps we should give him time to digest the more delicate issues and only tell him the absolute necessities tonight. We have him back now and can protect him better once he knows what's happening. There's no need to throw everything at him at once, is there?" Carlos met her eyes, but she simply stared at him in response. He lowered his eyes and placed both hands flat on the table, a move that looked almost like a bow.

"Carlos, I do not require your input at this time. Though I will admit you have a point, I'll consider your suggestion." As she finished, Carlos slid his hands from the table and looked up again, focusing his attention on me now.

"Caleb, there is much about our family that you could not imagine, and now that others have found you, your time of safety has passed. We have done what we could over the years to protect you, and now it is time that you take your place with us." Her tone was firm and her voice steady.

"I don't understand. What happened that put me at such a risk?" No one would meet my eyes, which made me regret eating as quickly as I did because it felt like my meal might reappear.

"Caleb," she said gently, despite her annoyed appearance, "I will gladly answer your questions, but first, let me tell you what you need to know. When you were born, your father and I knew that there was a possibility that we would have to send you away to protect you. Your father was in charge of our group, and that responsibility included the danger of attack from those who wanted to take what we had. Not everyone could control the group, and before we had you, we ran the risk of being overthrown. The day you were born, you proved that we had the right to rule, which was an even bigger threat to those waiting for us to fail." Her eyes had taken on a distant look as she seemed to relive the earliest days of my life.

What she'd told me made no sense, and before I could reign in my sarcasm, it leaked out. "So, you're what, like, royalty somewhere?" As the words escaped my lips, I remembered that I wasn't supposed to say anything, and the interruption snapped her back into the present. Rather than getting angry, she laughed, which made me feel better about my mistake.

"Not quite, though there is royalty in our bloodline; we are more like the CEOs of a large company or the head of a large, extended family. We make and enforce the rules, but our control is not absolute, and others can choose to leave the group if they want. Life without us is much more difficult, so most prefer to stay and do what we ask." Her blue eyes had warmed up now that she was back in the present again. She seemed to have a maternal connection to the group; perhaps her analogy was more literal than figurative. I suddenly missed the days of being an only child.

Four

"When you were a few months old, I left you in your crib alone to clean around the house for a few minutes. During that time, someone came into your room through the window and tried to kidnap you. You started crying, and I ran to the bedroom to get you. When I arrived, I found the window open and you sitting on the floor rather than in your crib. The person who tried to take you was a stranger, and we couldn't connect them to any of our known enemies. We found him anyway. Those who hired him to take you away from us had already killed him. He was a loose string, and they couldn't risk leaving it untrimmed. If we had found him and figured out who was behind the attack, we could have sent them away, or worse."

Her face was angry, and she seemed on the verge of snarling at the recollection. My mind was stuck on the 'or worse' part of her last statement, and I tried to figure out what that meant. I hoped I hadn't been reunited with my birth mother only to find out she was a serial killer.

"Why would someone want to kidnap me?" This whole scenario felt very melodramatic. The story my parents told me about my birth parents wanting to give me a better life seemed pretty dull now.

She looked at me for a few moments before responding, seeming to weigh her options or choose her words carefully. "They would have killed you to make a challenge easier."

Her words immediately impacted me, and I could feel the heat draining from my body as I realized how close I was to death at such a young age. I made a concerted effort to remain as calm as possible, but I could tell from the expressions on the faces around me that I wasn't doing a great job.

I started to ask another question, but the look she gave me silenced it before it was fully formed.

Lorelai continued with her story, "After that, we knew you were no longer safe even when your father and I were around. We fought it as long as we could, but giving you up for adoption was the best chance you had for survival. We contacted the McEllis family through a private adoption company and set up the adoption immediately." Her voice cracked with emotion, and tears began to run down her cheeks. "In a matter of days, you were taken away from us, and only your father and I knew where you were. When you decided to move back to San Diego, your parents contacted me, and I made the necessary arrangements for your safety." She reached over and took my hands in her's; they were smaller than mine but strong and unadorned. I looked down and realized that she was not wearing a wedding ring.

"What happened to my father?" I asked, squeezing her hands, trying to avoid showing my emotions swirling inside me.

The question seemed to cause a physical reaction, and she jerked away from me a little, but her voice was calm when she spoke. "I will get to that, but there is still more that I have to tell you while I have the time." Her tone was determined, and I realized there was no breaking her concentration, and taking a detour was not an option either

"We have been watching over you since you moved back to the area, and until recently, it had been working. Two weeks ago, Adam noticed someone else was following you, but they disappeared every time he tried to get close."

I looked up wide-eyed at Adam while she continued, "It's not unheard of for us to check out potential rivals, even without their knowledge. Many of the guests at your hotel could have been members of a rival group." She said it so flatly that I couldn't help but run through all the faces I remembered from the hotel.

Working the overnight shift didn't provide much interaction between the guests and myself, so it was easier for me to remember them than the day shift people. Lots of faces stuck out now because of their strange behavior. At the time, I assumed they were exhausted from traveling or drunk from one of the bars in the Gas Lamp district. The faces began to blur into something I told myself was far more sinister now than they had been originally.

"These rivals assassinated your father, and now they're coming after you. But until we know who they are, we can't do anything about it." She had been stoic the entire evening, but now I noticed the tightness around her eyes and the subtle downturn to her lips.

"Wait, he's dead? These people killed him, and you expect me to stand up against them? Who do you think I am?" My head was spinning, and my first response was anger. Who did these people think they were, dragging me into their messed-up world, where I could quickly be assassinated? After dealing with the anger, I tried to wrap my head around the fact that the father I never knew was now someone I could never meet. It felt like I had been punched in the stomach, and I gasped for air, trying to breathe around the pain. Tears stung my eyes, threatening to spill over at any moment, but I tried to blink them away. I wasn't sure how to feel about this new information. Admittedly, I didn't think I wanted to meet my birth parents, but when I found out I was going to meet one, I assumed I would meet the other.

"I know it's hard for you to understand, but you have to face this. We will all be here to support you, and no one expects you to understand or to adapt to this new information without some difficulty." She reached for my hands, but I pulled them off the table and clasped them in my lap.

"Why? Why do I have to face this? I don't know what's going on in your world, but in mine, you don't get to tell someone they have to face the possibility of assassination for no reason." My anger came back with a vengeance. How dare she try to force me back into this fight when she gave me up to get me out of this world in the first place. "And what do you mean by 'check out our rivals'? Who would consider me a rival, and what are they checking out?" She claimed she would give me every detail, but I was much more confused now than at the beginning of the night.

"Your rivals for Alpha," she said.

"Alpha? Am I also going to be doing a lot of calm and assertive behavior like Cesar Millán? Don't get me wrong, I love the *Dog Whisperer*, but I didn't think I had his knack for acting like a dog." Sarcasm spewed out of me without any hope of being contained, and it felt good to let it out, especially when dealing with the ridiculous crap she was telling me.

"Well, that's the other part; perhaps the most important part of the story. We have hidden it from you for long enough now, and it is time you learn about your true nature and what will be expected of you in the years to come. It's time you take your position within the group." As she spoke, the rest of the people in the room, who had been quietly listening up to this point, became much more interested in the conversation, and there was a noticeable build-up of tension in the air.

"Um…I hate to break it to you, but I'm gay, so I definitely can't take over the family business and give you grandchildren to play with." I was a little shocked by my forthright response, but I'd been out of the closet for far too long, and I was not about to lock myself in there again. I couldn't believe this was the second time in one night I was about to have this same conversation with someone.

"Caleb, this is serious, and much more important than something as trivial as attraction. You are not human." She looked straight into my eyes as she said the last part, and every ounce of joy left in my body disappeared. It was one thing to tell a person they don't align with your religious beliefs because of their sexual orientation, but to tell me I wasn't even human because of it was something I'd never expected to hear.

"I don't know what kind of crazy, ass-backwards things you people believe, but I am definitely human, and if you can't accept that you have a gay son, then you can let me go right now. I'd rather take my chances with the others." I pushed away from the table, stood up, and glared at her. The blood in my face made me so hot I started to sweat. How dare she say that to me, her only son, on the day we finally met!

She laughed at my anger, which seemed to be a common response with this crowd. I still did not find my temper quite as funny as they did. "Oh Caleb, my little drama queen, I didn't mean your being gay made you less human. I meant that none of the people in this room, yourself included, are human."

"I don't think I follow…" My confusion helped to calm me a little, and I figured I might as well get all the facts before storming out.

"Please sit down, you may not believe what I am about to tell you, and it would be best if you just listened." She continued, "I'm not sure how much you know, or think you know, about the supernatural, but we are part of that world. We appear human most of the time, but it is just the shape that helps us avoid detection. Evolution has helped us to conceal our true identities from those who would harm us."

I tried my best not to give her an 'okay crazy!' look, but it was difficult to say the least. "So what are we?"

"We call ourselves the Awakened, but we're what most people would call werewolves," she said.

My mouth fell open, and I stared at her for a second, then I laughed so hard I could hardly catch my breath. "Okay, now who's being a drama queen? Everyone knows that there are no such things as werewolves!"

"Carlos, if you please," she turned to him and gestured toward the sitting room to the right of the kitchen table.

"Of course, Lorelai," he pushed away from the table, removed his shoes and socks, and then stood and crossed the room. As he did so, he also began to peel off his button-up shirt and ribbed undershirt, his belt, and finally, his pants. Fortunately, he left his boxers on, though the exposed parts of his body were quite muscular for someone his age. I guessed he was in his sixties when I first saw him, but his body was that of a much younger man.

He closed his eyes, and a ripple went down his spine; then he flexed and stretched his hands. His back arched, and his legs buckled. By the time I stood again to see what had happened to him, his body was gone, and in its place was a gray wolf with a black chest. It padded over toward Carlos's chair and sat on the ground next to Rosa, who rubbed the wolf's head in a way that suggested it was familiar to her.

I swallowed audibly, "Okay, I will admit that the disappearing trick was cool, but I've seen magicians make airplanes, buildings, and elephants disappear. No big deal." I could feel my heart beat in my throat and was certain they could all probably hear it, but I refused to be made a fool of. Disbelief was better than accepting something as crazy as werewolves.

"All right, how about this?" Adam said, reaching his arm toward me. As he did, the nails on his fingers seemed to grow and curl, while his fingers receded into his hand and became thicker on the bottom. When he stopped moving it, his hand was a paw, but most of his arm was still his own.

I moved away quickly, almost toppling out of my chair onto the floor, but managed to grab the table at the last second to keep myself upright. I swallowed my shock and tried to stay calm, which was hard to do when surrounded by werewolves. "That's a little more impressive, but I can't do any of that. It must have skipped a generation." I hoped that calm denial and pretending not to be as freaked out as I was would help me get out of the house alive.

"The awakening doesn't occur until after the 18th year. Until then, our human-like bodies are growing and changing; the additional strain shifting from one form to another would cause a significant amount of unhealthy stress on our bones and tissues. Once you become 18, however, your body is mostly done growing, and your true self is ready to be awakened." She looked me in the face, as were all the others, including Carlos, who was still apparently a wolf.

"I'm sorry, but I still don't think I will be 'awakened'. I turned 18 months ago, and I feel just fine. No weird changes or pains that I've noticed, and no more body hair than usual," I tried unsuccessfully to joke. I was having a hard time accepting any of this, despite the visual evidence. There was every possibility that this was all a concussion-induced hallucination. Maybe I was at the hospital right now. Perhaps this is what would have happened in my dream if I hadn't woken up.

"Actually, you were born in January, but we told your adoptive parents that you were born the previous June, and then provided forged documents to prove it. We didn't want you to be traced to your new family, and a male baby born in January in San

Diego provided too short a list of other possibilities. They wanted a baby so badly that they were willing to overlook some obvious size inconsistencies. That's also why the adoption was closed, and a private agency was used. Technically, you will still be seventeen for another three months." I stared at her, my mouth hanging open. The hits just kept coming.

I remembered Adam's slip-up from earlier, but now realized I was the one with the wrong information. It felt as though my world was crashing down around me, and I was utterly helpless to stop it. I had been lied to my entire life, maybe not knowingly, but I had no factual information about who I was up to this point. I could feel my cheeks flushing and my stomach churning again, so I took a deep breath and sighed. "Maybe I just need time to think about all this information. It's a lot to throw at a guy in one night." I had to escape this whole situation, and part of me was clinging to the hope that this was just a dream.

She smiled at me, and the others seemed to relax. Rosa returned to fussing over everyone in the room and brought me fresh ice for my hand, which was aching. It was a consistent pain rather than the stabbing pains from earlier, making it easier to ignore. "Absolutely, Caleb, take some time to wrap your head around all of this, but please get in touch with me as soon as possible. We do not have any time to waste, and you are far from ready to battle for your leadership role with the pack. I'm sending you home, but Adam will stay with you to protect you for now.

And Karen will check in on you periodically, so do not be surprised if you see her around. I promise we are no more present than before, but now you may recognize the faces in the crowds around you. Ours and theirs."

I was ecstatic to hear that I'd be allowed to go home, and even if I didn't understand how I'd be safe, I wasn't going to ruin things by bringing up that detail. Returning to normalcy, whatever that looked like now, would be a nice change.

"Thank you. I promise to be careful and call as soon as I have dealt with all of this. Is it okay if I head home now, though? I've had a long night and need to get some sleep." I wasn't tired, but I had a lot to process, and home felt like the best place to do it.

"Of course you can leave. And please, don't worry about anything. I will take care of you, no matter what happens." She smiled at me again, and her blue eyes lit up, making me feel like maybe I could accept what she'd told me, and we could get through this together.

I tentatively hugged her and then waved goodbye to the others, except for Rosa, who swept me up in a hug that nearly crushed my ribcage. "Talk to you all later," I choked out. Then I turned and left, with Adam keeping pace behind me.

Five

As he pulled the door closed behind him, Adam smiled at me, enjoying my reaction to the news of what lay ahead of me. "Would you please stop smiling? This isn't funny!"

"You're right, this isn't funny, but you should have seen your face. It was hilarious! You looked like you were about to be eaten," he laughed. "It was classic!" His face brightened, his eyebrows lifting for the first time that night. He seemed younger now that he was laughing.

"I'm glad someone finds all of this shit funny. I just found out that my biological father was killed, and now I'm supposed to fight for the same position that got him killed, so it doesn't go to someone from a group you all hate. But no one seems to be considering the fact that I don't know how to fight or that I still haven't changed into anything but a new outfit." He laughed even louder now.

I was scared, and his smiling face, complete with the dimple, didn't help calm my fears; instead, it increased my anger, which was an okay response. Still, I was not a fan of violence and had never physically fought for any reason other than self-defense. That punch in the car was the first I'd thrown in years. Now, it seemed the whole pack relied on some innate fighting abilities I was expected to possess to defend a role I never knew I was supposed to have.

It was hard to believe that I was born into a family that was even remotely similar to royalty. Growing up, I remember watching movies with royal families and thinking how much I would have given to belong to one of those families. Later, when I began dating, I would fantasize that a Prince from some far-off place would somehow end up in the dusty streets of my small town and whisk me away to his mansion. At the time, those dreams mainly had been about getting out of the desert, but now I realize the idea of the title was also exciting.

Adam walked to the passenger side of his car and opened the door for me. "You're going to train me, right?" I looked him in the eyes expectantly. From this close, I could see his eyes had a trace of something wild behind the human surface. I shuddered.

"Of course, I will," he smiled again. "With my help, you'll be winning fights in your sleep." I hoped the one battle was all I would ever need. *Wasn't the point of being Alpha that you didn't have to continue to try to maintain that position?* I had a lot to learn about Awakened culture.

"When do we get started?" I asked after he had gotten in the car.

"Eager to begin?"

"Not really, but I figured I had better get as much training under my belt as possible before the change kicks in, and I'm not myself." In Hollywood, they looked cool, but there was also a lot of writhing and crunching in those depictions, and I'm a wimp when it comes to pain. "Huh! Some Alpha," I muttered.

"What did you say?" Adam looked at me in the rearview mirror; his eyebrows were arched in curiosity.

"Nothing, just talking to myself. Still processing all of this stuff, ya know?"

"It takes time; I knew from birth what I was, and when I reached my awakening, I had seen others do it for years, so I knew exactly what to expect. Coming from outside, having this thrown at you must be difficult, but you're handling it well." He smiled and rubbed my thigh with his hand, reassuring me.

"Th-Th-Thank you, Adam." My voice was husky and caught me off guard when I tried to speak. "What's it like? The awakening, I mean? Does it hurt?"

He looked at me again as if trying to weigh his answer before responding, as if looking for the best way to break the news. "It doesn't hurt, it is more uncomfortable than anything else. It feels like you've been on a long car ride and never got out to stretch. Your muscles are tight and sore. But when you finally stretch into your new body, you feel amazing!" His eyes lit up with excitement. "And anything that was a problem in your human form is fixed when you change. For example, your hand will immediately heal. If it didn't happen in your current form, it doesn't exist. So, since your wolf form didn't have a sprained paw, you won't have a sprained wrist when you change back. If you hurt yourself, you change that part of your body and get an instant fix." He smiled at my wide eyes and open mouth. All his talk about my wrist made it begin to throb again, and I wished I had asked for a fresh bag of ice before we left.

He continued, "That is handy since we can't go to the hospital to be treated for anything. And it isn't a cure-all. If we get sick, we're still sick, if we are too weak to change, we can't heal, and if the damage is too great, it just seals off the wound with new skin rather than healing the area, which is often worse."

I pictured all the types of wounds that might fall into the incurable category, and I wasn't happy with what my mind came up with. "Why can't we go to the hospital?" I asked.

"Our blood looks different from normal human blood once the change occurs. Before the change, everything is normal. After the change, our bodies are never the same, even in human form. Being awakened is the hardest because every cell in your body is altered into something less fixed."

"Um, sorry, but you may have lost me there." I had never been brilliant when it came to Biology.

"Okay, so you want the easy version? All cells in regular human bodies differentiate to form different organs, tissues, bones, or blood. Our cells are in that pre-differentiation phase, where they can take on the qualities of any cell necessary. It's like stem cells. They can be used to create any cell the body needs. Ours do the same, which is why we can change our bodies and heal ourselves so quickly. Rather than regrowing certain types of cells, we can use other cells to heal immediately. But it only works when we change forms, so we don't regenerate automatically." Adam looked at me for confirmation that some of that had sunk in. He would have had to look for a while.

"Oh, okay. Now I get it," I lied. "That makes total sense." I turned and looked out the window to hide my face from his gaze and saw the familiar lights of El Cajon come into view. We were only about 20 minutes or so from my apartment. When that thought crossed my mind, I was reminded that I would now have to share my apartment with Adam. I hope he didn't notice the mess.

We pulled into one of the driveway spots in my apartment complex, and Adam killed the engine. I kept trying to figure out what I would do once we got inside. Where would Adam sleep? And more importantly, how would I live my life now that I had an unexpected roommate? "Do you have anything you need to unload from the car to bring inside?" I asked.

"Nope, I left everything big at my place, but don't worry about me, I can get my stuff tomorrow. For tonight, let's just make sure that you're safe." Adam led the way to my apartment door, and I followed behind.

I started feeling around my pocket for my keys, "Oh shit, my keys were in my car. Oh my God, my car!" somehow, I had forgotten that Adam had blown it up earlier in the evening. I would blame it on the shock I experienced when I discovered I was a werewolf, but forgetting your car exploded was a pretty big deal.

"Don't worry, I have your keys right here." He reached into his pocket and pulled out my keys. "I got them out of the ignition before lighting your car on fire." He smiled at me as though he had done me a huge favor.

"Uh…thanks, I guess." He flashed what could only be described as a wolfy grin as he handed the keys over. I slowly opened the door to my apartment and prayed that the mess had somehow cleaned itself. But hoping for the dust to have cleared was something that had never worked in the past. "Well, it isn't much, but this is home for both of us now. So come on in."

Adam brushed past me into my living room, his nose working. Then he turned and looked at me, asking, "Has anyone else been here today?" His forehead was creased, and his dimple had disappeared, indicating that this was more than a simple question.

"I hope not," I squeaked out.

He continued to walk around the apartment, apparently checking out the sights and smells of the place. "I want to make sure I get familiarized with the normal scent of things, so I know what's out of the ordinary."

"That makes sense, I suppose. Have you picked up anything strange?" I silently hoped he'd say no.

Adam turned to stare at me and then went back to moving around inside and outside the apartment before responding. "Someone else has been in your apartment, but I can't tell if it was a human or a member of the other Awakened pack. I can smell something sweet near the door, but trying to track something sweet-smelling in the air is nearly impossible." I had to take his word for it because I always seemed to be able to follow wafting trails of food like a cartoon character, but that seemed to be a talent that only I possessed. Adam continued, "I'll let Carlos know in the morning so we can get additional people watching your place during the day, just in case." His face tightened a little, showing just how serious he was. "I guess it is a good thing I moved in tonight," he said.

He switched gears so quickly that I didn't have time to worry about a possible intruder. "Yeah, about that, how is this going to work? It's a one-bedroom apartment, and I only have one bed. While I don't mind sharing, somehow, I doubt your girlfriend would love the idea of you sleeping with someone else."

"I don't have a girlfriend."

"Your boyfriend, then," I smiled at him, my right eyebrow raised.

He laughed loudly at me, "I can sleep on the couch just fine."

My smile faded a little. "That's fine by me. I'll get you a pillow and some sheets. I don't have an extra toothbrush or anything, but we can go out and get you one if you need it."

Adam chuckled softly, "That stuff is out in my car. I said I left the big stuff at home, but I brought the essentials. I'll go get them."

When he returned, he was holding a box wrapped in silver paper in his hands. He set it down on the coffee table and walked toward the bathroom. "Aw, what'd you get me?" I held the beautifully wrapped box in my hands, afraid to damage the bow.

"I didn't get you anything. That's from Lorelai." He pointed to a small card I hadn't noticed earlier, indicating she had been the gift giver.

I slumped on the couch, "And here I thought you cared."

Adam smiled and shook his head before disappearing into the bathroom. While I had some alone time, I carefully unwrapped the box and pulled out a small leather-bound book with *The Awakened* stamped on the cover. I flipped through a few pages and realized it appeared to be a history book—just what I needed…homework.

I took the book to my bedroom and set it on my nightstand before returning to the living room. My emotions had run the gamut of possibilities, and I was exhausted. I leaned my head back against the couch and closed my eyes.

"Hey! You have your bed to do that in. If I'm going to sleep on the couch, at least let me be the one to do the sleeping," his chiding was gentle but tinged with exhaustion.

I opened my eyes to go into my room, and my breath caught in my throat. I had been around Adam for the past few hours, and based on how he looked in his clothes, I knew he had a nice body. But seeing Adam in his clothes hadn't prepared me for seeing him with his shirt off. My eyes locked on his chest, and my mouth went dry as I took in his muscular frame, with golden skin, a dusting of hair, and soft-looking pink scars that ran in multiple directions and ruined his golden perfection.

I imagined what it would feel like to run my hands over his chest and his firm abs, which were currently sparkling with droplets of water that he hadn't bothered to dry.

Adam cleared his throat, and my head snapped up so my eyes locked onto his. "Sorry about that. I might have just hallucinated there for a minute. I'll go and get you that pillow and sheet sex. I mean, uh, sheet set." I walked quickly out of the room with my head down. When I returned, sheets in hand, I looked anywhere but at him. I thought I saw him smirking out of the corner of my eye, but I didn't trust myself to check. "Well, goodnight."

I walked into my room and plopped down on my bed, slapping my forehead for good measure. I had always been cautious to avoid developing feelings for straight guys, and I didn't want to start now. Sure, he might have saved me from whatever was in the trees outside my car, and he had taken me to meet my birth mother, but he'd almost blown up my car. In the grand scheme of things, he was still someone I should watch out for.

My mind kept running in circles as I replayed the events of the evening. I saw the shadow detach itself from the side of the road again and again, and each time, I tried to remember if it looked like a wolf, a human, or something else completely. When I closed my eyes, the weight of everything I'd learned pressed down on me, and my heart would begin to race. My body started sweating, and the shivering from earlier in the evening returned, which made breathing difficult. I contemplated getting out of bed and asking Adam to keep me company, but the sounds of his snores through the thin walls of the apartment made it clear that he was not suffering from issues falling asleep like I was.

I finally decided to pull out the book Lorelai had given me again and try reading more about the Awakened. I turned on my bedside lamp and grabbed the book. Each page was carefully inscribed with drawings, stories, and details of past Awakened. One section caught my eye that detailed information for the newly Awakened, and it outlined tips on how to avoid detection when first going through the changes. The drawings showed people in various states of transformation, and since I hadn't actually seen Carlos change at the house, I was hoping that these were based on creative license, and that my arms wouldn't twist at that unnatural angle.

I continued to flip through the book, looking at photos and reading about historical figures until I finally fell into a dreamless sleep, the first good thing to happen to me all day.

Six

Around three in the morning, my eyes shot open at the feeling of extreme pressure on my chest. As the blur of sleep faded from my eyes, I recognized what was causing the pressure; Adam was lying on top of me with his hand clamped down over my mouth. This guy was the king of mixed signals, and I started to say something before he glared at me.

"Shhh! Someone's right outside your apartment. They've been pacing back and forth for the past ten minutes."

I tried again to speak through his fingers, but that only pissed him off, and he pushed down harder on my mouth. I continued to mumble, hoping to prove that I was not about to give up because he didn't want me to talk. Finally, Adam realized giving in was better than continuing to fight me.

"Thank you. All I was going to say was that these buildings look the same, and people constantly make mistakes. We all get each other's mail, food deliveries, and people thinking they're stopping by to see a friend when a stranger answers the door. Besides, if the person outside were Awakened, wouldn't they be able to smell us?"

"Well…" he blinked rapidly, "You have a point there." Adam sat up on my bed, putting most of his weight on my legs. "I guess I'm just a little jumpy knowing that someone else has been in here and was somehow able to hide their scent from me." He rolled off me onto the other side of the bed and stared at the ceiling. "Sorry," he said.

"Don't worry about it. I would rather you protect me first and ask questions later than worry about my being woken up and run the risk of someone finding me alone." I rolled onto my side and looked at him; he was now only wearing his boxer briefs, and even though there was not much light coming into the room, his skin seemed to glow. I suddenly found it much warmer in the room than it had been a moment ago, and my mouth went dry again, making swallowing nearly impossible. "Can I ask you something?" I asked, trying to take my mind off Adam's bronzed body lying next to me.

"Depends. Do I get to ask you a question in return?" He nudged me with his elbow and smiled, which seemed like a good sign given the situation.

"Sure, you can ask me anything you want. Although I think you know more about me than you let on. I just wanted to know a little bit more about being Awakened. I don't have much longer until my *actual* birthday, and I want to be sure I'm as prepared as possible."

"I understand," he said, "I'm happy to tell you anything you want about it." Adam rolled onto his side and faced me.

"Other than the quick healing, are there any other differences I should expect once I've gone through the awakening?"

"Well, there is that whole unquenchable hunger for raw meat that you might notice. But after you've eaten a few people or pets, you'll find it's pretty easy to control your cravings."

My stomach churned at the thought of eating not only raw meat but also literal food with a face. "Really? That sounds disgusting."

Adam began laughing so loudly that he had to smother his face in the pillow to keep from waking my neighbors. Apparently, live food was not on the Awakened menu either. Without warning, I grabbed my pillow and swung it so hard at his face that I almost lost my grip.

"I'm sorry," Adam gasped between laughs. "I've never had to train a newbie who didn't already know what to expect. I was just having a little fun."

"I don't mind fun, I love fun, fun is practically, well, maybe not my middle name, but I do like to have fun. And I appreciate your humor, but you are the only expert I know and have access to. And the book Lorelai gave me was great and all, but other than telling me fun facts about Romulus and Remus,

I'm still pretty clueless about how things actually work. So maybe the fun at my expense can be kept to a minimum, at least in the information department?"

"You're right, and I'm sorry. I promise to tell you the truth from now on, at least about the awakening." That last part didn't sit well with me, but I let it slide, for now.

"You will have heightened senses. Your first change will improve your hearing, sight, sense of smell, and ability to taste. They will be best in your wolf form, but you'll notice a difference even when living your life as usual. Though very beautiful when it's full, the moon does not hold any power over us. We change when we want to change, simply because we want to, not because we have to. And like I told you earlier, we can heal most wounds by simply changing shape, and the wounds that are too large to heal can be caused by anything." I must have given him a strange look because he sighed before continuing.

"Which means silver is dangerous to us, but only if it has been used to cause a fatal injury, not because it burns us or has some magical poisonous quality. I think that rumor started when someone shot a wolf, saw the skin reshape into human form, and thought the metal was causing more damage. Honestly, it probably wasn't even silver, I think that was probably our part of the embellishment of the myth."

"What do you mean?" I asked, adjusting my pillow so it was more comfortable.

"Silver's a pretty soft metal compared to other options, so if someone took the time to make bullets that were pure silver and you got shot with one, it would do a lot less damage than a normal bullet, making it easier to heal." He

I stared wordlessly at Adam while he nonchalantly explained the very real possibility of my being shot.

I closed my eyes for a second and tried not to think about what being shot would feel like, deciding to ask a new question to change the subject. "What about this whole Alpha challenge thing Lorelai was talking about earlier? When will that happen, and what do I have to do to win?"

He sat up and stared down at me as if trying to decide whether to tell me the truth or keep it to himself. The moon was coming in through spaces in my blinds, and the glow in his skin became even more pronounced where the light hit him. "The challenge can come anytime, from anyone who thinks they could take you out. Technically, they are supposed to wait until you undergo the awakening because you cannot lead unless you become a wolf. But, if they take you out before your wolf has been awakened, there is no chance for you to win."

His words sank in slowly, and I could feel a chill run down my spine. "Let me make sure I understand this: I can be challenged anytime between now and the rest of my life, and I will just have to accept them each time until I die or someone else wins?" I was already having problems with the idea of being the leader of a pack, but fighting regularly made the idea even less appealing. How the hell could I live my life if I was always expected to be ready for a fight to the death?

"Yes and no. When you become the Alpha, you will only be challenged by others who could maintain the position and lead. Until you take on that role, you are open to challenges from those trying to move up the food chain." I laughed at his wolf humor. I might have been losing it.

"If I survive the next few weeks and reach my actual birthday, go through the awakening, and then win my challenges, will I lead without any problems?"

"In theory, yes." He shrugged a little and smirked at me, which caused my heart to speed up, but my stomach to drop.

"In theory?" I wasn't thrilled with his vague answer, so I sat in bed to let him know that wouldn't cut it. "What do you mean 'in theory'?"

"As I said, once you're the Alpha, your challengers will be fewer but much more difficult to beat, especially since you will take power at such a young age. If you were able to progress through the ranks slowly, with fight training along the way, by the time you became Alpha, you'd be better suited to lead without challenge. Your path is not so simple, and you risk more challenges."

I felt like his weight was pushing down on my chest again, and I struggled to breathe with this new information filling my head.

"Caleb," he reached out and touched my shoulder, but even this physical contact did little to get me out of my mood. "Don't think about it right now. There is still time to train, and other people can take on challenges on your behalf. It's not worth worrying over at this point."

I tried to push my fear and trepidation aside and concentrated on what I could change and deal with right now. "What do we do until then?" I asked, trying to imagine what my life would be like until I turned eighteen.

"Now, we sleep. It's almost 3:30 in the morning, and we've got things to do tomorrow. But if you don't mind, I would like to sleep in here with you, just in case something happens." He stared into my eyes with a serious expression, and it was all I could do to nod. "Great, I'll grab my stuff." He left the room and returned a moment later with his pillow and the sheets I had given him earlier. He spread the sheets out on the floor and lay down. "Goodnight, Caleb."

I rolled onto my side away from Adam, angry that he had chosen the floor over my bed.

"Yeah. Night." Even my anger couldn't keep me up for long, though, and soon, I was fast asleep. This time, however, when I fell asleep, I was plagued by the same dream I had the day before. Darkness was swallowing me up; no matter how fast I ran, I couldn't escape it.

Seven

My phone's ringtone cut through the early morning quiet, and I frantically grabbed at anything nearby to shut it up. I finally found it in my pants pocket from the previous night.

"Hello?" I shielded my eyes from the light in my room and guessed it was around 7:00 a.m. I yawned and pulled the covers over my head.

"Bitch! That's all you have to say to me after last night? I have been calling you non-stop since we got disconnected, and all you can say is 'Hello'?"

I cringed in my bed, feeling like a dick for not calling Megan back at some point during the night to tell her I was okay. But I felt like I should get a free pass after what happened.

"I know, and I'm sorry," I began, "I had a bizarre night last night, and by the time we got home, I basically went straight to bed. I didn't realize I had my cell until right now. I thought it was still in my car." Talking about my car reminded me that it had blown up last night, and I groaned. I wondered if my parents' insurance policy for my car would cover a werewolf attack?

"That is the stupidest excuse I have ever heard in my life. And what do you mean 'we'?" There was a hint of a smile in her voice now, which meant she had moved on from being mad to hoping I had gotten lucky somehow. "Please tell me there are juicy details. Hot and steamy details, hard and muscular details you have not shared."

"I wish there were, believe me, I do, but I am nowhere near as quick to give it up as you," I joked with her, but realized that I did wish my night had taken a turn for the sensual rather than the science fiction. "There is a guy, but it's not like that." Then I remembered Adam was sleeping in my bedroom, and my eyes shot open. Oh, please god, tell me he was still asleep and didn't hear me say that. "Hang on a sec." I pulled the covers down and leaned over the bed. Adam's stomach was rising and falling at regular intervals, and he was making quiet snoring or growling noises. I figured either was a good sign and rolled back over to finish my conversation. The bed springs creaked as I did, and I held my breath for a second, waiting to see if I could still hear his steady breathing.

"Okay, sorry about that. Where was I?"

"Wait, is he still there? Did he spend the night with you? Caleb, you are holding out on me. I thought we were best friends," she fake-pouted.

"We are best friends, but it's not how it sounds. Nothing happened between us last night, I swear."

"I'm coming over to meet him." And with that declaration, the line went dead. It was no use trying to change her mind. Once Megan decided to do something, it would happen, no matter what it took. When we were sophomores, she decided that our fellow classmates needed a lesson in fashion faux pas. And she went out and bought fashion police tickets, which she used to write up nearly everyone in the school over the next few weeks. It was pretty hilarious to walk down the halls and see little orange tickets taped to the lockers, detailing the fashion crime that had been committed. However, the rest of the student population found her opinion annoying. That's why I loved her, though, and that was why I lay there and waited for the door to my apartment to open.

I should have thought about the sleeping bodyguard on the floor, who was expecting me to be attacked, but it was early, and I didn't function before ten o'clock at the earliest.

Fifteen minutes later, I had just started to fall back asleep when I heard the faint sound of the lock turning and my front door opening. A second later, Adam pushed me off the bed and onto the carpet and then burst out of my room, teeth bared.

Megan screamed my name, and I came running out of my room. "Adam, let her go. That's my friend Megan. She came over to make sure I was doing okay after last night." I rubbed my cheek, which felt bruised after smacking it against the floor.

He looked at me but stopped pinning her to the wall by her neck and arm, which was a slight improvement. "I'm sorry, Megan," he laughed and rubbed the back of his neck. "I didn't hurt you too badly, did I?" He had begun looking her over for any marks, and even though she was visibly shaken, I could also tell that Megan was as hot for my bodyguard as I was.

"She's fine, Adam, and my face is also fine. Thanks for asking." I walked into the kitchen to grab a bag of ice for my wrist, which was now sore from putting my weight on it to get up off the floor. I was beginning to see how helpful that healing ability would be when I finally got it. In the meantime, I would probably be icing my wrist for days.

Though she was no longer pinned to the wall, Megan had not moved too far from the door, but the look in her eyes told me it had more to do with the fact that she had probably forgotten how to walk since seeing Adam and less to do with any remaining fear.

"Megan, snap out of it!" I clapped my hands a couple of times, and she slowly blinked and then looked over at me, which apparently helped her remember why she had come over.

"Oh, my god!" she mouthed behind Adam's back. Yep, she had forgotten that he was ready to kill her only moments ago. She walked over, sat at the kitchen table with me, looked at my wrist, and then looked back up at me. "So, what exactly happened last night? What happened to your face? And where is your car? I didn't see it when I came in."

"Um…" I started, but realized I wasn't sure what I could tell her, so I looked at Adam for help. He came over and sat down next to me, which caused Megan to lose interest in me and probably forget her questions, but he answered her anyway.

"I was driving down the road last night when I saw a car in front of me swerve and drive off the freeway, so I pulled over and rushed to see if anyone was hurt. Fortunately, Caleb had only gotten slightly banged up, so I called 911 and pulled him out of the wreck." Apparently, the truth was acceptable; I wish he had told me that so I wouldn't have looked like an idiot. Adam continued to tell Megan about how he had to carry me to his car, but then the lies started.

"So I rushed him to the hospital," he continued, "because the ambulance was taking too long, and when we got there, I realized I didn't know anything about him or have a way to get in touch with anyone but the hospital doesn't let you leave without putting down information about the person. I put in what I could about myself, and faked the rest of the information about him. Then I returned and got his cell phone out of his car before it got towed away."

Since I knew he had blown up my car as we drove away, I was still confused about how my cell phone ended up in my pocket. It had been in a cup holder before the car flipped, but I was happy to have it, so I didn't care.

Adam continued to tell Megan all about our time in the hospital and how I was released to him because he claimed to be my brother-in-law and that he spent the night to make sure I didn't have a concussion. He made himself out to be a real saint, which was so far from the truth that I couldn't help but laugh a few times. Megan didn't seem to notice or care. When he finally finished, she told him how glad she was that he had taken the time to save her best friend and then conveniently slipped in that she would be happy to make it up to him in any way she could.

I just about gagged at her less than subtle attempts at flirting, so I excused myself and went back to my bedroom to lie down. It wasn't even 8:00 a.m., and I was still wiped from everything that had happened the night before. I could still hear Megan laughing every few seconds, meaning she started flirting in earnest. I buried myself in my comforter and fell back asleep.

I woke up about two hours later and found that I was alone in my bedroom, but I couldn't hear any voices or anything else coming from the other room. Reluctantly, I rolled out of the warmth of my comforter cocoon and walked out to the living room and kitchen area. Adam was sitting on my couch, flipping through a photo album my mom gave me when I moved down to San Diego. It was full of pictures of myself from birth through high school graduation. I cleared my throat, but realized he already knew I was there when he didn't even look up from the pages.

"You were cute when you were a baby," he said.

"Thanks," I said, smiling, "I'm not sure what happened after that." It was my typical response whenever someone told me that. Part of it was sarcasm, but part of it was my actual thoughts about my current appearance. I was like the anti-ugly duckling; I had been adorable when I was young, but I grew into a lanky young man.

Adam looked up at me after my comment and seemed to be analyzing my face, "I think you are still a handsome guy."

I could feel the warm flush of my blood rushing into my face, so I looked down to hide my red cheeks. "Thank you," I replied.

Adam closed the book and stood up, grabbing a piece of paper off the table in front of him. "Megan left about an hour ago, but she made me promise to give you this note when you woke up. I'm going to get ready, but then we need to go out and start training, so you are ready for the change when it happens." He walked into my bathroom and closed the door behind him.

Dear Caleb,

I forgive you for not calling me last night, especially since you were in the hospital; I'm glad you're okay! But you must have had a concussion if you were not trying to get all over

Adam last night! It would have taken a lot more than that to keep me from making my move on his fine ass! Call me if you need anything. You know I'm always here for you. And I'll try to check in with you after work today.

XOXO Megan
P.S. Tell Adam I said 'Hi.'

Well, that was pretty much what I expected; 'glad you're fine; Adam is hot; I'll call you later.' I was glad she accepted his story and didn't mention how he attacked her or still hadn't left. I sighed and went over to sit on my couch while I waited for Adam to finish in the shower.

A few minutes later, I heard the water stop, and he came out wrapped in a towel and steam. Water droplets cascaded down his sculpted chest and abs, and I had to swallow a few times before I could breathe again. There was no getting around Adam's attractiveness, and I was suddenly happy to know we would share such close quarters for at least the next few weeks.

"Just let me get dressed, and then we can head out." Adam came over to the couch to grab the clothes he had left there the night before, and I could smell my shampoo and something else on him that made me think of the woods. He smelled clean and earthy, which made me realize that I hadn't showered since before leaving for work. Since my accident, I hadn't even bothered to look at myself in the mirror.

"Take your time. I need to get cleaned up myself." I practically ran to get to the bathroom and shut the door firmly behind me. I braced myself and finally looked up at my reflection. I was surprised, in a good and bad way. That I didn't look as beaten up as I felt after flipping over in my car was good, but I also looked like I had been in a car accident and had my car flipped. My hair was sticking up in various places all over my head, and my eyes were so puffy that it looked like I had been crying for hours.

I turned on the shower and jumped in, letting the warm water flow over my face and chest as I imagined it washing away my physical pain, and after five or ten minutes of this, I turned around and let the warm water do the same to my back.

When I finally emerged, the water began to cool, but I felt so much better that I didn't mind that I'd probably used up all of my hot water in the process. When I looked at myself in the mirror, I actually did a double-take. My eyes weren't as puffy as they had been, and the bruises that had been on my shoulder and across my chest from the seatbelt had lightened a little.

"Caleb," Adam yelled from outside the door, "I'm not waiting around for you all day. Quit stalling!" His voice was enough to get me out of the mirror and on with my day. I wrapped a towel around myself and went to my room to get dressed for a fight.

Eight

Adam decided the best place to do some training would be in Balboa Park. There were a lot of open grassy areas, and it would give us plenty of space to try out different techniques. I figured he knew what was best, so I just went with the flow.

"Okay, today I am going to show you some pretty basic moves for self-defense in case someone tries to attack you before your awakening." Adam looked me up and down as though I were an animal he was trying to decide how to kill. It didn't make me feel any better about my chances.

"Well, fortunately, I am pretty good at defending myself and even know how to throw some pretty good punches. That's what growing up gay will get you." I preferred to brag about my ability to fight rather than focus on the necessity of learning how to defend myself at a young age.

"Perfect, why don't we just start with some pretty slow sparring, and you can show me what you already know. There's no sense in wasting time teaching you that." Adam looked like his opinion of me was possibly changing. "Based on the few things you did last night, you seem to have a good awareness of your body, which is important for fighting and shifting." He pushed his sleeves up his arms and got into a crouched position, ready to pounce. "Ready, go!"

Adam ran at me full speed, arms wide, as though he wanted to tackle me. I knew if he did, I wouldn't be able to get up, so I waited until he got closer and then ducked out of the way at the last second. He stopped and spun around quickly, kicking his leg and connecting it with my butt, sending me flying forward. By the time I stood up, he had wrapped his arms around me from behind, so I flipped him over the top of me, and he landed hard on his back. At this point, the teacher would typically have stepped in, so I was expecting him to stop, but he got back on his feet and charged at me again.

This time, when I tried to move out of the way, he expected it and changed his course right before he reached me, and I was on my back on the ground. He climbed on top of me and pinned me down; his teeth elongated, and he gently bent forward and bit my neck. I shuddered, but not from the fear I was sure that move was supposed to cause.

He released me a few seconds later and got off the ground, smiling down at me with his teeth back to normal. "Good job," he said, reaching down and pulling me to my feet.

"Good job? I got knocked down twice, and you could have torn out my throat!" I was a little winded by the exercise, but could feel the adrenaline and something else coursing through me. It felt good, powerful. It was like I was more aware of my body somehow.

"That's true, but you also avoided my first attack, and I landed on my back after getting hold of you." He smiled at me, which I took as a good sign, so I stopped arguing with him. "Now, you just need to fine-tune some of those things so you don't broadcast what you're about to do."

"What do you mean?"

"The second time I charged you, right before you moved, you looked in the direction you were going to move and moved slightly in the other direction to prepare for your action. That was how I knew which way you'd go. Also, you spun in the same direction, which is another thing you'll have to learn to avoid. You can't keep using the same moves over and over again. Other Awakened will figure you out and be able to attack you like I did. Let's try again, but this time. I want you to try to hit or kick me and avoid my attacks." Adam crouched down again and, without warning, came barreling toward me.

I jumped out of his way but stuck my foot out, so he tripped over it and lost his balance, and I chased after him, pretending to kick him in the stomach while he was down. He rolled onto his back and jumped up; his eyes had changed into his wolf eyes, and his lips pulled back in a silent snarl. The effect was immediate, and this time I lost my nerve. He charged again, and my mind went blank from fear. A second later, Adam was soaring through the air behind me and landed on his stomach in the grass, which was now ground into his shirt.

"How did you do that?" Adam's eyes were large and back to their usual color. He had walked back over to me, brushing the grass and dirt off his clothing as best he could.

"What do you mean? I was just standing there, too scared to move, and you flew past me." Adam's reaction was not what I expected, but it confused me even more because all I saw him do was jump and fly off to my left.

"I tried to tackle you, but you stepped out of the way, grabbed me in the air, and then threw me." His smile was so large that he was beaming at me, but I still had no idea what he was talking about.

"No, your little wolf act scared me so much that I just blanked and didn't know what to do. I couldn't think how to react, so I just froze." This whole werewolf thing was becoming just a little more than I could take, so I sat down where I was.

Adam sat down next to me and took his shirt off. "Here, look at this," he passed his shirt over to me. "There are little tears in the fabric where you grabbed it." I saw the small holes in the shirt he was talking about, but these couldn't be from me, could they?

"I don't know what to tell you then. I don't remember doing anything to you, and I honestly expected to end up on the ground again, so I gave up." I wasn't exactly proud of that, but it was true. I had just stopped trying.

"Let's try it again!" Adam was walking away before I could stop him, so I stood up and waited. He charged me; I stood there, and he knocked me down. He tried three more times, knocked me over on each try, and finally accepted that I was not going to repeat what I'd done. The powerful feeling from earlier had long since disappeared, and the only thing I felt now was sore.

"Maybe it was just a fluke. Maybe you tripped on something, and I just happened to move a little out of your way, so you landed on the ground." I was trying to explain away something that didn't make sense to me, but Adam wasn't having it.

"I know what I saw, and I know you can do this! You just have to believe that you can." Adam was looking at me, but I found it hard to meet his eyes.

"You weigh at least fifty pounds more than I do. I don't think I could throw you around at all, let alone a few feet away. Maybe we should just continue with the training, rather than trying to get this same reaction to take place. What do you think?"

"You're right, we should keep going. And who knows, maybe you will do something else to impress me." He smiled as he helped me back up.

We spent the next hour going through defensive moves, and he taught me how to avoid or deflect certain kinds of attacks. By the time we were finished, a small crowd had gathered around us, but we tried to pretend they weren't watching. I assumed it was because most of them were more interested in Adam's body than the actual fighting that had taken place. But a couple of women and even a young guy came over and asked Adam if he taught self-defense classes anywhere and how much these private lessons would cost. Once the crowd had thinned considerably, Adam and I lay back on the grass and enjoyed the sun setting as planes flew overhead.

"Can I ask you a strange question that has been bugging me since you first picked me up?" I looked over at Adam, unsure how to frame the question, but decided to be as direct as possible.

"Sure, go ahead."

"Well, when you were driving me out to meet everyone, I was fighting with you, and I thought you were going to punch me, but you kissed me instead. Why?"

Adam laughed loudly at the question, which caused me to blush and turn away.

"Never mind," I said.

"No, don't be like that. I laughed because I wondered how long it would take for you to ask me about that." He smiled at me, rolled onto his side, and looked into my eyes. "I kissed you because I knew you were gay. I had been watching you since you got to San Diego, and I put some things together after a little while."

"Okay, so I'm obvious. I get that." I laughed. "But that doesn't explain the kiss, just that you knew I would like it." As soon as the words were out of my mouth, I wanted desperately to take them back. I hadn't meant to admit to Adam how attractive I thought he was. I assumed he was straight and didn't want him to think I was hitting on him.

He laughed again softly, "You're right; I didn't explain why I kissed you, but knowing that you were gay was the biggest reason. I knew that if you thought I was going to hurt you, you wouldn't expect a kiss, and that it would probably keep you from continuing to try to attack me. If you had been straight and I kissed you, you probably would have fought much harder, so being gay did play a big role in my decision-making process. Plus, I would have been in even more trouble if I had hurt you as I told you that night."

"So, it was just to keep me from getting hurt?" I asked, a little disappointed.

Adam rolled over so he was lying right next to me and pushed himself up to look into my eyes. "I had to do something that would shock you enough to make you stop trying to escape and hit me while driving, and it was the first thing that came to mind." With that, he leaned down, kissed my cheek, and then lay back down.

"Can I ask you a question now?" He turned his head to look at me again; his eyebrows arched with his question.

"Sure, go ahead," I said, still a little in shock from the surprise kiss.

"You don't have to talk about it if you don't want to, but I wondered what brought you back to San Diego? Your parents worked so hard to keep you away from here to protect you, but you moved back pretty much as soon as possible. Why?"

"Well, it's not like I knew any of that before I moved here. And honestly, my ending up in San Diego was sort of luck. But getting out of my small town was something I absolutely had to do as soon as possible."

"Why's that?" he asked, shading his eyes from the sun.

"It's kind of a long story," I said. "But, I've got the time."

Nine

Fifteen Months Earlier...

"You won't believe what came in the mail today," my mom said as I walked into the kitchen.

"Okay, I give up. What was it?" I plopped my backpack down on the island and began rooting around in the refrigerator for something to eat. I could smell that she was baking peanut butter cookies, my favorite, which she rarely did, so something was up.

"A package for you from San Diego State!" I turned around and saw that she was holding an envelope in her hand and that her smile stretched from one ear to the other. I had been waiting to hear back from various universities, but moving to San Diego was my first choice.

San Diego State was my best option for getting out of the desert and away from the people who had made my life a living hell since I entered middle school. UC Riverside wasn't far enough, and anything in Los Angeles would have felt overwhelming.

"Oh my god!" I ripped the envelope open and pulled out the letter. Some of my friends had begun receiving their decision letters, so I knew that envelope size didn't mean anything. But I always thought the small envelopes contained bad news.

I started reading the letter aloud, "Dear Caleb, I am pleased to offer you admission to San Diego State University for the fall semester." My heart began to pound, and I couldn't stop jumping around the kitchen like a lunatic. "Based on your academic performance during high school, I am also pleased to offer you a merit award to help cover some of the costs associated with your attendance. You will receive more information from our financial aid office in the coming weeks, but you can begin the next steps now on our website." I looked up at my mom, and tears of relief started to pour down my face.

"I knew you could do it, Caleb. I'm so proud of you." She held me tightly to her chest, and we laughed and cried together.

"Thanks, Mom. I'm going to call Megan and tell her the news." I ran to my bedroom, closed the door, and dialed Megan's cell.

Being openly gay at school meant I was well-known but not necessarily widely liked. Even Megan's popularity couldn't save me from the daily barrage of verbal assaults and frequent threats of physical violence. I learned how to fight when I was young and defended myself, but the odds were never stacked in my favor when it was three or four guys against me.

"Hey, what's up?"

"I got in," I yelled. "I finally got my letter from SDSU today, and I got in!" I was still smiling, and I realized my cheeks were beginning to hurt from the effort.

"Congratulations, that is so amazing. Would they let us live together?" We both laughed at that. We'd discussed the possibility of moving off-campus together at some point if we got into the same school, but realized we would probably kill each other.

"Absolutely, and I'm sure if we moved into the male part of the residence hall, you would be the most popular one in that wing!"

"Are you, my best friend, calling me slutty?" she asked, disgusted.

"Yes."

"Thank you, that's so sweet." Megan liked guys a lot, and they loved Megan. She was the perfect mixture of beauty and intelligence. But she pretended to be a lot worse than she was, and I teased her about it constantly.

"I'm glad we both got in because I'm not sure I could do it without you." Since meeting the first week of our freshman year, we had never spent more than a week apart, and that was only because she took a family vacation every summer.

"You'd figure it out, but your life would be much less dramatic and fun without me."

"You took the words right out of my mouth," I said, laughing. My head was still spinning from the excitement. I felt like I had finally been given the freedom to be myself. Whoever that turned out to be. I had finally been accepted.

*****

As I finished telling him about the day I knew I'd be able to get out of my small town for good, I snapped back to the present and saw Adam staring at me as he listened to my story.

"That was a feeling I hadn't experienced in so long that I couldn't remember it very clearly. My parents were great, of course, but dealing with a daily barrage of slurs, taunts, and occasional physical abuse was more than anyone should have to deal with at a young age." I sat up and hugged my knees to my chest to keep myself from reliving the things kids had done to me in the past. "When I knew I had a way out, I was so excited that I never considered anything else. It was my chance to move to a big city where I finally blended into the crowd."

I realized that as the sun had set, the temperature had dropped pretty quickly, and I could feel my skin begin to cool as I sat there with Adam. "In the end, my merit award wasn't enough to cover all the costs of attendance, so I had to postpone my admission while I saved up some money. Moving to San Diego was already set in motion, so I still moved and have been here since I graduated from high school." I'd been talking, uninterrupted, for so long that I thought Adam was asleep or no longer paying attention. I finally stopped and looked over at him. His eyes were fixed on me, and they looked like they were beginning to shift from brown to a light greenish-yellow.

"I'm sorry you were treated that way, Caleb. You're right; no one should have to deal with those things at such a young age, and I wish I could have saved you from it. But everything happens for a reason, and as horrible as that time in your life was, it made you that much stronger, which will help you cope with the potential for future attacks." He leaned over, wrapped his arm around my shoulder, and pulled me toward him in a tight embrace. It wasn't until I was up against his chest that I realized how cold I had become, and I shivered against his body as his warmth spread into mine. More than the warmth, though, it was as if I could feel his acceptance of me spreading through my body, and I didn't want to move away.

"Thank you. I know you're right. I'm stronger emotionally, mentally, and physically having dealt with that crap in school. But," I said as my arms broke out in goosebumps, "it didn't make me immune to the cold, so can we get going?" I reluctantly pulled away, afraid that if I stayed in his arms much longer, I would begin to imagine things that couldn't be.

Adam's laugh was so deep that I could feel him shake from it, and it caused me to laugh as well, which helped lighten the mood. "Sure, let's go," he said, then he put his shirt back on, inspecting the green stains from earlier. "I'm still curious how you could throw me through the air and not remember doing it."

"What can I say? I'm just that good," I smiled at him.

"Right, that must be it," he countered as we walked back to his car to head home. On our way back to the parking lot, I could see Adam's gaze constantly scanning the space around us. I realized that I had completely dropped my guard and should try to remain as aware as possible of my surroundings.

"How do you do it?" I asked. I tried to focus my attention on a couple about a hundred yards away while walking and talking. It was more difficult than I thought it would be.

"How do I do what?" Adam looked at me, but I could tell he was still paying attention to everything happening in the park.

"Keep your attention on so many things simultaneously and still have the ability to carry on a normal conversation? I can barely walk and talk on the phone at the same time without running into things on the ground or tripping."

He smiled at me, and I noticed his eyes were returning to the warm brown color I had enjoyed. "Practice and heightened senses. I don't have to see or hear everything to know what is happening, which leaves me enough attention span to talk to you or kiss you and drive safely." He smirked at me as my cheeks flushed, and he probably looked like I had spent a couple of hours in the sun without sunscreen.

"Okay, I'm sorry I asked about the kiss! I was curious, not trying to declare my undying love for you." *Although if you kiss me again, I might be willing to declare it at that point.* I stomped ahead in mock indignation and tried to follow his movements using only my hearing while looking straight ahead. I had gone about 50 feet before my foot caught in a hole in the grass, and I began toppling face-first toward the ground. Rather than smacking into the dirt, I somehow found myself somersaulting, and I rolled back up onto my feet without missing another step.

I could hear Adam running when I started to fall, but as I corrected the issue, I heard him slow down and then start chuckling softly. "It looks like you have some tricks up your sleeve that you didn't tell me about during practice. Next time we train, I'm pushing you even harder!"

I groaned at the thought, but then I tried to figure out how I did that. I'd never done anything like it before, and there was no reason I would suddenly start rolling around on the ground now. Maybe some wolf habits began appearing before the shift, and no one remembered to tell me about them.

"Hey Adam, how do you know when the awakening is coming? I mean, do we start acting like wolves or something? Does extra hair start sprouting up in previously non-hairy areas? Dogs suddenly start running away from you for no reason?"

I could tell that my line of questioning had thrown him off, but he was trying to keep himself composed. "No, there isn't any hint that you are getting close to the awakening, other than your 18th birthday approaching. Remember, this isn't some magical curse or anything like that. You shift because you want to, and your body just gains the ability to be able to handle that change."

"Gotcha. That makes sense, I guess. I just wondered."

"Caleb…"

"No, it's true. I was just curious."

"Caleb…stop."

I looked up at him and realized he was staring at the couple I had noticed before, but they were somehow in front of us, standing near Adam's car. "What's wrong?"

"Just don't move. Wait right here. I'll be right back." With that, he started to circle slowly around the couple until he was standing downwind of them. After a few seconds, I could see his face relax as they got into their car and drove away. It looked like he was being a little overly cautious until he looked back at me. I could see him yelling something, but I couldn't hear what it was, and by the time I realized what he was saying, I could feel a hand grip my shoulder and squeeze hard.

Sorry, Adam, but I don't think I can run now.

I looked behind me at the man holding me in place and noticed his wolf eyes before seeing his long teeth, which seemed out of place in his human mouth. "Hello Caleb, it's nice to meet you face-to-face."

Ten

"Hello." I mentally slapped myself for my response and turned back to try to find Adam, who had disappeared.

"Looks like your protector isn't doing his job very well. What do you think, Caleb? Do you feel protected?"

"Do I need to be protected?" Answering a question with another question was probably not the best idea, but my mind blanked, and I didn't know what to do. Where was Adam?

"You'll have to be the one to answer that, I guess. In the meantime, why don't you walk with me to my car? It's just over there," he pointed to the far side of the lot, which was shaded by some of the large trees in the park, making it much darker than the surrounding areas and hard to see.

"You know, I think I'd rather not, I'm…"

"Start walking," he growled into my ear as he pushed me forward.

"All right." I knew this was a bad idea, but I was also seriously underprepared, and the guy was a good four or five inches taller than me and 100 pounds heavier, easily.

He pushed me towards his car, never releasing my shoulder, so it looked like we were two guys hanging out together, not that it mattered. I looked around for other people in the area, but Adam was still missing in action, and no one else was within earshot. So much for making a scene and hoping for a Good Samaritan to step in to help me out.

I knew that I was on my own, and I would have to do something to stop him from forcing me into his car, or I was as good as dead. When we finally reached the shadows surrounding his car, I spun around quickly, bit his arm as hard as I could, and pushed him backward. Within seconds, he reached for me again, but I was ready for it this time, and I slipped out of his grasp a few times. Each time he missed me, or I was able to escape, I could see him becoming even angrier. His features were shifting into something much more deadly. His face elongated, giving room to the sharp teeth I had seen before, and his nails grew into claws.

Though he was still mostly in human form, he got down on all fours and started running at me, mouth open. I looked around for help, but the small crowd from earlier had left, and in the seconds I had to look around, I didn't notice anyone. I knew there was no way I would be able to slip out of his teeth or claws without sustaining some sort of serious injury. The knowledge of that and the fear of being attacked caused my mind to empty yet again, but I could stay mentally present this time. I realized that I could see more detail than before, and he seemed to be running in slow motion now. It was easy to step out of his way on his first pass, and when he swung around for a second, I stepped aside and kicked him in the ribs as he passed.

He flew into the trunk of a nearby tree and lay there for a few seconds before shifting into something much more human in appearance. He sat up and shook his head for a second, then reached down and gently pushed against his ribs where I had kicked him.

"Anything broken?" Adam's voice came from behind me and caused me to jump.

The man shook his head again, "Nope. Probably just bruised." He pushed himself back onto his feet and walked toward Adam, who shook his hand.

"Good to hear. I thought he'd gotten you when you flew through the air," he said with a deep laugh. His laughter surprised me. I was bracing for another attack when Adam turned and looked at me.

"Caleb, this is Brent. He's part of our pack. I asked him to come by tonight to help me with the training, but he showed up late. When I finally saw him, I wanted to put your skills to the test in a real situation, so I let you handle things on your own."

"You told him to attack me?" I was sure I had been about to be abducted for the second time in a week, and it was all part of a plan. To say I was pissed would have been an extreme understatement!

"Not at all. I just walked into the trees to see what you would do. Brent was walking with you, then you attacked him."

"He was going to make me get in his car! How was I supposed to know he was part of the pack?" I was furious now. Adam was supposed to help me, not get me attacked!

"You weren't; that was the point. He wasn't attacking you, but you still defended yourself against someone you saw as a threat. And even though you didn't throw him, you still sent him flying!" Adam laughed at that, and Brent groaned a little.

"Sorry if I scared you, Caleb. I wanted to see what you had learned already. It seems like you picked up a lot." He was smiling down at me with his hand extended.

I shook it and winced as he squeezed harder than was strictly necessary, "Nice to meet you. I'm sorry I kicked you into a tree."

Adam started laughing again, and I couldn't help but join in. After a few seconds, Brent laughed along with us, and I finally relaxed.

The three of us continued talking in the park for a few more minutes until I started to shiver again, and Adam agreed that we'd better head home. On the way, we stopped for some burgers and fries. When we got home, I changed into something warmer, lay in my bed, and was out for the night.

The next day, my muscles protested so hard that I fell back into my pillows when I tried to get up. Adam's workout affected me, but I wasn't sure it had been entirely positive. I might be able to defend myself a little better, but if I were this sore after mock fighting with him for a little while, and facing down Brent, fighting the other Awakened, who were trying to kill me, would be a lot worse.

I had been in bed long enough and hadn't gone back to work since finding out who I really was. If I thought the physical pain from my workout was bad, it would be nothing compared to the financial struggle of no work and no money in my bank account. I rolled to the edge of my bed and maneuvered my body into a standing position, but with my first step, I tripped and fell face-first onto the floor.

"Ouch!"

"I'm so sorry, Adam, I completely forgot you were still sleeping on the floor." I flipped over and looked back at him. He was not amused at being woken up by me falling on top of him. But when I saw his grumpy face and disheveled hair, I couldn't stop myself from chuckling softly. And when my stomach muscles reacted to the movement, I sucked in a quick breath and stopped.

"I don't believe you..." Adam glared at me, and his eyes had shifted to his yellow-green wolf eyes, which, for some reason, caused me to laugh even harder.

"Ow, ow, ow, ow!" I cried. "Don't make me laugh. It hurts too much!"

"Oh, really? Does it feel like someone is kicking you in the side and then landing on your diaphragm?"

"Yes!" I was still laughing and holding my stomach from the pain.

"Good." With that, Adam rolled onto his side and covered his face with one of his pillows.

"You know, you can sleep in my bed if you want." Adam peeked out from under the pillow; his eyes trained on my face.

"Caleb, I think you may have gotten the wrong idea yesterday. I..."

"I meant right now." I managed to get out through the pain in my chest and stomach that had nothing to do with my aching muscles. "I'm awake. You can have it to yourself."

He watched me closely as he seemingly tried to read my face, which I hoped was more neutral than it felt. "Oh, okay. I'd appreciate that, thank you." He got up from the floor, pulled my covers up, and lay down on top of them.

I forced myself to look away from him and went to take a shower, where I could hopefully wash away my physical and emotional pain. Once the warm water washed over my body, I finally started to relax, which is when my mind started going a hundred miles an hour.

"What did he mean? I never thought he was attracted to me," I lied to myself. "I was just being nice. He didn't have to be such an ass about it. Next time I'll just let him sleep on the floor!" My embarrassment had firmly shifted into anger, and it was so distracting that I didn't realize the water around me started to feel warmer than it had a few minutes before. "I'll show him what I think about him the next time we spar when I claw his face off," I thought, swiping my hand in front of me. What I saw there scared me so much that I stumbled backward and fell for the second time that day.

The crash was loud enough that Adam knocked at the door and yelled for me moments later. Not wanting him to see me, I called back, "I'm fine. I just uh...dropped the shampoo."

"Are you sure you're okay? I thought I smelled a wolf right before the crash." Oh god, then it wasn't just my imagination. I looked down at my hand, everything looked normal, but moments before, I could have sworn I had long, sharp nails on the tips of each finger.

"Yeah, I'm fine," I said in a shaky voice. "Go back to bed." How could this be happening to me? I was still months away from my actual 18th birthday, and Adam said I wouldn't change until sometime after that.

I didn't want to worry Adam if it was to be expected, but I also didn't want to show him how scared I was. He was supposed to protect me, but I had been taking care of myself for a long time, and I wasn't about to stop now.

The rest of the shower passed by without incident, though my hair did feel a little thicker and coarser than the day before. I was sure I was overreacting and feeling things that were not there. When I stepped out of the bathroom with my towel wrapped around my waist, Adam had already gotten up and was nowhere to be seen.

I opened the closet to get dressed, where I found Adam as he quietly whispered into his cell phone. When he heard me, he spun around and looked at me. Of course, I would be in a towel! I let out a little yell, backed up, and slammed the door shut.

Adam was talking to someone and didn't want me to hear. I was beginning to doubt that I would be able to trust him. His actions lately had been confusing, and he had sent mixed signals.

It took him a full minute before he emerged from my closet, cell phone in hand. He had a serious look on his face. "Caleb, we need to talk," he said.

"You're right. But since I have work to do and can't do it in a towel, you will just have to wait until I'm dressed." With that, I marched past him into my closet and shut the door behind me. Then, I remembered the light was on the outside, and I couldn't see a damn thing without it. I just stood there and tried to decide how I could turn on the light without looking like an idiot, but about ten seconds later, the light turned on. I rolled my eyes and smacked my forehead. This was not the way I wanted to portray myself. I pushed it out of my mind and quickly got ready for work.

"Okay," I said as I opened the door, "You can say whatever you need to say while I get ready." I walked past Adam, sitting on the end of my bed, and headed back out to the bathroom.

"I need more of your attention than that." He spoke calmly, making it hard for me to hold on to my anger, but I wasn't going to give in that easily.

"Then you'll have to wait." And with that, I closed the door to the bathroom while I finished brushing my teeth, doing my hair, and generally making myself presentable. Tonight would be a long night, and not just because I had a lot of explaining to do when I got to work.

I found Adam waiting for me in my living room when I was ready to go. "I need you to please give me a ride to work. We can talk on the way. That way, you'll have my undivided attention, and I won't be able to escape." After hearing what I'd just said, I regretted pointing out that I couldn't escape the talk.

"That's fine, let's go." He had his keys in hand and was out the door before I could figure out a way out of the car ride that had started as my idea. I followed him out of the apartment and locked up before walking to his car.

"As I said, we need to talk," Adam began as he pulled onto the main road. "When you walked in on me on the phone, I was talking to Lorelai."

That got my attention, and I asked him, "Why were you talking to her?"

"I check in with her or Carlos every day. But while we were talking, I heard the crash in your bathroom, and I told her about smelling a wolf." He paused and waited for me to acknowledge what he was saying.

"Right, you thought you smelled a wolf before I dropped the shampoo. But that was just an accident, slippery hands or whatever." Lying wasn't something I did well, and I never knew when to be specific or keep things vague.

"Exactly, but what I told her that I did not say to you was that *you* were the wolf I smelled."

My breath caught in my throat, and I felt my pulse speed up. I hadn't imagined things; I had begun to transform in the shower. "I don't understand. I'm still months away from when I'm supposed to be able to change for the first time." I didn't confirm that I knew what he meant about my changing.

"That's why I'm concerned. And your mother agrees with me. You shouldn't be able to shift until you're at least 18. As you said, that's still several weeks away, but the truth remains, I smelled your wolf. And Caleb, I know what a shampoo bottle sounds like when it falls."

Busted.

Eleven

When Adam dropped me off, he told me that I needed to call Lorelai on my break to discuss what happened when I was in the shower. He tried to drive me straight to her house, but I refused to miss another day of work for something I wasn't even supposed to be able to do yet. I was barely through the sliding glass doors of the hotel before my manager called out to me.

"Caleb, glad to see you could make it to work today. Please come with me," Robert said as he walked toward his office behind the front desk. He was in his thirties and pretty cute for someone older than me, but I couldn't tell if he was straight or gay. He never talked about his personal life at work and didn't wear a ring or have family photos on his desk. My instincts told me he was straight, but he occasionally looked at male guests longer than I thought a straight guy would, so who knows?

"Caleb, I'm sure you know why we are sitting here. Why don't you tell me exactly what happened to you that kept you from showing up for work for the past few nights?" His face looked relaxed, so I figured I would tell him as much of the truth as possible and hope he bought the little white lies along the way.

"I completely understand, Robert, and you know I would never usually miss work without letting someone know. I've always been early and haven't even called in sick." He nodded, so I continued. "I was on my way to work three nights ago when a motorcycle came out of nowhere, and I swerved to avoid hitting it." I leaned in and gave him my most honest expression as the lies began. "I'm sure you saw something in the newspaper about the car on the 163 freeway that flipped over after driving off the side of the road."

"Oh my god! That accident was you? Are you okay?" Robert looked at the parts of my body he could see from the other side of my desk.

"Yes, yes, I'm fine. I was wearing my seatbelt, fortunately. I have some cuts and bruises on my chest, stomach, and legs and a pretty big knot on the side of my head, but fortunately, nothing was broken."

He pointed to the splint on my hand, "What happened there?"

I had forgotten about that and looked down at it guiltily, "Oh, um...I hurt it after the crash, actually.

Which is why I missed my shift the next night." I felt my stomach clench, and my heart fluttered as the lies piled up. I figured changing the timeline was okay as long as I kept the details accurate.

"Someone broke into my apartment while I was gone, and when I came home, they were still there, trying to steal my laptop, Apple TV, and PlayStation. I didn't know what to do, so I just started swinging. I'm not good at fighting, clearly." I laughed a little to try and sell it.

"You were in a car accident, and then you got in a fist fight with a burglar?" His frown showed that my last addition had pushed him into the realm of disbelief.

"I know, this week has been pretty crazy! But I do have a note from the hospital for both visits." I handed him the fake hospital forms Adam had printed for me earlier in the day. Thank goodness he was adept at lying and scheming because I was crap at it. "I realize I should have called in for work, but I was honestly just so out of it with pain medication and stress that I completely forgot." That much was true, at least.

"Well, I'm sorry to hear about your car accident and the break-in, and I am glad to see you are doing all right. I'm glad to have you back. Now go clock in and get up to the front." Robert filed away my hospital forms and smiled at me. Hopefully, he didn't check on those visits too closely, or I'd be screwed.

Being back at work was a relief. Finally, there was something normal for me to do that I was good at.

The guests all fell into the same groups as always: the ones that were regular visitors and had their routine, the smiley out-of-towners, the 'nothing is right, give me free things' people who complained the moment they stepped into their room, the business travelers, and secret rendezvous couples. I recognized them the moment they hit the door, and their familiarity helped me relax.

In addition to recognizing them, I also had a particular way of handling guests based on their group membership. The routine guests were easy to spot and deal with because they knew the process, and I regularly upgraded them when possible. The smiley out-of-towners were fine, and I tried to give them the best views or rooms available to keep the magic going. The complainers were automatically downgraded so that when they complained and I gave them something 'extra,' it was still less than a regular guest received. It was my way of getting back at people who want something for nothing and expect nice hotels to cater to their every whim. It was terrible, and I knew it, but I couldn't help myself.

The business travelers, I usually booked in rooms closest to the business center in case they needed access to our printers, fax machines, and computers. Finally, the secret rendezvous couples got rooms on the lowest levels when possible because they were not there for the view, and it gave them easy access to the stairs if needed.

My first four hours of work flew by with a lower-than-average number of check-ins during that time, but it was a slow tourist season in San Diego, so that was not unusual. When the door slid open and I saw four people walking toward me, my immediate reaction was excitement because I would at least have something to do for the next couple of minutes. My first thought about the group was that they were business customers because they were dressed nicely and did not seem to have any familial or romantic connection with each other. But they moved as though they were bored and knew what to expect, like a regular.

However, these faces were all new to me, so I greeted them as politely and professionally as possible.

"Good evening, and welcome to The Cameron, San Diego. How may I assist you this evening?" My smile was big and bright, but my skin was covered in goosebumps that spread quickly as the group got closer.

The woman in the lead locked eyes with me and gave an almost imperceptible sniff of the air as though she was trying to see if she could smell me. "We've been going from one hotel to the next, trying to find rooms, but everything is completely booked. Do you have any rooms available?"

As she spoke, the other three, two men and another woman, moved up to the front desk, looking around and sniffing the air. Something didn't feel right about the four, but her lie about everything being booked was the most obvious issue. We were less than sixty percent full, and I knew that the hotels around us in the Gas Lamp district were similarly empty.

I lowered my eyes to check our reservation system, "I'm sorry to hear that you had problems finding accommodation. Let me just check my system here." I tried to remain calm. So far, they hadn't tried to do anything, and I was probably just having weird feelings because of my own drama. "Yes, we do have some availability. How many rooms would you like?" I smiled up at the woman, hoping that it was still cheerful and did not give away my discomfort.

"Four," she said flatly.

"Let me see what I can find on the same floor for you," I said, and I clicked around on the computer. "Would you like a specific view of the city?"

She blinked at me, and her lip looked like it was curling into a snarl, but she seemed to realize that and seemed to force it into what was supposed to be a smile. "That won't be necessary, just four basic rooms."

"Okay, I have four rooms, with two queen beds each. Would you like to pay for those as a group or separately?"

"All together," she said sharply.

She was not going to be much of a conversationalist, which put my awkward meter into the red. Not to mention that it was not helping to calm my nerves. "Great, I just need a photo ID and credit card on file for any incidental charges, and I also need to know how long you plan to stay with us."

She placed her license and credit card on the counter, and I took both of them from her. "We will be here for one night."

I made sure to input all of the information from her license and triple-checked her name on her ID and her credit card to confirm they matched. "All right, four rooms for one night each, that will be $1,125.65. Check out is at 11:00 a.m.. Is there anything else I can do for you in the meantime?" I was hoping she would say no, but it was then that one of her companions stepped forward.

"Are you the only night person working right now?" He moved in front of me and began looking around the desk to see if someone was on the other side with me.

I lied immediately without thinking about it. "No, sir. My manager is in the back, and another person will return from his break in just a few minutes. Did you need to speak to one of them?"

He sniffed the air as I finished speaking and then turned to look at the others, all of whom smiled. When he turned back to me, he was smiling the same strange smile the woman had used, where it was more teeth than anything else. "No, I just wondered if someone would be available if we had a problem with our rooms. Thank you." With that, they grabbed the keys I had laid out on the counter and walked together towards the elevator.

"Okay, that was awkward," I said quietly under my breath. When I looked toward the elevator, they were all looking at me as if they had heard me say it, but when I noticed, they went back to waiting silently for the doors to open.

I watched quietly until they all got onto the elevator, and the doors slid closed before I finally looked away. Then I immediately called Adam.

"Hello?" He said after a couple of rings.

"Hey, it's Caleb..."

"Yeah, I know, I put your number in my phone. What's up?"

Normally, that would have made me feel a certain kind of way, but I didn't have the time to focus on that right now. "Four people just walked into the hotel, and I got a bizarre feeling from them. It looked like they were literally sniffing around the front desk area. As my bodyguard or whatever, I just figured that you would want to know." I spoke quickly into my cupped hand at the base of the receiver.

"They did what? No one should have been able to track you yet, so they shouldn't be any danger to you unless...shit. I'll be right there." And with that, the line went dead.

Great, just what I needed, a curse and then a dial tone. My dad was notorious for that; he would be done with the conversation and just hang up rather than saying 'bye.' It bothered me, but with my dad, I never felt like I was in danger after he hung up. In this situation, that could be a different story.

I figured now was as good a time as any to call Lorelai, so I went behind the desk since nothing was happening out front, grabbed my cell, punched in her number, and waited for her to pick up.

"Caleb, how nice to hear from you! I wasn't sure when you would be able to call. Adam told me we have a lot to talk about." Her voice was kind, reassuring, and firm, reflecting her power in her world.

"I'm happy to discuss all the ins and outs of wolfdom with you sometime, but for now, will you answer a question for me?" I didn't want to start worrying until I knew I should, and I figured she was the best place to get information on my transition.

"Of course. What's on your mind?" I could hear the laughter in her voice, and I figured it was a good sign that she was in a good mood.

"Let's just assume for a second that I did shift early; that somehow I was able to change before it should be possible. Would other people like us," I said quietly, "be able to tell what I was?"

"If you have transitioned into a full-fledged wolf, hypothetically, then yes, they could smell you, and they would have a physical response to you, which would also be a beacon for them." She spoke with conviction, which was nice, but it made the already sick feeling in my stomach change into that feeling you get when you are on a roller coaster and suddenly fall out of the sky. I wanted to scream and throw up at the same time. "Crap."

Twelve

In shock from Lorelai's information, my knees buckled under me, and I slid down the wall to sit on the floor. It wasn't until a full minute later that I remembered I was on the phone and realized I hadn't heard a word she'd been saying.

"Caleb? Caleb, can you hear me? Are you there? Hello!" Her voice was concerned but didn't contain the edge of panic that mine did.

"Yeah, sorry, I thought I saw a guest enter the lobby, so I had to check." I closed my eyes and let my head hit the wall behind me. "Sorry, but I had better get back out there, just in case. I'll call you on my meal break; I promise." We said our goodbyes, and it was nice to know someone still said them.

I walked back around the corner and almost smacked into a guest from a few minutes prior. "Oh, my goodness, I'm so sorry, sir, I didn't see you there," I apologized automatically, without realizing that he was behind the front desk, almost in the back area, and not where he should've been.

"You weren't at the counter, so I came to find someone. It looks like I found you." He 'smiled' again, and a fresh set of chills ran down my spine.

"I'll be happy to help you, but I have to ask you to please move back around to the other side of the counter. Guests are not permitted behind the desk." I moved forward to open the gate that led to the employee area, but he didn't budge. I continued to hold the little barrier open until he gave in.

He let out a soft grumbling noise that sounded suspiciously like a growl. He walked back around to the front and glared at me. Behind him, I heard the front sliding doors whoosh open, and he reacted quickly to the sound. His nostrils flared, and his gaze sharpened as he spun around to face the new guest. Fortunately for me, it was a face I was relieved to see.

"Good evening, miss, I'll be with you in just a moment," I smiled at her and hoped it wasn't immediately evident that I recognized her.

"No problem," she said politely.

I turned back to the now red-looking man in front of me, who was breathing so roughly that he appeared he might explode from the effort. "I'm sorry, sir. What was it that you needed help with?" I was nothing if not good at this customer service act.

He mumbled something under his breath, waved his hands dismissively, and backed away from the desk toward the elevator. I waited until he had gotten on the elevator and was well on his way up to his floor before I started laughing and finally gave the new guest my attention.

"Karen, I'm so happy to see you!" I finally breathed again, and my excitement had me smiling like an idiot.

"Calm down, Sparky," she laughed at me. "Adam called and said I should get down here as soon as possible. I was closer than he was, so I came to see what was happening."

I had only met her once before at Lorelai's house, but her short, curly hair helped give her a unique appearance that many women would have been afraid of or unable to pull off. When we initially met, she had been all business, but in her casual clothing, it was obvious that she wasn't much older than I was, maybe twenty-one or so. Her coral-colored top accentuated her dark skin and made her smile even brighter.

"What were you doing before Adam called you?" Her tight-fitting jeans and gold hoop earrings helped her blend into the college-age crowd that frequented the Gas Lamp district.

"I was across the street at the coffee shop. It's close enough that I can see who is coming and going in the hotel without being so close that I draw more attention to you than you do on your own." Her expression told me she was joking with me.

"What can I do? I'm hard to ignore."

"I'll say." She rolled her eyes and laughed again. "Well, as long as I am here, you might as well tell me what happened here that got Adam's boxers in a bunch."

I did my best to let that image fade away from my mind almost as soon as it entered. I ran down the last few minutes and the creepy feelings I was getting from the group that had checked in.

"That is strange, but it's hard to say whether they were actually from another pack or just weird regulars."

"Regulars?" I looked at her quizzically.

"That's what I call people who can't do what we can. I don't like to call regulars 'human' because that implies that we aren't human, and I don't believe that."

"Oh." I hadn't thought about it. Lorelai said that we weren't human, so I just accepted that. I never thought about what I would call people who didn't shape shift, but I definitely still thought of myself as a human. I'd have to figure out what I would call them, but 'regulars' had a nice ring to it and made me sound special. "Well, I've dealt with my fair share of strange 'regulars,' and these four were different from anyone I've ever met, especially the guy who was up here when you walked in. Did you get anything off him?"

"Do I look like your own personal bloodhound?" Her eyes started to shine, and all humor drained off her face.

"Wha...n-no! I just thought maybe..."

The light returned to her face, as did her smile, "I'm just messing with you, Caleb. Brent said you were gullible, but I didn't expect this. Calm down, kid. We're not all out to get you."

Apparently, my fear was still the most hilarious thing the pack had ever encountered, and everyone was determined to get their scare in. "F-you, Karen." It took all of my control to keep my tongue in my mouth and walk away from her.

She continued laughing at me, "I'm sorry, I just had to see it myself. Though seriously, I didn't notice anything strange about him, he didn't look at me, and I wasn't close enough to get a good whiff."

"Maybe one of them will come back down. If you wouldn't mind staying to keep me company, you can check them out if they do." She agreed, and we spent the next few hours discussing our lives. I asked her about her family, and when she found out, she could change into a wolf. Only Karen's mom had been able to change, and her dad hadn't been part of their lives, so there wasn't anything she had to hide. I was surprised to learn that it was not necessary to have two Awakened parents to inherit the gene. If it were a dominant gene, I figured there would be more of us around. When I asked Karen about it, she laughed and asked what made me think there were only a few of us. I didn't particularly like the sound of that.

She asked me about growing up without being part of the pack and what it was like living with parents who didn't know about my ability. That reminded me that I still hadn't told my parents about my accident, finding my birth mother, or the whole wolf thing. I was probably going to keep that last one to myself for a while.

Karen told me about my birth father, though she had only known of him, never actually met him in person before he died. According to her, everyone in the pack respected him, and he was a good leader, something I hoped I could be, assuming I lived that long. I wasn't sure what it took to be successful and respected as a leader, but I was pretty sure no one would let my head get too big. If the teasing I was dealing with now was any indication, I might never be respected by the pack unless I got control of my fear.

My break came and went, and I knew I was supposed to call Lorelai back, but I didn't want to make Karen sit alone in the lobby for so long, so I split the food I brought to work with her, and we ate at a small table near the front. Only one couple came in while we were eating, but Karen looked unconcerned as she ate some of my veggie chips, so I figured I had nothing to worry about.

By the end of my shift, we had discussed our childhoods and my plan for college, and I shared my "coming out" story with her. Karen was working on her MBA already, and I felt so lame for having to put off college for a year, but her mom was helping her out a lot, so I didn't feel as bad as I would have if she were doing it on her own.

"You should consider USD. I think you might like it. Classes are small, and they have some pretty good financial aid packages."

"Yes, but USD is also a private Catholic school, and I'm not private…or Catholic. I don't think I'd fit in." I smiled at my joke, but she didn't seem to understand. "C'mon, that was funny!"

"Um, it wasn't not funny." Her use of the double negative was unusual and made me laugh, so I couldn't be mad at her for not laughing at my joke.

"Whatever," I rolled my eyes. "So, what now? Do I just go home, or am I staying with you today?"

Her eyes filled with something between panic and disgust. "You aren't staying with me. I have work of my own to get to, and you'll still be with Adam today. We just have to wait for him to show up."

As she looked out the front windows, I heard the familiar ding of the elevator, which had been going off all morning as guests came and went. This time, however, my stomach instantly dropped. Without turning around, I knew exactly who was about to step through those doors, and every hair on my body felt like it was being pulled out of its follicle. "Karen," I managed to choke out, "it's them!"

She turned and looked at the elevator, and I followed her line of sight. "Stay here."

When I turned back around to ask what she was planning to do, she had disappeared. I seemed to end up alone an awful lot for someone who was supposed to be receiving protection.

I stayed in the lobby chair but turned my back to the elevator, knowing that this was public enough and I should be relatively safe from harm. I tried to locate Karen by scanning the lobby with my peripheral vision, but she seemed to have vanished.

I could hear the group check out at the counter behind me, and I could see their reflections in the plate glass window as they appeared to be looking around the lobby for me. It didn't take them long to realize I was only a few feet behind them. Their eyes seemed to glow when they made eye contact with me in the reflection, but I quickly averted my gaze, hoping they wouldn't get any closer. Then I heard a familiar laugh as the automatic doors slid open.

Karen and Adam walked into the hotel and went straight to the front counter, where they created a physical barrier between the others and me. I ignored the whole scene as much as I could until I saw Megan's car pull up out front. She had some fantastic timing! I got up from my seat and practically ran to her car before jumping in, "Drive, Thelma, drive!"

"What?" Megan looked at me like I was crazy.

"Never mind, just go!" She peeled out, and I was finally able to breathe again.

Thirteen

Once we were a safe distance from the hotel, I took a minute to breathe and then turned to my best friend, "Megan! What are you doing here? And, can I just say, you have perfect timing!" I leaned across the front console and hugged her.

She laughed and hugged me back with one hand. "Glad to see you're feeling better. I figured you'd be back at work last night since you're too much of a goodie-goodie to use the perfect excuse of your car crash to take some time off. I figured I'd stop in to give you a ride home since you're stranded."

"Very much appreciated. I had this creepy group check-in, and one of the guys came down again to talk to me. They were all checking out when I walked out."

"Uh oh, maybe he wanted a little 'extra' attention that only you can provide," she laughed.

"Ew!" I couldn't stop the image from popping into my head. "That's so gross!" I hadn't even thought about that, plus he was not my type. Tall, dark, and handsome are great for some, but since I am tall, pale, and cute, I don't think I'll ever snare someone like that.

"Oh, please, you know you have more perks in this job than just discounted travel, right? Please tell me you at least flirt with the hot guys that come in." Megan looked at me hopefully.

I laughed, "Fine, I'll admit it. I flirt, sometimes more than I should, but I have never gone beyond that." Wanting to change the topic, I figured the only sure-fire way to do that was to talk about her. "Anyway, how've you been? I feel like I haven't talked to you in forever." In reality, it had only been a couple of days.

"Well, it's now officially over between Nate and me. He just wasn't living up to my very high expectations." This was not uncommon with Megan, who had a new guy every other month or so.

"What happened?" I loved listening to her stories about her failed attempts at love, mostly because it helped me feel better about being eternally single.

"He threw his food at me." She looked at me seriously.

I burst into loud laughter; thankfully, I was sitting, because had I been standing, I would have fallen on the floor. "What!?"

"Caleb, this is serious! We went to dinner, and I drove, so when I was dropping him off, we got into a little fight, and he threw his leftovers at my car." She was laughing with me, "I swear, Caleb, I don't know how I do it, but I attract all the freaks!"

"Who does that?" I had heard weird stories about Megan's ex-boyfriends, but this was, by far, the most hilarious one.

We spent the entire car ride back to my apartment talking about some of her past relationships and the various ways they had ended. I was still laughing when there was a loud knock on my front door. I tried to pull myself together, but when I looked out the peephole, all the humor drained from my body anyway. Staring at me from the other side of the door was Adam, who looked pissed.

"What the hell happened last night? Did they do anything to you?" Adam was practically yelling at me. When he saw Megan standing there, he faltered and tried to contain his visible anger. "Oh, uh, hello again."

Megan swooned in front of me, and I knew that Nate was already a distant memory. Somehow, I had a feeling that, thrown food or not, their relationship was going to end because Megan was already lusting after Adam. "Hi," she said, fluttering her eyelashes.

Shoot me now!

"Hi, Adam," his attention snapped back to me. "Megan just stopped by my work to give me a ride home and tell me about her recent breakup." Megan elbowed me so hard in the ribs that I oofed. "And I told her about the really weird group that checked in last night, and the even stranger guy from the group that came back down later and tried to get in the back room." I gave him as much of the story as possible without raising any suspicions, though I doubted Megan was even listening to me.

"I told Caleb the guy was probably just trying to get into *his* 'back room,' if you know what I mean." Apparently, she had been listening.

"That was nice of you to give him a ride," he smiled at Megan, who responded with her sexy smile.

"And I was telling him how this evil guy broke my heart and then trashed my car," she pouted. I rolled my eyes at her new version of the story. Somehow, I felt that she was not the broken-hearted one in that pair, but I kept my mouth shut.

"I'm sorry to hear that. Is there anything I can do?" Adam was either incredibly gullible, or he was playing dumb for Megan's benefit.

Her smile spread, "Well, if you have some time right now, I could use a coffee or something."

"Sounds good. I'm ready when you are." I stared at Adam, my mouth agape. Had he really just rushed over to protect me and then hardly spoken one word to me before agreeing to leave me alone again? What an ass hat!

Megan looped her arm through Adam's and led him toward the door. "See you later, Caleb," she called over her shoulder. I was too angry to respond, but not surprised that she went in for the kill so quickly.

I couldn't really blame Megan for doing what she had. Adam was extremely hot, and if I thought I stood a chance, I'd have tried something too. Not that ballsy, but something.

Now that I had some free time on my hands, I figured it was as good a time as any to call Lorelai.

"Hello, Caleb," she picked up on the second ring, sounding wide-awake and cheerful. It was nearly 6:30 in the morning, and even though I wasn't tired, I still felt that she had more energy than I did.

"Hi, sorry I didn't call you back sooner. It was a crazy night at work, and I never got a chance." I sighed and started looking through my pantry for something to eat.

"Not to worry, I understand that work is important to you. I'm glad we get this chance to talk, just the two of us. Now then, why don't you tell me what happened last night?" She sounded concerned, but mostly like she was ready to get to business.

"It wasn't really that remarkable; I was just angry about something, and then when I looked down at my hand, it looked like it was a claw. I freaked out and fell over." No point in lying to her since Adam had already told me he knew I was lying about the shampoo bottle. "By the time I got back up, my hand was fine, and Adam was knocking on the door."

She was quiet for a moment before continuing, "Did you happen to notice anything else? Feelings, sensations, pain?" This sounded a little too touchy-feely to me. Who knew being Awakened meant you had to be in touch with all those extra things in your life?

"Um--I think the water might have felt hotter, but it didn't feel uncomfortable. I don't think I was in pain. I was just embarrassed and angry, like I said."

"Did the anger seem more intense than it has in the past? Did you feel like you were losing control of it?" Her line of questioning was beginning to scare me a little. Was I going to lose control of my temper? I read paranormal books; I knew what happened to a werewolf when he got angry.

"Not that I recall. I was angry, but not to the point where I thought I was going to go crazy and punch a hole in the wall or something."

"Oh, good. I wouldn't worry about it then. You *are* almost 18, and the change is bound to be a little different for you since you didn't know about it until recently. As I'm sure Adam has explained, most of us grow up knowing what will happen when we come of age, so it's not a surprise." She sounded sure of her answer, and since I didn't have a better one, I was inclined to believe her.

"I'm glad that's settled then. What would it mean if I changed earlier than I was supposed to?"

"Well..." She seemed to think about her answer for a long time before continuing. "It has only happened once in the past that I know of, but that was a long time ago. That person was not only the Alpha for her pack, but she became the Alpha for every pack."

"How many packs are there?"

"No one knows the exact number. We've lost count since they grow and fracture all the time. There's usually one dominant pack in each country, but in some places, like Western Europe and parts of Africa, there is one pack for a couple of countries because of the population of wolves in a given area. Here in the U.S., there are packs for every few states.

"How can one person control all of those people all around the world?"

"She lived in France in the 16th Century, so as an Alpha there, she would already have had to rule a large area, but when she changed at 15, the rest of the Awakened knew something was different. She became the most powerful one of us in the world. She was not like a queen, who made the rules for everyone, but when she traveled, she was always respected and feared by those with whom she came into contact."

"That doesn't sound like a bad deal at all," I pictured myself being loved and respected or even feared by everyone I met, and it felt good.

"It wasn't, for a while. But then some Alphas grew tired of bowing down to her, and they decided to use her power rather than submit to it." Her voice seemed to get faraway as she continued. "They approached the girl and suggested she create a council, led by her, that would oversee all of the packs in the world to make sure we all stayed in line."

"Wait," I interrupted, "I thought you said she didn't control everyone or make rules for all the packs."

"She didn't, but the Council did. The Alphas that approached her wanted more power and control, so they manipulated her into believing they were helping the others when they only created fear and panic among the packs. Some packs left Europe for North America, and we've been here ever since."

"What happened to the girl?"

"Nothing, she lived for a long time, longer than anyone had before her, and the older she got, the more obsessed with the power she became. Her early years with the power-hungry Alphas had also changed her into someone who craved power. Eventually, she died in a fight for dominance, but no one has been able to hold her seat on the Council since."

"The Council still exists?" I couldn't believe that something like that was still in place.

"Yes, to some degree. Today, they have no real power because no Alpha controls everyone. New Alphas are chosen to hold a seat and act as a figurehead for their area's packs. They cannot control behavior, but they do their best to keep stories of the Awakened from getting out too often."

My mind had started to wander with the information she was giving me; I had begun to imagine what the council would look like, what their rules would be, and the kind of power they had, so I almost missed what she said. As it was, it took me a few seconds before it clicked into place.

"What did you say?"

"Our pack is in line to have a representative on the council within the next few years, which means you would be on the council. But if others challenge you and they win, they would become our Alpha and sit in your place."

"I don't understand why someone in our pack would do that?" The food I had barely touched lost all its appeal, and I pushed it away.

"Not from our pack, from any other pack. Any wolf can challenge you; if they win, they become Alpha. Most years, this doesn't happen because when an Alpha is selected for the council, they are typically older and more powerful. It's only when an Alpha is young and about to gain power that an immediate challenge is likely." She said all of this with such emotional detachment that it seemed she was talking about a plant's evolution, not my future.

"In other words, I'm screwed."

Fourteen

Late the next night, I checked my watch for the millionth time. Only three hours of work left before I could go home and feel safe again. I'd never been this uneasy in my entire life, and I didn't like it. I heard the whoosh of the door, and my stomach jumped. I'd hoped it was Adam, but what I saw caught my breath in my throat. Walking toward my desk was perhaps the most attractive guy I'd ever seen. He looked to be about my age. He was a little shorter than me, maybe 5'10" tall, but he was a bit bulkier than me as well. His hair had different streaks of color throughout, making it look like it had bits of the sun with it at all times. When he got closer, I saw that his lips were full, but since the bottom one was a little bigger than the top, he seemed to have a slight pout.

It wasn't until I met his golden-brown eyes that I realized I hadn't yet said anything, and he had been in the lobby for a full minute. "H-Hello, sir, how may I help you?" I mentally slapped myself for staring and then stuttering. I'd always been pretty shy when meeting new people, but working in customer service was fixing that until tonight, apparently.

He smiled at me, and my stomach flipped. "Hi, I was wondering if you were hiring?"

Yes! Not a guest! I did a little dance in my head, but on the outside, I remained quiet. "Do you know what type of position you are looking for?" I started chanting 'overnight!', 'overnight!' in my head, hoping he would choose something that would let us work together.

"I'm not sure; maybe I would be interested in the front desk or the restaurant." He leaned against the desk, and I leaned forward toward him before I realized what I was doing. He smiled again, and I suddenly realized I was closer than I should have been.

"I would be happy to print the application for you if you'd like, or you can just fill it out online and submit it there." I straightened up. "I'm not sure whether the restaurant is hiring. I know we are looking for someone to work overnight in the front, though." If he wasn't going to choose it on his own, a slight nudge in the right direction from me couldn't hurt. It was a lie, of course, but maybe someone would quit, and he'd get an interview or something.

His smile never wavered, even though I'm sure I got a faraway look on my face as I thought about our working together. "If you wouldn't mind printing the application, I could just fill it out and give it to you if that's okay. Maybe you can tell me about the job at the front desk."

"Sure!" I said, too happily. I pulled up our application on my computer and then clicked print. I turned my back, waiting for the application to pop out of the laser printer. I took a couple of deep breaths, tried to calm down a little, and avoid hyperventilating. When I turned around, he wasn't there anymore, and my face fell. I looked around a little, then practically jumped out of my skin when he stood up again.

"Sorry about that," he said, laughing softly as my breathing returned to normal. "My shoelace was untied."

So much for calming me down, "No problem, I'm just a little--" I wasn't sure what to say, so I smiled and pushed the form toward him. "Here you go."

He looked down at them as I did. "Great, thank you." His hand brushed mine as he took the pages, and it felt like electricity coursed up my arm. He pulled back quickly, his eyes wide, and his smile faltered.

"Sorry about that," I said, mortified. "Sometimes the static builds up back here because of the carpeting, and I shock people," I lied.

"No worries, it was just a little jolt." His smile was back, but didn't reach his honey-colored eyes. "I've survived worse."

I laughed politely, trying to hide my discomfort and struggling not to rub my arm, which was still tingling. "Oh, good, maybe you can tell me about that sometime."

He looked at me strangely, his head tilting to one side.

I realized what I had said and rushed to cover the mistake. "If you get the job working nights, I mean. We have a lot of downtime." I forced out a laugh again, but was rolling my eyes in my mind at how stupid I was acting.

"Oh, okay, that makes sense," he replied. Again, his smile didn't reach his eyes. "I'd better get started on this," he held up the form as he stepped back from the desk.

"Oh," I couldn't keep the disappointment out of my voice. "Okay, not a problem. Anything else I can do for you, just let me know. My name's Caleb," I said, hoping to keep him there even a few minutes more.

"I'm Gabriel. Nice to meet you, Caleb."

"Nice to meet you too, Gabriel."

He walked to a chair in the lobby and sat down to fill out the application. I tried to concentrate on work while he was still in the vicinity, but found it nearly impossible not to sneak glances at him. Occasionally, I would look over at him, and he would see me, so I would just smile politely and pretend I was checking the doors for new guests.

After sitting there for 20 minutes or so, I brought him a glass of ice water, which was just an excuse to be closer to him again. I'd never felt this way before, and for some reason, I couldn't help it.

"I thought you might be thirsty," I said, smiling down at him.

"Thank you." He reached for the glass as I was setting it down on the table, and it seemed like he brushed his finger on the back of my hand on purpose as he did so.

My hand felt like hot wax had been poured everywhere his finger touched, and he winced as he pulled his finger away. "Is there anything else I can bring you?" This time I couldn't keep from rubbing my hand and wished I still had the cool glass so I could use it to soothe my burning skin.

"No," he said, rubbing his finger along the glass to cool it. "This is all I need," he held up the application I had just printed. "Thanks again for the water, though."

"All right. I will just let you finish that on your own." My smile felt fake, and the ache in my hand was slightly more painful than the one in my chest. I started to walk back to the front desk, a little disappointed.

"What's it like?" He asked.

"What's what like?" I responded. Yeah, I'm quite the conversationalist.

"The hotel. What's it like working here?"

"Oh, it's fabulous. Well, most of the time, it is. The guests are usually nice, and the night shift keeps things interesting." I gave him a look that said there was more to the answer than I was saying aloud.

"What do you mean?"

"Well, there are the normal 'crazies' who stumble into the hotel after a night of drinking in the Gas Lamp, tourists who haven't adjusted to the time change yet, so they end up in the lobby at strange hours, and then there are the people who are just good for people watching. I have a whole system down; everyone falls into groups. If you get a job here, maybe I can teach you my categories and how to spot them," I smiled down at him, loving the idea of us working closely with each other.

"Sounds like fun. I'm not really a 'people watcher,' but I'd love to hear more about your system." His eyes seemed to catch the light from a nearby lamp and began to give off a honey-colored glow. I blinked a few times, thinking I'd imagined it.

"As I said, I'm happy to help you learn. And who knows, I might make a people watcher out of you along the way." I laughed a little, hoping I didn't sound as desperate to him as I did to me. I don't know how to flirt, and right now, I was crashing and burning in my attempts to keep our conversation rolling. "Well, I'd better let you finish that application, or I might keep you here with me all night long."

He chuckled softly, and although it was a pleasing sound, I was a little miffed that he was laughing at the thought of spending the night talking to me. "I should be finished soon, and I'll let you get back to your people watching." He winked at me, and I blushed so much that my face felt like it was overheating, and I worried I would become a sweaty mess.

"Thank you, I will…uh…I'll just be over there if you, uh…need me, er…um…anything." I stumbled away, rolling my eyes at my stupid brain. Of all the times to run out of words, it had to be in front of one of the hottest guys I'd ever met.

I spent the next ten minutes pretending to work while sneaking glances at Gabriel. He kept his attention fixed on his cell phone and the application. Just before 4:00 a.m. he appeared at the counter, which caused me to jump a little because I hadn't heard him approach.

"I'm all done. Thanks again for your time. I hope we get to work together; you seem like a cool guy." He slid the application across the desk to me and then reached out his hand to shake mine. I was a little hesitant because of earlier pain, but I wasn't going to ignore him, so I mentally prepared for the shock and grasped his hand in mine.

The electricity was still present, but now it was almost so hot it was numbing, and I didn't realize I'd held on to his hand for longer than was socially acceptable until I could feel him struggling to break the contact. I gave him a small apologetic smile and then picked up the application from the counter.

"I'll make sure to get this to my manager when he comes in later this morning. You should hear something from him within a week or so."

"Okay, great, thanks a lot for your help. I hope you have a good night, Caleb."

"You too!" And with that, he walked out of the hotel and disappeared into the darkness of downtown.

Fifteen

The rest of my shift passed without any incidents, but I still felt incredibly uncomfortable the whole time I was there, so when my replacement showed up, I rushed through my closing procedures and left a few minutes early. The sound of downtown San Diego in the morning assaulted my ears, which had become used to the soft jazz music playing in the lobby. The smell of the city this morning was particularly pungent, and the gasoline fumes, coffee, and breakfast smell all mixed together caused my stomach to growl and lurch at the same time.

"Caleb!" Adam yelled at me from across the street. I started walking over to him, happy to see that he hadn't entirely abandoned me, and froze as a car horn blared at me from a few feet away just before it was about to crash into me. I reacted automatically and jumped out of the way, landing in a crouched position on the other side of the street near

Adam. "Holy crap! Are you okay?" Adam ran over to where I was standing and looked me over for any signs of damage.

"Yeah, I think I'm okay," I said, checking my body for any cuts." I don't know what happened. I didn't even see that car coming. How could I have been that stupid?" I was terrible about jaywalking, but usually smart enough to make sure no cars were coming. "Did anyone see what I did?" We looked around to make sure no one was going to rush to my aid.

"Looks like they didn't see or didn't care enough to stop on their way to work," he said, grabbing my elbow as I made my way to the table.

I sat down quickly, trying to avoid any further attention. "I thought you'd left me for good. You never came back yesterday after disappearing with Megan." I smiled, but there was still some pain in my voice as I said it.

Adam sat back down but kept facing the street, making sure there were no more surprises this morning. "I was just trying to get her away from your apartment. If other packs knew she was attached to you somehow, they could try to use her to get to you. When she said she wanted coffee, I knew I could get her away from your place without raising suspicion."

It made sense for him to get her away safely, and I was a little embarrassed that I'd gotten as angry as I had yesterday when they both ditched me. Admittedly, hearing that he wasn't as interested in Megan as he seemed last night was strangely comforting. I shook the feeling off because I wanted

Megan to be happy, even if it meant she got the guy who had saved my life. I wasn't sure Adam was the right guy for me, even if I did still dream about kissing him sometimes, which was a nice change from the usual inescapable darkness.

I didn't want to think about it anymore, though, so I changed the subject. "Did you get a chance to talk to Karen about the strange people in the hotel? Who were they?"

"They're from another pack on the west coast; they usually stay in the northwest, but since your return, they've been spotted throughout California and most recently here in San Diego. The group the other night was the Alpha and her guards; she cannot officially do anything to you until you've awakened, but that won't stop her from seeking an opportunity to scare you off from the challenge before it takes place."

Great, I can't be outright attacked, but I can be scared to death, basically. "And what happens if I were to die 'by accident?'" I used air quotes to reference my car accident, which had most likely been the other pack, and my stupidity, which nearly got me run over.

"There's no punishment if there is no proof. But since you lived and I rescued you, they know you're being watched and protected by our pack, so they probably won't try anything." Despite his assurances, I knew there was no way to guarantee my safety. I had to prove that I could handle myself in a fight before I would be relatively safe from attack.

Adam's cell phone started to ring, and it snapped me out of the negative thoughts I had begun to have. "Hello?" His face paled, and he turned away slightly, covering the mouthpiece. "When? Where did it happen? Okay, I'm on my way, and I'm bringing Caleb." He hung up his phone and grabbed his things without looking at me. "We have to go."

I stood up, my feet protesting since I had spent the past eight hours on them, but I followed behind him quietly. Once we got in his car and he was speeding toward the freeway, I finally got up the courage to find out what was happening. "Where're we going?"

"Karen's house," he said quietly. Seeing Karen again so soon sounded great, and I thought it would give me a chance to spend some time away from Adam for a change. I was much happier than I had been moments before.

"Oh, okay, but can we stop at a drive-thru on the way?"

"No." He said it with such finality that I almost didn't say anything, but my big mouth and I have never backed down from lousy timing.

"Why not? I'm starving!"

"Caleb, Karen was killed last night." Adam was on autopilot now, driving and speaking without thought or emotion, and his declaration of Karen's death hit me like a slap.

"What?" My mind felt like it had shut down, and I was shocked into silence, which Adam did not fill with an explanation. I was left to think things through on my own. I was sure her death had something to do with me since she was a member of my pack and had protected me the night before.

It didn't take long to arrive at her house on the outskirts of downtown. Its cheery yellow exterior, complete with white, red, and pink rose bushes, made it seem like we were there for a party rather than gathering at the site of a murder. There were cars in the driveway and parked in front of the house, but there was a noticeable lack of police presence, so I was expecting things to have been cleaned up and all evidence cleared away. But when I walked into the house, my nostrils were assaulted with the scent of blood. Lots of blood. There was a sweet, coppery scent to it that I'd never noticed before. Even with the not altogether unpleasant odor, I was glad that I hadn't eaten breakfast. Underneath all the blood, I could smell another scent that was familiar to me. It was the man who had tried to corner me in the back at the hotel.

I turned to Adam, "I know who did this."

"So do we. But there isn't anything we can do about it right now. There is no way to prove who started the fight between Karen and Dominic, the other Awakened. If we retaliate, they have the right to attack us at will, which means they could attack you. This is a warning to us. We need to be much more careful. They knew that Karen was connected to you, and they attacked and killed her. Now none of us are safe."

As Adam was describing how the people close to me were in danger, my mind suddenly went to Gabriel. Could they have been watching us interact? Would they know I found him attractive and use him to hurt me even more? I remembered the electricity that seemed to ripple up my arm when we barely touched, and I started to rub my arm where the sensation had traveled.

"Are you okay?" Adam looked at me a little too critically, which meant I had done something wrong. I dropped my arms to my side.

"Yeah, just shaken up by all of this," I gestured to the too-quiet house. "I've never known anyone who died from something other than old age, and I'm just trying to cope with the fact that she's dead."

"I understand. Take your time. I'll be right back." Adam left me standing where I was and went to talk to the others in the tiny house. The only two I recognized were Brent and Carlos. I assumed the others were also in the pack, but I wasn't in the mood to make friends.

I looked around her living room, where everything seemed in order and still had a homey feel. The outside of the house was bright, but the inside was muted. Pops of crisp white accessories accented soft blues and tans. Even though I didn't want to see what had happened to Karen, I forced myself deeper into her home. The door to her office was open, and Carlos looked around inside. He nodded at me as I entered. I moved through the room slowly, careful not to touch anything, including Karen's body. It was covered with a sheet that thankfully protected my mind from storing the image of her ravaged body in my subconscious.

It was clear from the amount of blood splattered around the room that this was where the fight occurred and that once she walked into the office, she never left. Her desk had been knocked over in the struggle, and broken glass and paperclips were strewn all over the ground. Her laptop had been snapped in half and had bloody fingerprints on one side. I hoped she had gotten in a few good shots before passing away.

Anger suddenly flowed through my body, and the fire I had felt earlier was nothing compared to the intense heat that filled me now. I could hear a soft growling from down the hall, but I didn't bother looking to see who it was. I closed my eyes and tried to calm down before doing something I regretted.

"Are you okay?" Adam reached out and grabbed my shoulder.

My eyes shot open, and my vision seemed to blur and get fuzzy as I tried to get my anger under control. "No, I'm not," I managed to choke out. "Karen died because she protected me, and now I have to live with that forever."

He gripped me harder, digging his fingers into my shoulder, "I can smell your wolf again. You need to calm down."

His words hit me like cold water, shocking me out of my anger almost instantly. I looked back at him, afraid of what would happen if I changed too early. "What am I supposed to do?" Tears pooled in the corners of my eyes, streaking down my cheeks when I blinked. Now that the heat of my anger had vanished, it was replaced by an ache in my chest.

Adam released his grip on my shoulder and took a step back, "I'm not sure, but we should get out of here. I'm sorry I brought you. We don't need to be here for this. There isn't anything I can do to help out."

I wanted to protest, but I knew I was probably more of a distraction than a help, so I agreed. I apologized in my head to Karen for not being able to do something to save her and then said goodbye to Carlos, who continued his search through the house.

Sixteen

Adam spoke with Lorelai about what happened, and they decided it was best that we didn't go back to my apartment, and after seeing what happened to Karen, I didn't disagree with them. Lorelai and the other pack members met at her house and decided they would shift me from one place to another over the next few weeks, and today I would be stationed in Adam's apartment downtown. The whole feeling of the place was different from what I'd expected for some reason. He looked like a stereotypical surfer guy when he wasn't dressed in his work clothes, so I expected something right on the beach. When I walked through his door, I found dark, masculine colors and exposed brick walls that spanned the entire length of one side of his home.

It was the kind of look that should have screamed bachelor, but the minimal decorations and total lack of gaming systems, pizza boxes, and posters of curvy women with barely-there clothing made it look like this bachelor was much older than his 21 years. His black leather sectional was flanked by dark wooden media towers filled with a variety of action and horror movies, including three shelves of nothing but werewolf films. I raised my eyebrow at him and smiled.

"What? Everyone has hobbies," he said, sorting through some mail he'd picked up when we walked into the building. "Mine just happens to be watching Hollywood's take on shifters. Most of it is so far off, but they will occasionally get something right, which usually means someone involved in the film is an Awakened."

My mouth dropped open. "Why would they give away real information?"

"Relax, it's never anything that could hurt us by getting out. And anyway, the funny thing is that most of the movies that get it completely wrong have Awakened writers whose sole purpose is to continue the myths by adding fake additions to the legends."

"So I guess getting my facts from the American Werewolf movies was probably not the best idea?"

Adam just laughed at me and shook his head as he walked away. "Great movie pick, though."

"Hey, I didn't know…I just figured I'd start somewhere, and I love those movies!"

I could hear his laughter from down the hall, but I wasn't sure if I should follow him, so I stood in the living room and looked at the few pictures he had hanging on the wall. Most were black and white landscapes that had a gritty appeal. "Nice photos," I said before remembering he had left the room.

"Thanks." His response was so close to my ear that I jumped and swung out with my arms as I tried to escape him, but I managed to fall onto the couch. Adam stood smiling down at me. "You weren't paying attention, Caleb. I was barely trying to sneak up on you, and I shouldn't have been able to get as close as I did without your noticing."

Trying to play off my reaction, I smiled back devilishly. "Who says I didn't know you were there? I could feel you lean close, but it didn't bother me, so why move away? Why do you think I spoke so quietly?" The lies poured out of me so quickly that I surprised even myself. "I watched you leave the room. Why wouldn't I yell to you if I didn't realize you were close?" I could feel the confidence grow in my voice, and it caused my smile to become more forceful. "I just liked having you close to me." I winked at him, then stood and ran a finger down his chest to his belt buckle.

I could see him fighting to keep from backing up as he processed what I had just said. It was an impressive response for a straight guy. Most of the guys I knew in high school would have already thrown punches well before I touched them. "Oh," was all he managed to say.

I burst out laughing, unable to stay in character. "I'm totally kidding. You scared the crap out of me! I don't usually flail around like that when I am fully aware of where other people are in relation to myself."

He seemed to relax, and his goofy smile returned, which meant the dimple on his left cheek made a rare appearance. "Well, I'll give you this: your ability to lie is improving. Your heart didn't speed up at all. You became more relaxed and comfortable as you spoke, which usually means you're telling the truth."

"I'm finally gaining some control over how I react around you! It's about time!" We both laughed, and the tension that had begun building in the room dissipated quickly. "So, what now?"

"Now, we see what you're made of." The heat coming from Adam's eyes made me start to sweat.

"Wh-What do you mean?"

Adam lifted his shirt over his head, exposing the muscled planes of his chest and stomach. "Let me show you." He reached out and took my hand, pressing it into the middle of his chest. A little bit of hair that he had tickled the sides of my fingers.

My mind immediately went blank, and I tried very hard to concentrate, looking only at my hand and not the golden skin beyond it.

"Show me what?"

"There is so much to being Awakened that has nothing to do with fighting for power. We possess what some might call animal magnetism. In reality, it is a unique ability to influence those around us by touch or scent."

"Which means what exactly?" I could feel my hand heating up against his skin as it continued to rest there. "I can make someone love me just by touching them?" It was a dumb joke, but leave it to me to take things there.

"Why don't you try it?"

I looked up at him finally, convinced he was making fun of me again, but his eyes held no trace of humor, so I allowed myself to believe it. "Okay, what do I do?"

"You have to imagine the thing that you want; that desire, need, or hunger flowing from inside you and into the other person."

I still didn't believe him, but I figured there was no harm in trying. I closed my eyes and thought about my attraction to Adam. I imagined that attraction was a physical thing that I held inside. Then I imagined it moving from my brain, heart, and stomach and getting channeled down my arm and into his chest. I willed him to kiss me.

He reached out and lifted my shirt, exposing my stomach, and he placed his hand just above my hipbone. My cheeks flushed, and the skin in contact with his hand began heating up. It was as though I could feel the energy moving from inside me to his chest and coming from his hand into my body. When I opened my eyes, he was leaning toward me, and my breath caught in my lungs.

His face crept closer to my own until he was so close that I closed my eyes, waiting for the kiss that I was sure would happen. And then I felt his lips against my ear as he whispered, "I want a cheeseburger."

I was so confused that my mind wouldn't even allow rational thought to enter it. And it was a full ten seconds later, when my stomach began to growl, that I fully understood what had just happened.

"You asshole! You told me I could make people fall in love with me!" My face was hot from embarrassment and anger, and I thought about punching him, but I knew that it wouldn't do any good, and he would probably just laugh even harder.

"No, you asked if you could make people fall in love with you, and I told you that you should try it out. I never said it would work." He was smiling down at me, but was gracious enough not to laugh in my face.

"Well, you implied that it would work, and now, instead of love, I have an overwhelming desire to eat cheeseburgers." Adam did start laughing at this point, and I couldn't blame him, so I laughed right along. "I hate you."

"No, you don't. You want me. I could feel it, remember? And what did you expect? You haven't awakened yet."

"Wait, then how did you know what I was thinking?" Now I was really confused.

"Just because you haven't awakened doesn't mean I haven't. Remember that day we first trained in Balboa Park? You told me why you moved back to San Diego and leaned into my body. Do you remember feeling anything coming from me?"

I thought back and remembered feeling his acceptance, which I had assumed was my interpretation of the situation and not a genuine feeling he was sharing with me. "I didn't realize that was real…" I stared at him, not sure what to think anymore.

"But let's get one thing straight, you don't love me. You were just trying to get me to kiss you again. And trust me, that comes from something a bit south of the heart." The realization of what Adam had just said sank in, and I was immediately red again.

"Okay, I can't make you fall in love with me. What can I do?"

"You can't make anyone do something they wouldn't usually do, for example, make a straight guy fall in love with another guy. But you can cause someone to find you more attractive if they are already interested. You can convince people, or other Awakened mostly, to follow you, the Alpha, if they are not interested in being the Alpha themselves."

"I don't have to fight off everyone then, only the ones who would have challenged me anyway?"

"Right, you can let them know you are the Alpha through your scent; that way, they will treat you as the Alpha you are. They'll leave you alone if they aren't also high in their pack's rank."

"How do I send out a scent that says, 'I didn't want this, please don't kill me'?"

"That you can't do—you were born an Alpha, and you cannot be anything but an Alpha, no matter what you do."

"Which means…?"

He hesitated before answering me. "You lead, or you die."

Seventeen

Two weeks had passed since Karen was murdered, and we were still no closer to stopping things from escalating than we were when we first found out about it. Adam continued working with me on my defense training, trying to improve my fighting. Except for the few times I got lucky, I didn't think I was any better now than I was when we started.

He and Brent were trading off watching me, but would often leave me alone at work, so I could still have some space and normalcy, or as much as possible. I assumed that meant someone from the pack was around, but I didn't ask. I had seen other people at Karen's house helping to sort through what was there, but I hadn't seen any of them since. And when Adam asked if I wanted to meet more of the pack, I decided against it. Losing Karen had been hard enough, and I had only spent a few hours with her. I wouldn't be able to handle it if more of the pack were hurt for protecting me, especially since I was supposed to be their leader.

The one good thing that had happened was Gabriel getting a job at the hotel. Since I'd been lying about the overnight front desk position, he had been offered a valet and bell desk attendant job. He was on a rotating schedule, so we only worked together a couple of days a week, but I tried to shift my breaks to match up with his so we could spend time together.

He wasn't kidding about not being a people watcher. He never even looked out at the street for more than a couple of minutes. Meanwhile, I had problems trying to stay focused on just him, even given the extreme level of attraction I felt. When other people were around, it was as if I were a puppy, and they were shiny new toys. I was at a constant level of mild paranoia, which I thought was healthy given the situation.

However, tonight was not one of Gabriel's night shifts, so I was at the front alone, not paying attention to the current valet guy, who was probably smoking around the corner of the building anyway. When the front doors swooshed open, I felt the mild panic I always did now, but when I saw my parents' smiling faces, it was quickly replaced with an overwhelming sense of joy.

I hadn't seen my parents since I'd moved to San Diego and it was good to see them again. After my accident, I hadn't had much free time to call, so having them come to surprise me was the best thing I could have imagined.

"Mom! Dad! What are you doing here?" I walked around the front of the desk and hugged them both.

"We had nothing going on at home and hadn't seen you in so long that we figured we'd surprise you." My Dad's hazel eyes had a kind of sadness that never seemed to go away unless he was looking at my mom or talking to me. That was when I noticed that he looked happy. It made me miss them both even more than I already did.

"I'm so glad you're here! How did you know I was working?" I hadn't given them my new schedule, and I usually would have been off tonight.

"Sue told us. We stopped by your apartment, but you weren't there, so we went down to say hello to her, and she told us you were working tonight." Sue didn't technically know my schedule, but since I was reasonably sure she was keeping an eye on me for my mom, she probably realized my hours had changed and started keeping a record. Hopefully, she didn't also mention that I was conspicuously absent a lot, and there were suddenly new people around she'd never seen before.

"Mom, you need to tell her to stop watching out for me so closely! I am legally an adult now; I don't need another mother keeping tabs on my comings and goings." I laughed so she knew I was kidding, though the thought of moving did sound good. "But, I'm glad she told you where to find me! What are you planning to do while you're in town? And how long are you staying? Where are you staying?"

"We're just here for the weekend. We thought we'd find a room at a hotel near your apartment." My dad said, yawning quietly.

"Why don't you stay here? I can comp you a room for the weekend." I couldn't, but what they didn't know couldn't hurt them. And in the grand scheme of lies, this seemed like the most forgivable.

"Caleb, you know that's not why we came here…" my mother began.

"I know, Mom, but let me do this for you. I'm working right now anyway, and you're already here. I'll get you a room, you two can get some sleep, and we can all go out for breakfast in the morning." I had already walked back to the desk to check our reservation system to find out where I could afford to put them. After a few clicks, it was done, and I got their keys ready for them. "Here you go. Your room is on the 6th floor. I want you both to go and get some sleep, and I'll come and wake you up in the morning for breakfast." I returned to the front of the check-in desk and handed my father the room keys.

"Thank you so much, Caleb. I wasn't sure your father could make it back to Mission Valley without falling asleep." My mom reached out and pulled me into her arms. It had been so long since someone I loved had held me that I found I was practically melting into her embrace. After hugging my mother, my father pulled me into his arms and held me tightly.

As I told my parents goodnight, I heard the front doors slide open. My nose immediately wrinkled, and all of the hair on my neck stood on end. I turned around quickly and went back to the front desk, where a familiar-looking man was waiting.

"Carlos! What are you doing here?" I sighed.

"Hi Caleb, I just stopped by to see how you were doing. I hadn't seen you since Karen's..." he seemed to be searching for a word to use, but had come up short. "Well, you know."

"I understand. I haven't been feeling much like seeing other people lately. I feel responsible for her death, even though I wasn't the one to do it, and facing the pack isn't something I think I can handle right now."

"Caleb, you shouldn't blame yourself. Everyone in the pack knew the risks they were taking on when we decided to help you. Karen did what she did, knowing full well that she may lose her life for trying to protect you." He looked me in the eyes as he said it, but there was no warmth and indeed no feeling of comfort from his words. "But that's not why I'm here, and there's no need to bring up what has already passed. Your mother sent me to ensure you are doing all right."

"You can tell her that I'm doing fine and I'm still working hard to be the leader she wants me to be." I couldn't tell Carlos I wasn't getting better at fighting. If he told Lorelai, she would only worry more and send more bodyguards to their deaths to protect me.

"She will be glad to hear that." He smiled at me, but there was still less warmth than I'd hoped for. "Who were those people you were helping earlier? It looked as though you knew."

"Oh, those are my parents." It felt strange to tell someone who knew my birth mother about the people I considered my real parents. "They surprised me by driving in from my hometown, so I got them a hotel room for the night."

"I'd love to meet them while they're here! Maybe we can get together for dinner tomorrow night; you, your parents, and the pack."

Having my parents meet the whole pack at the same time I do? No thanks. "Yeah, we'll see. I'm not sure what they have planned for tomorrow, so I can't guarantee anything, but I'll let them know when they wake up in the morning."

"That sounds fine. I know my Rosa would love to see you again, and I promise the pack will be on their best behavior." He stepped back from the front desk and glanced around the lobby as if he were looking for someone. After a few seconds, he seemed satisfied, winked at me, and strode toward the door. "Hope to see you tomorrow for dinner," he called. As he left, the sounds and smells of downtown San Diego filled the lobby. Buses rumbled by, the distant sounds of music pouring out of bars, and a hint of cinnamon and sugar from the all-night bakery down the block all assaulted my nose.

I smiled and waved as he walked out the door, happy to be alone again but feeling even lonelier than

I had before. My parents showing up reminded me of my life with them, which didn't feel compatible with my new reality with the pack. I knew I'd have to meet them eventually, but I didn't think I could do it with my parents in the room. How could I tell them that the boy they raised would soon be a monster?

Eighteen

Blood was everywhere I looked. It covered my hands and my arms, and even though I couldn't see them, I could feel that my face and neck were also sticky from it. Its rich coppery taste filled my mouth, and although it wasn't an unpleasant taste, I tried to spit out as much as I could.

Three weeks had passed since Karen's death, and we were no closer to finding a way to stop the attacks from the other pack. Fortunately, there hadn't been another attempt on my life lately, but Lorelai worried it could happen at any time, so I was forced into intense fight sessions where I had to face numerous people from the pack at once. It hadn't been going well so far, and my body ached constantly, but I knew I had to keep trying if I wanted to live beyond my birthday.

"Again!" he yelled from the shadows, and I knew the pain was far from over.

They all ran toward me again, their claws extended, reaching for the soft, pale skin that covered my ribs. I sidestepped one easily, but the other one was used to this and compensated. She easily grabbed me by the throat and bit down on my shoulder. Luckily, her teeth were not any sharper than a normal human's, so she only left an imprint on the skin rather than tearing open my flesh.

"Enough!" I yelled into the darkness. "I can't do this anymore. I'm tired. Please, leave me alone."

The pack members laughed, but they were cut off by Adam's voice. "That's not going to happen," he said angrily. "You're not calling the shots here today. I am. Again!"

I could see their eyes glowing as they watched me, tracking my every move. It had been three hours of nonstop fighting, and I still hadn't been able to avoid being pinned. The only positive thing about the afternoon was that I was learning to tap into my anger. One of the pack members had tackled me to the ground, and while he gloated, I bit down so hard on his hand that I drew blood. I guess he figured that blood for blood was fair, so he broke my nose. Adam had to remind him that, unlike them, I wasn't able to shift to heal myself. After that, they'd still pushed me hard but hadn't done any real damage other than maybe causing a few bruises.

Now they had begun shifting to prepare me for that as well. Some remained mostly human, while others had entirely changed into wolf form. One seemed to be stuck in the middle. He was the one who had been glaring at me from the shadows and was now running full speed toward me, his mouth open. His hand had healed when he shifted, but his grudge was still apparent. I guess, even with Adam's reminder, he didn't feel we were even.

I could see that his teeth had sharpened with the change, and I knew that if he bit down, it would leave more than just an imprint. I tried to shut my brain off and let my instincts take over, but it kept screaming for me to run away. It turns out my fight or flight instinct chose flight first and foremost. I guess those years of bullying from high school taught me that it was easier to walk away when things got physical. But this wasn't high school anymore, and these weren't bullies trying to push me around for being gay. These were werewolves, and they were trying to kill me.

I stared him down as he ran toward me and saw saliva drip from a lengthened canine before landing on the ground. As I watched, everything around me seemed to slow down. The air was already heavy with the scent of blood and sweat. But now, it seemed to become even thicker, making it appear like he was moving through mud. I knelt on the floor to create a solid base for myself, and when he got close enough, I exploded upward. I imagined my fist punching through the soft skin under his jaw and through the top of his head. As that happened, his momentum brought his arms forward, allowing me to dislocate one at the elbow.

When I opened my eyes, I could hear someone screaming. I looked around the room, trying to find out what had happened. Thinking it was perhaps me making the noise, I covered my mouth but realized that my lips were closed. I looked behind me and saw the wolves shifting back into their human form, and the others surrounding the man who had attacked me. He was lying on his back, and his arm was bent at a strange angle, but I could see from where I stood that his face and skull were in one piece.

"What happened? What did I do? Is he going to be all right?" No one looked at me, and no one answered. They just sat there in stunned silence as the screaming continued. I moved closer, "Can he heal? Is he going to shift?" Again, my questions were met with silence.

"Perfect, Caleb, you have a natural ability to protect yourself. We just have to work on how you tap into it." With that, Adam opened the door behind him and left the room. All that was left was me and five werewolves.

I looked back at the group huddled around their injured friend and figured now was the best time to leave to avoid fighting the rest. I had only met the pack in its entirety the day before, and now I felt like I was making an impression I might not be able to live up to.

As I walked out of the small space and wandered down the hallway, I couldn't help but think back on my life just a few weeks prior. My biggest concern back then was whether or not my new boss hated me, and now I felt as though I would be lucky if I survived long enough to celebrate my birthday. I followed the hallway until I found the door leading to the outside and freedom from fighting for the afternoon.

"Caleb! What happened to your face?" Lorelai was sitting on her back porch, which faced the building I'd been fighting in for the past few hours. When she saw me walk out into the sunlight, her eyes widened, but there were no other signs of concern. I guess that comes with the territory.

"I'm fine, I've been sparring, and things got a little out of control." I reached up and wiped my hand across my face, but when my thumb brushed the tip of my nose, the explosion of pain reminded me that I needed to get this set fast. "Is there someone here who could set my nose? I think it broke during one of my practice fights."

Before discovering I was Awakened, I had never broken a bone or even sustained any serious injury. The first night I entered this world, I sprained my wrist trying to punch Adam in the face, and now my nose was broken. My 17-year streak of near-perfect health had come to an end.

"Of course! Rosa," she called into the house, "please ask Olivia to come look at Caleb's nose." As I got closer to the house, I could hear Rosa speaking frantically in Spanish on the telephone.

"Come here and let me see what happened to you." Lorelai's eyes had lost their shocked expression and changed into something softer without losing their sharp edge. I sat on the rickety chair next to her and tried to relax. I could tell that when the chair was first made, it had probably been a light shade of blue. Age and exposure had worn it down to its natural wood color, and only the most stubborn paint still clung to hidden edges and deep crevices that marred the chair.

"This looks serious. Who did this to you?"

"It doesn't matter who did this. I'm sure that if they hadn't been part of our pack, I would've suffered much more than just a broken nose."

"You're right, but that doesn't mean I don't worry about you. I am your mother, after all, even if I didn't raise you."

Lorelai had been a little uneasy since I told her my parents had come to town. I knew she appreciated what they had done for me, but I could also tell from her reaction to the news that she felt like they were intruding on the life she was trying to build with me. "I'm not saying you don't have to worry, just that there's no reason to be upset about something as small as a broken nose when my life and the lives of everyone else here are in danger."

She focused her eyes a little closer on my face, and a hint of a smile played on her lips, "That's something your father would have said. I wish you could have known him; he was a great man and leader."

"I wish I could have met him too…maybe then some of this would be easier. I wouldn't have to fight so hard to catch up to where I'm expected to be."

She reached out and took my hands in hers. "Caleb, I know this is hard, and I wish I could make it easier, but we are all here to help you."

"I know that, but I'm supposed to lead this pack, so I need to learn how to take care of myself." I thought back on all the sparring I'd been doing lately. I was being forced to fight without input until I gave up or caused enough damage to stop the group long enough to escape. However, today was the first time that had happened. When it was over, Adam, Brent, or Carlos would talk to me about the things I had done wrong and the one or two things I was doing right. Today's comment from Adam was the most positive so far. Probably because today was the only day I walked out relatively unscathed.

"We are dedicated to training you to take control of the pack. I know Adam and the others will do everything in their power to make sure that happens, even if the methods are somewhat harsh."

The sound of tires crunching along the gravel driveway pulled our attention to the front of the house, and I hoped Olivia had finally arrived to fix my nose. Breathing from my mouth was starting to annoy me.

"Back here, Olivia!" Lorelai called out. She must have seen the confusion on my face. "Her tires make a unique sound, and I can smell her." That was another good reason to get my nose back in order.

Olivia walked around the side of the house, carrying what looked like a cross between a purse and a doctor's bag. "Hi Caleb," she smiled at me, and I was surprised at how young she looked. I vaguely remember her face in the crowd when I finally met the whole pack, but I never expected she would be the one coming to help.

"Uh…Hi, Olivia. How are you?" I tried to recover from my confusion quickly, and if she noticed my staring, she didn't mention anything.

"Better than you from the look of things," she gestured to my blood-covered shirt and arms. "Let me see if I can fix that for you." She set the bag down and started pulling a few things out. Among them was a pair of gloves, two hollow tubes, and a nasty-looking chisel-type object.

Oh god, what was that for?

I watched as she put the gloves on and picked up the tubes. "Okay, I can do this fast, or the slightly less painful but longer way. Which would you rather have?"

"The one without the chisel!" I looked at the offending equipment and held my hand out to keep it away from me.

She and Lorelai laughed. "The fast way it is then. Do you want to put some ice on it before we start?" I was still trying to figure out how the chisel was the less painful option, so I almost missed her question.

"Will that help?"

"Not really," she answered honestly. "It just makes your skin a little more numb and could stop you from swelling up, but once it's fixed, you shouldn't have much swelling anyway."

"Then let's just get it over with. I'll ice it after if it hurts." I could feel my stomach clenching up, and I thought I might get sick, so I tried to concentrate on my breathing.

"All right, let's do it." She put on the gloves and got something that looked like skinny needle-nose pliers, an appropriate name for the occasion. She stuck the ends into each nostril and expanded them while looking up both sides. "It looks like it's a fairly easy fix, considering…Caleb, I'm going to count three and then push on each side, trying to align them. I need you to sit perfectly still while I do that."

I wasn't sure I could sit still while parts of my face were being forced in different directions, but I nodded anyway, "I'll do my best."

She placed her thumbs on either side of my nose, "Ready? One, two." As I waited for three, she had already forced the two parts of my nose back together. In addition to the pain that immediately hit me, my eyes began to water to the point where I found it nearly impossible to see. I blinked rapidly, trying to clear the tears from my eyes, and as I did, I heard an almost imperceptible pop.

"There we go, good as new." Olivia took a step back to admire her handiwork. "Breathe in through your nose for me."

I took a careful breath through my now-fixed nose, and the air passed through without obstruction, but it stung like crazy, causing my eyes to water again.

"Perfect!" She picked up some gauze and the little green tubes. "Okay, I'm going to put this up your nose to keep it from slipping back out of place. Give it a couple of days, and we'll see how everything looks."

When she finally finished, I felt like I had the worst cold ever, and my nose still hurt. "Thanks for your help, Olivia," I said. "I think I'll take that ice."

Nineteen

Later that afternoon, I felt something was missing in my life, and I realized it was Megan, whom I hadn't seen in quite a while. Since Karen was killed, I hadn't spent much time in my apartment, which meant I hadn't been near Megan lately either. I knew she would probably hold a grudge, and I figured I also knew the way to smooth things over. Adam. I decided a little retail friend therapy was just what we needed.

I dialed her number and was surprised that she actually answered on the first ring. "Hey Megan, I know you're probably pissed at me for not calling, but…"

"Pissed! Pissed? Why would I be mad?" Uh oh, I was in for it. "It's not like my best friend completely disappeared on me suddenly and refused to return my phone calls."

I wasn't surprised by her anger, and I didn't want to dismiss her emotions, so I let her yell at me for a few more minutes before she finally gave up. "Do you feel better?"

"Yes. Thank you." I could hear the smile in her voice, which was a good sign, and my cue to continue.

"Glad to hear it. I apologize for my very un-BFF behavior; I have been a huge flake and impossible to get in touch with, and I'm truly sorry. I'd like to make it up to you by taking you on a date. A three-way date, if you will." I knew this would get her attention.

"Caleb, you know I'm kinda kinky, but even that sounds a bit outside my comfort zone." Her joke was proof that she had already forgiven me, and what I was about to do would make up for messing up really badly in the future. Or earn me the right to ask for a big favor in the future if I needed something.

"I'm not sure that it is. I know who and what you've done in the past. Meet me at Fashion Valley in an hour and make sure you look good for me and our date." I hung up before she could ask any questions and ruin the surprise. Then I went to the bathroom and checked my gauze. Still hanging in there, no pun intended. It was barely noticeable unless you looked right up my nose. The bruising under my eyes from the break was starting to fade already, and it looked like I was more tired than battered. Maybe Lorelai would have some concealer I could use to make myself look more presentable for the public. I'd have to ask before heading out.

For now, I needed to shower badly. Once Olivia finished with my nose, I rinsed off my arms and face in the sink, but I was still grimy. Based on the way I looked, I assumed the smell wafting from me was strong, so I carefully removed my shirt, which was soaked in blood and sweat, and threw it in the garbage. There was no returning from that much nastiness, and even if there were, I wouldn't wear it again. I was about to take off my pants when the bathroom door opened and hit me in the back.

One perk about living alone—no one walks in on you in the bathroom, so you don't have to lock the doors. I had to remember that it wasn't my house, and locks always needed to be engaged before nudity occurred.

"Oh, sorry about that." Adam's voice caused me to snap back into the present and grab the door before he could close it.

"Actually, I'm glad you found me." He gave me a strange look as he peeked around the door and saw me in the middle of undressing. "Not like that." I rolled my eyes. "I want to hang out with Megan today, and I'm hoping you'll come with me."

His face lit up a little too much for my liking, but I had to deal with the fact that guys always preferred Megan to me. It was just an unfortunate truth about them that I needed to accept. "Yeah, that sounds like something I can handle."

"Great." I let go of the door and nudged it shut with my back. "Then get out of here and let me clean up."

Thirty minutes later, we were out the door and speeding down the freeway toward San Diego again. As we got closer, the familiar sights of the city made me feel homesick and miss my little apartment, even if it was a little rough around the edges.

"When do you think I'll be able to move back into my apartment?" I asked Adam, hopeful that he would be able to give me a timeline for my return.

"Never." He said it so matter-of-factly that I was confused, thinking I had missed a conversation about what would happen next.

"What the hell? Why Not?"

"Caleb, be realistic. It's easier to watch out for you if you live with the pack and easier to hide you from other Awakened along the way." He looked me in the eyes, seemingly trying to will me to understand.

"I get that, I do. But why don't I get a say in this situation? If I'm supposed to become the Alpha, why don't my opinions matter to anyone?"

He lifted his hands from the steering wheel and gave a little shrug, "This isn't my call. You'll have to take it up with your mother and Carlos."

"Fine, I will." I crossed my arms and slid down in my seat, fully aware that I was pouting but not caring enough to snap out of it. I had been living independently for months, and having that taken away from me without anyone bothering to tell me pissed me off.

"If it makes you feel better, the pack is still paying for your apartment, so you can still hang out there with pack protection, and if things blow over in the future, maybe Lorelai will let you move back." He gave me a small smile, trying to cheer me up.

"That's a plus, I guess." I sat up again and uncrossed my arms. "Can we run by there after the mall? I need to get some stuff for work before we head back out to the boonies."

He laughed at that, "I don't see why not."

I was starting to feel a little better about the forced abandonment of my home, so I put on my happy face and tried to imagine Megan's reaction when she saw Adam and me. I pictured her running in slow motion toward us. Her shopping bags flung carelessly to the side. Soon enough, I was laughing so hard that I couldn't contain it.

"What?" Adam looked at me, confused.

"Nothing, just the things in my head…" I left it at that and smiled at him when he gave me a sidelong glance. "Hurry up. We're supposed to be there in 15 minutes!"

"No problem," he got a wicked grin on his face, and I felt like I would have to get a spatula to peel myself off the seat due to his rapid acceleration. Fortunately, we arrived in one piece, with five minutes to spare. It only took me two minutes to regain the ability to walk without shaking, so we were right on time when we finally saw Megan waiting outside the Carolina Herrera store.

"Caleb!" She yelled a bit too loudly. "There you are! I was beginning to wonder." She had pasted a perfect look of concern on her face. "Oh, Adam, I didn't even see you there." Her giggle was so fake that I wanted to gag, but he seemed pleased with her attention, and since she barely looked at me, I knew I was forgiven for disappearing on her.

"Can we go to the Apple Store? I want to check out the watches." I was moving in that direction already, but when I glanced behind me, I noticed that neither of them had moved from where we all met up. "Hey Adam, I'm going to the Apple Store, okay?"

"Yeah, sounds good," he called over to me, not bothering to look in my direction.

I'm not sure what it was about Megan, but it worked on all men, no matter the breed. That thought had me picturing Adam curled up as a wolf at her feet, and I could barely contain my laughter as I walked away.

The store was packed, of course; it always was, so I pushed my way gently through the people milling around at the different tables and found a watch station that wasn't being used by anyone else, so I started over in that direction. Just before I got there, a guy walked up to it, and I was so bummed that I almost didn't realize I knew him.

"Hey, fancy running into you here," I said. Gabriel looked up from the counter; his smile was unforgettable.

"Caleb, hey! How are you?"

"Doing well, thanks. I was just coming over to look at the watches, but you stole the one I was going to look at." I smiled at him so he'd know I was messing around.

"I'm happy to share with you," he said as he moved to one side, making room for me to get closer.

"Aw, thanks." I moved into the space he had just vacated, and his scent still hung in the air. It was a mixture of chocolate and something rich and musky. "Mmm, I like your cologne. It smells amazing."

Gabriel gave me a strange look, "Um, thanks, but I'm not wearing cologne."

"Really?" I automatically leaned in and smelled the part of his neck that connected with his shoulder before realizing what I was doing.

He tilted his head to the side, which I assumed meant he didn't mind the invasion of his personal bubble. The scent was even stronger up close and made my mouth water slightly. I leaned a little closer, and my nose grazed the skin on his neck. The familiar electric shock that always seemed to happen when we touched shot up my nose. My eyes began to water, and it felt like my nose had been re-broken. "Ow, shit!"

"Are you okay?" Gabriel grabbed my shoulder, but there wasn't any electricity flowing between us this time. He was staring at my face, waiting for me to reply.

"Yeah, sorry about that. I broke my nose recently and just accidentally hit it on your neck. I'm fine."

"Are you sure you're okay? Here, let me see," he reached over and tilted my chin back, but when his hand touched my chin, the electric shock was there again, and he pulled his hand away. "Damn, one of us needs better shoes because we always have an electric charge to give off." He bent down slightly and looked up at my nose while my head was still leaning back.

"I can't see anything but some white stuff up there. How could you smell anything at all? It looks like both of your nostrils are completely blocked?" His question caught me off guard. I hadn't been able to smell much of anything since Olivia plugged up my nose with the gauze, but I knew I could smell him.

"I have no idea…maybe it was just in my mind." I laughed, trying to play it off, but he didn't look convinced. I attempted to move the conversation in a different direction while still trying to clear the tears from my eyes. "You want the new watch too, huh?"

"Definitely! Now that you helped me get the job at the hotel, I have money of my own."

"I know what you mean, I've been trying to save all my money for school next year, but I figure I deserve a little something for being so responsible."

"I'm not sure blowing all your money on a gadget is being responsible, but I'm doing the same thing, so I can't say much." He looked like he was going to touch me, but seemed to think better of it and dropped his hand back down.

The disappointment in me was swift and confusing. It seemed that I was now a glutton for punishment if I was willing to withstand electric shock for some physical contact. "On second thought, my birthday is coming up soon, so maybe I'll add it to my wish list."

"Good idea. And if you don't get it, you can blow all your money after your birthday." His smile was contagious, and I found that I was trying to figure out excuses to continue to talk to him.

"Exactly! Hey, I'm here with a couple of friends, wandering around the mall. Do you want to wander with us?"

"If your friends wouldn't mind, I think I could join you. I'm just killing time before work anyway."

"Great!" My excitement may have been too much, and Gabriel took the tiniest step backward. "Sorry about that. I think maybe my nose is messing with my hearing as well." *What?* That didn't even make sense; I mentally slapped my forehead.

He laughed at me, "Yeah, must be."

"Anyway, my friends are waiting outside if you're ready to go."

"Yep, let's do it." His choice of words held some hint of double-entendre, but I tried to let it go and concentrate on walking so I wouldn't smack into someone on our way out.

Adam and Megan were practically in the same place I left them, only now they were sitting on a bench, and Megan was laughing and playfully hitting Adam every few seconds. Gabriel and I walked up and stood there for a full minute before either of them noticed our presence.

"Oh, hi Caleb, we didn't see you walk up. Who's this?" I noticed that as Megan addressed us, she also scooted closer to Adam's side.

"Adam, Megan, this is Gabriel. He's a friend from work. I just ran into him a couple of minutes ago." I looked Megan in the eyes and mentally sent her an 'Isn't he cute?' message, then did a subtle head nod in Gabriel's direction.

They both reached out their hand to shake his before I could warn them about the electric shock, but neither one seemed to notice anything after their greetings.

"Nice to meet you both," he said before turning to me. "Now I understand why you asked me to stay, Caleb, you didn't want to be the third wheel." I was so surprised by the lack of electric shock that it took me a second to process what he had just said.

Adam looked a little uncomfortable, but Megan smiled from ear to ear. "They aren't a couple, Megan and I have been friends since high school, and Adam and I..." My voice trailed off, still unsure how to explain why Adam and I were together.

"I saved Caleb from the car wreck he was in a little while ago," Adam spoke up, saving me from myself.

"Wow, that's cool of you. Most people wouldn't stop." Gabriel seemed comfortable, as though he didn't mind that he had just made a mistake assuming they were a couple. Maybe his confidence would rub off on me, and I wouldn't care so much what other people thought.

"All right, enough chatting, let's get our shop on." I turned around and headed for the rest of the mall with my friends in tow.

Twenty

After a few hours of intense shopping, we were finally ready to call it quits. Megan had tried on countless outfits, each a little more revealing than the last. Adam seemed content watching us all, but I noticed every once in a while that he sniffed the air and kept the three of us in his line of sight. True to his word, Gabriel was just killing time before work and didn't purchase anything. I bought a work shirt at Macy's, but the rest of my day was spent window-shopping and watching Gabriel when he wasn't looking.

"All right, I should probably get going," Gabriel finally said. "Will I see you later tonight at work?"

"Yeah, I start at ten, but I might come in early to hang out."

"That sounds good. I think I'll probably take my break around nine. Maybe we could eat together?"

His easy smile and the invitation to eat together had my stomach fluttering.

"I'd love to!" I realized I sounded too excited about dinner, so I tried to play it cool. "I mean, yeah, that'd be cool." God, I felt like a dork.

"Great, well, it was nice meeting you," he turned to Adam and Megan, and shook their hands again. "And I'll see you later tonight, Caleb." He reached out and wrapped his arms around me in a hug that I was happy to return. As our cheeks touched, the electricity flowed between us and quickly spread from the tip of my head down to my feet. After a few seconds, the shock and pain went away and were replaced by a feeling of warmth and comfort. When Gabriel stepped back and released me from the hug, he seemed to have felt the same thing I had and stared at me as he walked away.

"What the hell was all that, Caleb!?" Megan asked, looping her arm in mine as we both watched Gabriel leave.

"I have no idea what you're talking about," I said, "I just gave him a friendly hug." I hoped my lie sounded more genuine to her ears than it did to mine.

"Right, and I'm a virgin." She gave me a look that caused me to bust out laughing.

"You're a virgin? I have to say I'm a little surprised." Megan gave me a fake offended look and slapped my arm, which caused me to laugh even harder. By the time Adam made it over to the two of us, we were wiping tears from our eyes.

"What's so funny?" He asked.

"Oh, nothing," I said, "just an inside joke."

Adam didn't look convinced, but he was smart enough to leave it alone. "Okay… If you want to stop by your apartment before work, we should probably head over there now. I'd hate for you to be late for your date tonight."

I looked over at him, my mouth wide open, and he and Megan were now laughing at me. I guess I deserved that for forgetting that Adam could hear everything I was saying.

We left the mall and headed to my apartment, which was fortunately just up the road. I decided I wanted to wear my new shirt to work, so I turned the shower on high heat and hung it up in the bathroom to steam. While that was happening, I decided I had better clean out my refrigerator since I wouldn't be here to eat any of the food, and I didn't want it to go bad.

"Hey, do either of you want any of these cookies or some slightly green cheese?" Adam and Megan had made themselves comfortable on my couch, but they moved into my tiny kitchen at the mention of food.

"Sure, no reason to let good food go to waste," Adam said, taking a couple of cookies out of my hand and grabbing a slice of cheese without bothering to remove the moldy parts.

"Ew!" I said as he raised it to his mouth. "I was kidding about the cheese, don't eat that!" I slapped it out of his hand and threw the rest away before he could take another slice. Megan took one of the cookies and returned to the living room with them. Adam grabbed the rest and made his way back to the couch.

"Make yourselves comfortable. I'm going to get ready for work. There's water and soda in the refrigerator. Help yourself." I walked into my bedroom and closed the door behind me.

It felt like it had been months since I had been in my bedroom, even though it had barely been a few weeks. I went over and lay down on my bed; the mattress was so firm that it refused to let me sink into it more than an inch. I'd forgotten how firm it was. Maybe living with the pack had some perks I needed to remember. I thought back to my hug with Gabriel earlier and how the electricity seemed to go away. I was happy to feel it go because touching him was like being forced into reparative therapy, no thanks! But no one else seemed to experience the shock like I had. Adam and Megan were fine when they shook his hand both times. If this were another wolf thing, I should probably figure that out. Maybe Lorelai could help explain it to me. I'd have to remember to call her about it later or ask her in the morning when I got back to her house.

Maybe it was a warning sign, telling me to be careful around him. Perhaps he was genetically engineered to be attractive to me and then destroy me. The thought gave me a weird feeling in the pit of my stomach. I was probably blowing this entirely out of proportion; stuff like that didn't happen in the real world. Of course, most people would say that the Awakened didn't either, so what did I know?

There was no point worrying about it now; he hadn't given me any reason to suspect he was dangerous, and Adam hadn't gotten any weird vibes off him that he'd told me about. All this worrying was depressing. I had a semi-dinner date tonight, and I was going to enjoy myself, damn it!

I looked around in my closet for my pants that were maybe a little too tight, but still fit. They created what Megan and I liked to call 'drapery,' meaning they clung to my butt and then went straight down to the floor. They weren't obscenely tight, but they highlighted some positive things. Fortunately, they were wrinkle-free, so I didn't have to worry about throwing them in the bathroom to steam, which reminded me that my shirt should have been good by now.

I walked out of my room and went straight toward the bathroom, but movement in my peripheral vision made me stop. I wasn't sure what I had seen, but it looked like Adam had jumped from one end of the couch to the other. I looked over, and Megan was on one side, playing innocently with her hair. Adam struggled with the remote, trying to get the TV to work. They both looked a little red for such innocent behavior. I just smiled and went into the bathroom to shut off the shower.

"Looks like it got pretty steamy in there," I said as I walked back to my bedroom.

"No! Wait, what?" Megan was trying to cover up her guilty conscience.

"I said it must have gotten pretty steamy in the bathroom. My shirt came out perfectly." I tried to avoid laughing but couldn't keep it in, so I faked a cough instead.

"Oh, I thought you said…something else." She refused to make eye contact with me, and the lipstick smudge on Adam's neck told me everything I needed to know.

"Hmm? Oh, hey Megan, would you come in here for a second? I need your opinion on what I should wear tonight." I could hear a very soft kissing sound come to an abrupt end as she, I'm sure, detached her lips from Adam's.

"Yep." She rounded the corner and shut the door after her.

"Oh my god!" I mouthed to her when she looked at me. "You were totally kissing him!"

"I know!" She made a high-pitched sound and clapped her hands together.

"I was thinking these pants with this new shirt," I said a little louder than was necessary. "Was it good?" I whispered.

She nodded her head, her eyes going wide. "Yeah, I agree. That's a great combo, and it really brings out your eyes." She was a bit more melodramatic than needed, but it wasn't like Adam didn't know what we were saying. Not that I could tell Megan.

"Thanks for the help," I winked at her, "slut!" I mouthed.

"Jealous!" she replied quietly with a smile, "Of course, my pleasure."

God, I loved this girl; I hoped I could tell her what was happening soon so I didn't have to keep so many secrets from her. I felt like she could handle something like this, especially since Adam was also involved. She had dated some terrible guys in the past, so a werewolf was nothing to worry about.

A couple of minutes later, I finally walked out of my room. "I hate to break up the party, but I need to get going." The two looked over at me, still smiling, and stood together. If it weren't so cute, I might have thrown up on them, and if there weren't still a tiny part of me that was attracted to Adam, I would have been ecstatic for Megan. As it was, I returned their smiles and shooed them out my front door, so I could lock up before we left.

Since Megan met us at the mall, she had her car at my apartment. Adam walked her to her car, opened her door, and closed it for her. Meanwhile, I waited impatiently by his passenger door, nervous about a hopefully undisturbed hour with just Gabriel and me. I had no idea what we would talk about. What if we had nothing to say to each other? My mind raced for a while; then, I realized I'd be eating in front of him. What was I going to eat? I needed something that wasn't too messy, so I didn't end up wearing part of it, but it also couldn't be too smelly.

Adam finally reached the car and unlocked it using his key fob. "What? No five-star treatment for me?" I joked with him.

"You don't look as good in a dress as she does," he quipped.

"I won't argue with you there, although I've never worn a dress, so I can't guarantee that." We both laughed, which helped calm some of my nerves, which had slowly moved from my stomach to my legs. They were now bouncing around on their own as we drove toward downtown.

Twenty-One

I made Adam take me to a local fast-food Mexican restaurant so I could grab a quesadilla combo before finally heading downtown. I figured I could be trusted with the relatively drip-proof food, but it would still fill me up enough to last the whole night. "Will you be my bodyguard tonight?"

"Not tonight. Carlos wanted some of the other wolves to cover the area so no one realizes I'm here to watch over you. But I'll still come get you at the end of your shift and take you back to your Lorelai's house." I felt uneasy knowing he wouldn't be around, but I needed to be willing to accept that I wasn't always going to have the protection of other wolves.

"What do I do if something happens?"

"The others'll be watching, but you can always call the house or my cell. I'll get someone over here fast." I hated to admit it, but hearing that made me feel more comfortable than I did moments before.

"Okay, good," I said as I got out of the car. "Now, wish me luck. I need something to go my way!"

Adam laughed as I closed the door, "Good luck, Caleb, go get him." He waved at me before pulling out of the hotel driveway and speeding into downtown traffic.

Here goes nothing. I took a deep breath and looked around for Gabriel. It was just before 9 pm, so he shouldn't have gone on his break yet.

"Caleb!" I saw Gabriel slowly jogging toward me from the valet lot. "How's it going?" He was so calm that it almost irked me. I was a bundle of nerves, and he looked as relaxed as ever. But when he smiled at me, my slight anger disappeared, and I grinned at him like an idiot.

"Good," I said automatically. "I mean well…it's going well. How're you?" *Smooth.*

He laughed warmly at me, "I'm good. Are you ready for dinner?" The other valet attendant looked over at us but didn't say anything.

"Uh, yeah. I've got mine right here," I held up my plastic bag of food, "I'm ready when you are."

"Kasey, I'm taking my lunch break. I'll be back in an hour." Gabriel grabbed his cell phone from the attendant stand and headed toward the employee lounge.

I was happy to see that we were the only people in the break room at the moment. Having our first date in front of other people would have been incredibly awkward since it was at work. If this even was a date, I hadn't asked Gabriel what he considered this dinner. Maybe he thought it was just us hanging out as friends, or perhaps he wanted to talk to me about Megan. It wouldn't be the first time a guy made me think he was interested just to get at my best friend.

"You know I'm gay, right?!" I practically yelled at him, catching him off guard a little.

Gabriel laughed at me as he walked to the refrigerator to retrieve his dinner. "I figured that out, yes. You know I'm gay, right?" He cocked his head to one side, lifting an eyebrow as he asked it.

"Of course," I laughed, trying to play it cool. "I just wanted to get that out there, so it wasn't, you know…awkward." *Awkward?* I was the only thing that was awkward here. God, I was hopeless at dating. I may never have had food thrown at my car like Megan, but at least she had the confidence thing down.

"Glad we got that cleared up," he smiled at me again, set his plate of food down at the table, and then sat down next to me. Our legs brushed against one another, and I winced a little, afraid of the shock, but nothing happened. It seemed like the electricity between us was finally giving way to sparks of another kind. But right as I had that thought, the back of my hand touched his exposed wrist as I opened my bag of food, and the pain from the contact radiated up through my shoulder.

"Ouch! What is that? Why are we always shocking each other?" I shook my hand, trying to make the pain go away.

He laughed again, "I assumed it was my charming, electric personality." I blinked a couple of times at him, and we both started laughing so loudly that a bartender who was walking past stuck his head in the door to see what was going on.

The rest of the dinner passed by without any other incidents, and fortunately for me, without any other zaps to my body. He told me that he had just come out about a year ago and that his mom was disappointed initially, but came around to the idea. I told him I had been teased for years for being gay before even knowing what that meant, but that my parents had fortunately been open-minded and accepting. He was taking a year off from school, then wanted to go on to college somewhere, but he didn't know where. I told him about moving to San Diego for school and finding out I couldn't afford to go.

We talked for almost the entire hour, and I was sad when his cell phone started beeping to signal the end of his break and the start of my shift. I grabbed his phone out of his hand and started adding my number to his contacts list.

"What are you doing?" He was playfully trying to take the phone back, but I noticed that he avoided touching my exposed skin.

"Just give me a minute here. I'm trying to learn all your secrets," I responded, turning my back on him.

"Oh, if that's all," he grabbed my sides and lightly squeezed, making it impossible for me to type since I was frantically trying to get away from him. "You should have just said so."

I finally finished and hit the 'save' button before handing it back to him. "There, now your secrets are out, and you have my cell phone number in case you ever want to call or text me."

He looked at his phone and smiled, "Thanks, Caleb. I'll definitely use it."

"Cool, well, I'd better get going, or Robert will yell at me for being late again, even though I've been here for over an hour."

"And I better get back out to the front, or Kasey will take all my tips." He smiled at me as he walked out the door, "Thanks for having dinner with me. It was nice to talk to you without worrying about people showing up outside."

"I had fun too." I smiled back at him and then went to the sink to wash my hands before clocking in. When I was finally ready for the night, I walked out to the front desk and checked the list of guests who had checked in before going through my usual process for the night.

My head snapped up automatically as the front doors slid open, and a weird feeling settled into my stomach, but I smiled through it at a couple waddling toward me with their overfull suitcases and braced myself for whatever the night had in store. *Here we go!*

About an hour into my shift, I realized I hadn't seen Kasey or, more importantly, Gabriel walk in with a cart full of bags from outside, so I peeked out the sliding glass doors and saw Kasey on his cell phone, but didn't see Gabriel anywhere. I reached into my pocket to see if he'd sent me a text, but still nothing. I had to remind myself it had only been an hour to keep the disappointment at bay.

I kept glancing outside for the next couple of minutes without any sign of Gabriel, but I did notice a familiar face making his way toward the front doors, and my stomach dropped. Dominic, the man from the other pack, was back and headed toward my hotel lobby. If Adam had been here, he would have recognized him right away, but whoever the other pack members were wouldn't have seen him before, and I had no idea if they would realize what was about to happen.

I fumbled for my cell phone again, but he was already at the desk before I had a chance to scroll through my contact list to find Adam's number.

"Good evening," I managed to squeak out. My heart was pumping so hard, and there was no way he didn't know I was nervous. Half of downtown San Diego could probably hear it beating out of my chest. That visual was a little too close for comfort, given how Karen had been killed, so I tried to think of something else as I concentrated on slowing my pulse.

"Hi."

Even his clipped address sounded more growl than a greeting.

"How may I help you?"

"I need a room, something close to the ground floor, and something with easy access to the stairs." He stared directly into my eyes as he barked his requirements, and they seemed to hover halfway between human and wolf.

"Of course, let me see what I have available." I had to close my eyes to break the hold his stare had on me and quickly searched through the list of available rooms. There was something on the second floor, but I didn't want him that close to me. "I have something on the sixth floor. It's near the ice maker and the emergency stairs."

"Nothing lower?"

"I'm afraid not," I said, sweat dripping down my face as I lied to him.

"Fine, the sixth floor will do." His nostrils flared, and he looked over his shoulder. I followed his gaze and saw Gabriel at the valet stand again. The man had a strange grin when he turned back around. "Please send him up with my bags," he pointed at Gabriel, and my stomach dropped.

"O-okay." My response was automatic, but what I was thinking was 'Hell no! I'm not sending my possible future boyfriend to your room after you murdered someone!' I was trying to stall while I scrolled through the list of people on my phone. I finally found Adam and managed to open a text message to him before being caught.

"Am I interrupting your phone time?" His eyes were narrowed and looked even more yellow than they had a minute ago. His nose was also twitching, which I assumed meant I was sending out some guilt-related pheromones.

"Of course not, excuse me. I have your room key right here, Mr. …?" I let the question hang in the air.

"Great," he said, ignoring my question, as he swiped the card from my hand. "Send up my bags, and do not disturb me for the rest of the night." He started to walk away from me, but I wasn't quite done with him.

"I'm sorry, sir, but we need a credit card number for the room in case of any incidentals."

He spun around so fast that I thought he had possibly slipped on something, but then he was moving back toward me with a look of pure hatred on his face. "Here's $500," he practically threw the money at me. "That ought to cover any incidentals." He turned on his heel and walked toward the elevator, ignoring my attempts to call him back. No demands from me were bringing him back, and I knew it.

I finally gave up on texting and called Adam, it went straight to voicemail. "Karen's murderer just checked in again, and no one I recognize has come in to help me. Come back now!" While I was talking, I ignored the sound of the doors swishing open, and it wasn't until he was already stepping onto the elevator that I realized Gabriel was holding luggage and going up. I tried to wave frantically at him, motioning for him to come back down, but he only glanced down at me and waved before the doors opened on the sixth floor, and he was gone.

Twenty-Two

After ten minutes, Gabriel still hadn't come back down, and I began to worry. I tried to call up to the room, but the phone rang without any answer. The elevator remained on the sixth floor, taunting me with Gabriel's disappearance. I pictured him in pieces, his blood covering the hotel room floor, and I started to feel sick from the thought.

Adam still hadn't called or texted me back, and there was no sign of help from anyone else in the pack. I decided I would have to handle this on my own, so I called Kasey in from the valet stand and asked him to cover the front desk while I ran upstairs to check on something. I made an extra copy of the room key and sent Adam a text telling him what I was doing in case I died; at least someone would know I went out trying to fight for someone I cared about. I pushed the elevator call button, which seemed to take forever as it slowly made its way down to the lobby.

Once I was inside, I tried to concentrate on my nerves. I willed them under control and slowed my breathing to focus on finding Gabriel. The elevator dinged, letting me know I had run out of time to calm myself and had to take action. I took a deep breath and stepped out into the hallway. There was no sign of Gabriel or anyone else, so I walked slowly toward the room in question. When I finally got to the door, I pressed my ear against it and listened for the sound of a struggle, talking, or maybe the television. Everything was completely silent, even after I waited for a few seconds. Slowly, I inserted the keycard into the door reader and flinched when it beeped and lit up green, letting me know the door had been unlocked.

I turned the handle and was surprised that I could ease the door open, which meant that the deadbolt hadn't been engaged. I pushed past the point where the security latch would have stopped the door and did my best to see into the room without making myself vulnerable to anything or anyone inside. The gauze prevented me from taking any deep breaths through my nose, so I couldn't tell if there were any apparent smells in the room, but everything inside was completely silent.

Finally, I threw the door open, prepared myself for what might have happened, and walked into the room. What I found was even more unnerving than I had been ready for. The room was empty. There was no sign of any luggage, no Gabriel, and Dominic was also missing. I took a few cautious steps inside, afraid he might have been hidden around the corner near the bed, and as I was about to jump into the main part of the bedroom, my cell phone started to ring. I had no way to sneak in now, so I ran into the room and turned to face the corner with my hands up like I was holding a gun, just in case.

No one was in the room, so I reached into my pocket and saw that Adam had finally sent me a text: "On my way, wait for me!" I rolled my eyes at his timing and then backed out of the room. I made sure there was nothing I had missed in my initial inspection and then closed the door. As I left the room, I noticed that the entrance to the emergency stairs wasn't shut all the way, which should have triggered the alarm, but it was eerily quiet except for the low hum from the ice maker.

It all clicked into place at once.

Gabriel had been taken.

I pulled my phone out of my pocket again and called Adam while I ran down the stairs.

"Caleb? What's happening?"

"Gabriel's gone. Dominic took him. I think they left through the emergency stairs that lead outside the hotel. I'm heading down there now. Where are you? And why isn't anyone here to help me?" I was scared and angry, which filled me with a sense of power and an inability to reason.

"There was a mix-up. Carlos told me he wanted someone else to cover you tonight, but he thought I'd still want to be there, so he figured I'd get the people I wanted to come with me. I thought he was assigning someone to watch you for me, so I didn't ask anyone."

"Are you telling me there's no one watching the hotel?" I asked, as I continued descending the enclosed staircase.

"Unfortunately. I'm on my way now, but I'm still half an hour away." I could hear traffic whizzing past him as I imagined him speeding down the dark freeway toward downtown.

"That's not good enough, Adam. I'm going after him. He took Gabriel!" I made it to the bottom of the stairs and rushed out the side door, causing the alarm to go off, its shrill sound piercing the quiet until I slammed the door shut.

"What the hell was that?" Adam yelled into the phone.

"The emergency door. I'm outside," I tried to sniff the air, but the gauze got in my way again. I braced for the pain and ripped the gauze out of each nostril. The smells of downtown flooded my nose. Strangely, there wasn't any pain, but there was a faint scent of chocolate, which made me think of Gabriel. Maybe he'd been forced to come this way. Underneath the sweetness was something darker, wilder, but I couldn't place it. I was still trying when I realized Adam had been talking to me, and I completely ignored him.

"…him, whatever you do. You can't risk it." He sounded serious, but I had no idea what he had said.

"Okay, I won't." Agreeing was faster than waiting for him to explain whatever I'd missed again. I walked along the side of the hotel and tried to listen for the sound of struggling, talking, or even the movement of two sets of feet. Adam was still talking in my ear, but I had tuned him out so entirely again that it took him yelling my name a few times before I realized what was happening. "What? Did you say something?"

"Caleb, what are you doing?" he growled in my ear. I could almost feel his nerves through the phone, but I didn't say anything. It made me happy to know he was concerned about my safety, but I didn't have time to waste.

"I'm checking the perimeter of the hotel. I won't go very far, but I'm hanging up now. If I get close, I don't want them to hear me talking." As I was pulling the phone away from my face, I could hear the objections starting, but I pressed the 'end' button on my phone's screen and put it on silent before I slipped it into my pocket. I could see the hotel dumpsters, which sat right at the front of a little alleyway between one row of buildings and the next. I checked the ground around me for anything I could trip over or accidentally kick before carefully walking toward the alley. The smell of the garbage had started to overwhelm me, but the hint of chocolate got stronger as I got closer.

I paused in front of a large metal bin, afraid to take a deep breath, but I forced myself, and the smell of chocolate overwhelmed me. The sweetness hung in the air; it teased me but was also mixed with the scents of rotten food and bleach, which caused my stomach to turn. I gritted my teeth, prepared for the worst, then pushed the lid open to look inside. I felt a sense of immediate relief at the lack of a human body in the dumpster, but after looking closer, I realized that some of the clothes Gabriel had been wearing were there and appeared to be blood-stained. My body kicked into overdrive, and I could feel my senses heighten. It suddenly got brighter, and things seemed to move in slow motion, even though I was still moving at regular speed. I noticed footprints on the ground, two sets that I hadn't seen before, and followed them into the darker part of the alley. I could smell chocolate and blood now, but wasn't sure if it was the remnants of what I just smelled or if it was actually down the alley.

I ran full out, determined to find Gabriel and his attacker. I wasn't going to let someone else die for me, especially not someone completely separate from this world, my world. As I ran, I saw something dark smeared along the back wall of one of the buildings and knew the smell of blood was coming from this direction. I hoped for Dominic's sake that Gabriel was still breathing, or he would get to experience his own blood loss.

I finally cleared the alley and ran out onto the sidewalk, then turned the corner and ran right into the man I was looking for. I backed away quickly, snarled at him, and checked around him for signs of

Gabriel. He wasn't there, and the scent of burnt rubber suggested he had been taken away in a car.

"Where is he?" I growled.

"He has been taken care of by now, don't you worry," he had a strange glint in his eye that made me uncomfortable, but I pushed that feeling aside. I preferred the anger that had already begun to course through my body.

"If you hurt him, I swear it will be the last thing you do." I took a cautious step forward. I was angry, not stupid. He had likely been the one who had killed Karen, and I was not about to make myself an easy victim.

"I'm surprised the young alpha cares so deeply for someone like *him*." What was it about the Awakened that they felt so different from ordinary people? I dropped my guard at his question, and he lashed out at me. His kick sent me flying back into the darkness between the two buildings. I got to my feet, shaken, and pressed lightly against my chest, feeling for any broken bones. Nothing happened, so I figured I was okay.

"I kind of hoped you'd do something stupid." I flashed my teeth at him, motioning him toward me into the darkness. "You want me, come and get me, *wolf*."

He ran full speed at me, and I quickly stepped aside to avoid him. But unlike in my practice fights, he didn't give me the same amount of time to turn and prepare myself. Before I knew what was happening, he'd turned and slashed my arm with his newly changed claws. Pain ripped through me as deep wounds opened along my underarm. I could feel the warmth of my blood as it flowed down my arm, but I refused to look at it or even acknowledge the injury. I closed the distance between us and used my other arm to punch upward toward his face. It connected with his nose, which exploded in a shower of blood.

He sneered at me, which was somewhat unnerving because his mouth was filled with his blood, making it appear as though the blood came from there instead of a little bit higher. Then I realized he was laughing and watched as his entire face elongated as he started to change. The blood stopped flowing, but his extended jaws and the longer, sharper teeth remained. "If you can't shift, you can't heal, and if you can't heal, you can't win." He half spoke, half growled through his new mouth, no longer intended for speech.

He ran at me again, and this time I grabbed one of his outstretched arms and used it to flip him over my back. His lower jaw connected with my shoulder as he was flipping, tearing into the flesh there. I had him on his back, but my blood loss made me dizzy, and the increased senses had disappeared. I put my knee on his throat to avoid being attacked by his razor-sharp teeth, but his claws still damaged other parts of my body. Most of my clothing was completely shredded, and my skin wasn't faring much better. The night was getting darker around me, making it more challenging to see, and my strength had diminished with the light.

"Where did you take Gabriel?" My anger returned, and with it, some of my strength. I grabbed both of his arms, pinned them down as best I could with my injured arm and shoulder, and head-butted his snout.

"He's with us now…" he choked out.

I increased the pressure on my knee and asked again, "Where did you take Gabriel?"

A sound near the front of the alley caught my attention, but because of the shadows and my diminished ability to see in the low light, I found it impossible to see what had caused it. My attention was snapped back to the man below me as he pulled his arms free and slashed me across the face with one of his paws. I covered my face with both hands, allowing him to push me off of him. I landed hard on the ground, and before I could react, he was on top of me, his nails digging into the wounds he had already inflicted.

"As I said, young alpha, you can't beat me if you can't change." As he spoke, he continued to use his nails to open new wounds and worsen current ones.

The pain had begun to overwhelm me, and I could feel consciousness becoming a distant hope as the night seemed to close in. It was like the dream I had been having for months. No matter how hard I ran, the darkness always took over. The faces of my family and friends started flashing through my mind. All the people I'd never see again and never be able to say goodbye to. The last face was the one that made me smile, even through the pain. Gabriel came into crystal clear focus. His smile, his laugh, and the way his eyes seemed to see something inside me that I didn't see. All our small touches, even laced with pain, felt precious to me.

Distantly, I could hear Dominic say, "Goodbye, little wolf," and as I prepared to die, I held tight to the memory of hugging Gabriel when the pain ended, and all I felt was comfort.

"Goodbye, Gabriel," I whispered before the darkness took over.

Twenty-Three

An annoying beep cut through the silence at regular intervals, and as much as I tried to ignore it, I couldn't think of anything other than that horrible sound. I tried to roll over but couldn't get the lower half of my body to cooperate with my top half. I turned my shoulders, but my hips stayed glued in place. I kept rolling back and forth, willing my body to turn over, to escape the annoying beep, but the sound became more insistent even as I tried to escape. I gave up on rolling away and decided to muffle the sound with my pillow, but when I tried to lift the side of the pillow to cover my ears, my arms felt like they weighed an additional fifty pounds each. As all of this took place, I became more aware of my surroundings, the soft noises of life began to get louder, and the smells of food and something sharp floated through the air and into my nose. My mouth was dry, and my tongue felt like sandpaper as it ran over my lips, trying to moisten them.

I attempted to speak without luck, but I wasn't sure what to say, even if I could form words. What was left to say when you were dead? I sat there silently, unmoving, for another few minutes before the thought that should have been obvious finally slammed into my brain. Dead people don't think, and my mental capabilities, although slower than usual, were still functioning, which must have meant I didn't die in the alley. I tried to open my eyes, but it felt like they were glued shut. No matter what I tried, they remained closed for the time being. I gave up on my eyes and concentrated on speaking again. Surely this wouldn't be as impossible as opening my eyes had been.

"H-h-h…" Nothing yet, but I kept trying. "I-I-I," my throat burned with the effort.

I felt hands on top of mine and attempted to pull away, but moving my arms was difficult, and they barely even flinched. "Shh… Caleb, you're all right." It was Lorelai. Her voice was calm, but there was a tinge of sadness and something else I couldn't identify without seeing her face. "You're safe now, but you've been badly hurt, and you need to rest now. Olivia will give you something to help you sleep, and when you wake up, we'll be here waiting." As she was talking, I could feel something cold begin to flow through my right arm, which had been sliced open during my fight. Within seconds, I was out...

*****

My eyes opened before I was completely awake, which caused them to burn from the effort. Lorelai sat on a chair in the corner of the room I'd been using at her house. There was an IV stand on my right, and on my left was a machine that let out a faint but regular beep, which I assumed was keeping track of my heart rate. I tried to sit up, but when I did, it felt like someone punched me in the diaphragm, and I fell back onto my pillow. Lorelai's eyes snapped open at the sound, and she was at my side before I even had a chance to smile at her.

"Here you go, sip this slowly." She held a cup of water out to me with a straw. I took a little water in my mouth, which quickly got to work smoothing the sandpaper feel of my tongue. When I finally swallowed, I immediately wanted more and leaned forward to take another sip.

"What happened to me? How did I end up back here? I thought…I thought I was going to die," I could form words now, thank goodness, but my throat was sore, so I tried to keep the questions short.

"Caleb," she said quietly, "you did die. Adam found you bleeding out on the street behind your work. He went to the front desk to find you, and the employee there said you had disappeared thirty minutes earlier." She set the cup down and held my hand in hers as she continued, "When Adam found you, he said it looked like you had been in a fight with someone and lost. Your heart had stopped, and you weren't breathing, but somehow the wounds on your body were slowly closing." Her words confused me. I wasn't able to heal yet; I couldn't even change, so healing shouldn't have been possible. But somehow, I'd done something to cause the healing to take place.

"How did it happen?" I coughed, and she held the cup of water for me again. I greedily swallowed a few more mouthfuls before lying my head back down.

"We aren't sure. Olivia looked at you when you got back to the house. You still weren't alive, but most of your wounds had completely closed."

"When did I…" I searched for the right word, "come back?" The question was strange; the thought that I had died and come back to life was beyond what I believed possible.

"Just a few hours ago," she replied. "The first time you woke up and I told you that you needed more sleep was the first sign of life you exhibited. We didn't know what to do with you, so we laid you on the bed and hooked you up to the heart monitor to see if you had even a slight pulse, but there was no sign of any activity." The emotion returned to her voice, and I watched as tears streamed down her face. "You'd stopped healing after a few hours, but still showed no signs of life. Then the beeping began, slowly at first, and then it picked up speed until there was a regular pulse. A few minutes after that, you started moving around. I wasn't sure what to do, so I asked Olivia to put you under so your body could rest while we tried to figure out what was happening."

I was still confused but so happy to be alive that I didn't want to jinx it by asking additional questions. I listened silently as she recounted what had happened to me over the past few hours.

"Now you're awake again, and other than the bruising, you look good." Her tears had stopped falling, and her face was filled with wonder, which was the emotion I couldn't place earlier from the sound of her voice alone. It was strange for me to be in this position, especially with someone I had never expected to meet.

Now, more than ever, I wanted my parents to be with me, holding my hands and helping me recover. Lorelai was great and had been supportive through everything, but they were my family, and I missed them. I made a mental note to call them as soon as I was able to do so.

"I don't know what happened," I croaked, "but I'm glad it did." I smiled and could feel it reach my eyes. I tried to think back on the evening's events, but they were foggy at this point. I remembered the fight and my senses coming and going. I remembered the darkness closing in on me and faces and memories appearing in the dark, but the rest was utterly blank. That made sense, I guess, since I was dead at the time. "Adam?" I managed to get out before losing my voice to another coughing fit, followed by drinking more water.

"He's here. Would you like to see him?" When I nodded, she looked out the door and waved him in from the hallway. "Here he is, Caleb, but try not to talk too much. You need to rest your voice."

Adam filled the doorway as he entered and knelt next to the bed. "If you hadn't been dead when I got there, I probably would have killed you for going after Dominic on your own!" His eyes were beginning to glow with emotion.

"Adam!" Lorelai's response was swift and sharp, but it didn't cause a reaction in him.

"Sorry," he said, his head dropped slightly, and his eyes returned to normal. "I told you not to go after him no matter what, and you agreed. Then you did what I told you not to!" I had the good sense to look embarrassed but didn't try to reply. His anger seemed to flow out of him, and he rested his head against the side of the bed. "I'm glad you woke up. I'm not sure what we would have done without you."

I figured this was as good a time as any to ask the one thing I'd been wondering since coming back to my senses, and he was probably the only person who might have an idea. "Where's Gabriel?"

Adam looked up at Lorelai, who gave the tiniest of nods, and then he looked back at me, "We aren't sure. I followed Dominic's scent as far as the next corner, but he either got picked up or had a car there. He disappeared from there."

The pain in my chest was immediate. I had followed them to save Gabriel, but he was gone, with no hope of being recovered. Tears burned my eyes as they began to well up, but I refused to wipe them away. I was going to find him somehow, and then I was going to finish what I started with the Awakened that took him.

As if he could read my thoughts, Adam leaned over and whispered, "Don't worry, we'll find him, and this time I'll help you make sure they don't get away."

I made sure not to react to his words but whispered in return, "Good."

Twenty-Four

The following day, I woke up, and the clock on the table beside the bed said 11:15. I needed my rest to recover from the night's craziness. I tried to roll over again, and this time I could feel the lower half of my body responding, but it was also protesting against the movement. My whole body felt like it had been run over by a bus three or four times. I hadn't felt this bad after being in an actual car wreck, so I had no accurate pain comparison, but a bus sounded about right.

I groaned and complained as I worked to get my body off the bed. I eventually had to wriggle to the side of the bed and force my legs over the side, which sort of cantilevered me up off my back and into a sitting position. My head swam from the sudden change in direction, but I felt good after a few seconds, so I tried to stand up. The first try was laughable, as I didn't even get my butt off the mattress. The second attempt was a little better, but I still ended up stuck on the bed. By my fifth try, I made it up to my feet without any issue, but my first step caused me to fall forward toward the chair Lorelai had occupied the night before.

Fortunately, I caught myself on the way down, but I was now feeling even worse, and I had more than just pain on my mind. It had been over twelve hours since I had last gone to the bathroom, and my bladder felt like it was going to burst. Very carefully, I pushed back into a standing position and slowly walked into the bathroom, where I could finally relieve one small part of my overwhelming pain. Bladder empty and hands washed, I made my way back to the bedroom, where Olivia was waiting for me.

"Hi Caleb, it looks like you might be doing better than expected this morning. I was afraid you might have been bedridden for a few more days, but you're already up and moving around. Good for you!" Her enthusiasm was not contagious, and I felt tired just listening to her. I returned to the bed and sat down so she could check me over.

"How's everything looking?" I hadn't even glanced at myself in the mirror, scared that I might look as bad as I felt, which would probably cause me to feel even worse.

"You look about the same as you did a few hours ago, still bruised but no longer bleeding from your wounds. I'm checking for any signs of bleeding under your healed skin, in case the wounds closed without actually stopping the hemorrhaging." *Okay, hemorrhaging? That sounded gross.* "But so far, everything looks good."

"That's a plus, right?"

"Of course," she said as she continued to look things over. "We're all thrilled that everything seems to be healing nicely, even if we have no idea what's causing it." She smiled at me while checking my pulse, pupil dilation, and reflexes. "As far as I can tell, you seem to be healing. I'd still recommend that you take it easy, and if your body hurts, that is its way of telling you that you are doing something you shouldn't be. A little soreness or stiffness is okay, but pain isn't." She looked right in my eyes as she said it, seeming to gauge my reaction.

I shrugged my shoulders, not wanting to let her know that nothing was keeping me from going after the other pack and Gabriel, "No problem. I'm not much of a fan of pain anyway." She smiled at that, apparently agreeing with my statement. I swallowed my pride and winced at some back pain as I moved my body a little on the bed.

She seemed almost pleased that I had trouble moving. "Take it easy, Caleb. We need you healed completely for your awakening. Otherwise, you may do more damage than your body can handle."

"I thought once I was awakened, everything would heal when I shifted?" I was trying to remember what else Adam had told me when I first asked about the process.

"That is usually true, but you've never shifted before. The first change is stressful on the body, and attempting it when you're injured wouldn't be advisable. There's no telling what could happen." This was new information that would have been helpful to know last night, but it was too late now, and I was already committed to finding Gabriel.

"I understand," I said, "I appreciate your help, Olivia." I lay back for a few seconds before the sound of the front door opening and slamming shut got Olivia and my attention. She helped me up, and we moved as quickly as possible to the living room, where Adam and Lorelai spoke in hushed voices. "What happened?"

Adam turned and looked at me, his face ashen. "Carlos and Rosa are gone."

I could feel the blood rushing from my face as the news sunk in, "Are they…" I couldn't finish the sentence, but my meaning was obvious.

"No, at least not that we know of. I went to their house this morning to talk to Carlos about a plan of attack, but when I got there, the front door was open, and there was no sign of them inside."

Olivia pulled me over to the kitchen table and helped me sit down, so I could process everything without remaining on my feet. I pictured the kind face of Rosa as she doted over me since my return to the pack. Though she wasn't much older than my mom, she felt like a grandmother to me—someone who would love and understand me, no matter what

I did. The idea of her being attacked by the other pack pushed me over the edge.

"Was there any sign of a struggle?" Lorelai asked.

"No, and no note indicating that they left on their own. Right now, we're assuming they were forced out of their home and that they didn't fight back for whatever reason." Adam continued, "The bed wasn't made, and no clothes seem to be missing, so we think they were drugged or taken while asleep, but we don't know that for sure." Adam paced back and forth between the kitchen and the table where I was sitting. The frustration was evident in the set of his shoulders and the concentration on his face. "I've already called a few people to get the word out. See if anyone has seen them and can report something back. I went through their whole house, but nothing seemed out of the ordinary, and there weren't any unfamiliar scents."

Lorelai gently grabbed Adam by the arm to stop his pacing. "Call everyone and ask them to gather here at the house. It would be safest if we were all together right now." Adam nodded and left the room, then she turned and looked at me. "And Caleb," she said softly, "I'd like you to tell your parents to go away somewhere while this is happening. It doesn't matter where, as long as it's hard to track their movement."

"Why?" I didn't understand what my parents had to do with any of this. They definitely weren't the ones behind the disappearance of Carlos and Rose.

"After they came to town and surprised you, the other pack may know who they are, and they may have been followed back home." Her face was serious, and I could tell this made her uncomfortable.

There was a pain in my chest thinking about them being in danger, and a sudden pit in my stomach. I hadn't thought about the risk of my parents being followed home. "Oh my god, I told them to stay in the hotel, I hugged them in the lobby! If we were being watched, it would have been so obvious! Not to mention the fact that we went out to breakfast that next morning and they spent the next night at my apartment." I dropped my face into my palms to hide the tears that had started to fall. "I'm so stupid!"

"No!" Lorelai said, placing a hand on my shoulder. "You didn't know they were going to come to the hotel and surprise you. That wasn't your fault. And it wasn't their fault for wanting to spend time with you."

She continued to rub my shoulder while I attempted to get my emotions under control. Eventually, I stopped crying, and while I didn't feel better about what had happened, I tried to put it out of my mind so I could do what needed to be done.

"I'll tell them I won a trip and want to give it to them for their anniversary. It's not for another few months, but I could probably make it work. How far away do they need to be?"

She and Olivia shared a look, "I'd say at least a plane ride away; otherwise, it'd be too easy for them to be followed. And Caleb, once you figure out where you're sending them, don't tell anyone, not even one of us."

"I understand, and I'll make sure they are gone by tomorrow." Getting my parents to drop everything and leave town without any notice was going to be difficult, but I would tell my dad that he had to force my mom to go and relax. He was much more likely to be willing to take a trip than she was.

Adam came back in the room and nodded at Lorelai, seemingly to indicate that he'd finished the request to the pack to come to the house.

"Good. Now, we have to get the house and guesthouse ready for everyone's arrival. Adam, Olivia, you know what to do. Caleb, why don't you eat something here and then take a shower? You look like need it. And you can also take this time to figure out where to send your parents."

I smiled and nodded at her, then mouthed, "Thank you," which earned me a smile. Then she and the other two were off to make room, and I was left alone to eat and scheme.

I filled a bowl with cereal and fired up the laptop on the kitchen table. I pulled up a few travel websites to find the best plane ticket prices and then pulled up my hotel portal to check the friends and family rates I could get on such short notice. After about fifteen minutes of web searching and deal-hunting, I was done and sent a quick e-mail to my dad with all the details. I told him everything was non-refundable and needed to be now or never. Hopefully, he would be able to talk my mom into leaving, but I couldn't worry about that now.

I deleted my web history, just in case, wolfed down, excuse the pun, the rest of my cereal, and then moved as quickly as I could to my bedroom to get ready for what I had to do today. Stepping into the shower was painful and relaxing at the same time. I felt like I had gotten a bad sunburn, and the hot water irritated it. After a minute or two, my muscles relaxed, and I felt better in the heat. I was as thorough as my body allowed me to be, trying to pay attention to the difference between soreness and pain. After getting as clean as possible, I shut off the water and grabbed the softest towel I could find to dry myself off.

I threw on some clothes and shut and locked my door before picking up my cell phone and calling the hotel. I knew I would get chewed out for leaving last night and never coming back, but I needed to see if they had heard from Gabriel or not. Someone answered on the second ring, and I was connected to Robert, my manager.

"Caleb, you'd better have an amazing excuse for walking out last night without telling anyone!" His anger was under control, which either meant someone else was in the room or he had already decided what he would say to me, no matter what I said.

"I was attacked in the alley behind the hotel last night, but that's not why I'm calling."

"You were what?" He cut me off as I was about to continue. "Attacked by whom?"

"I'm not sure who it was. It was so dark I couldn't see. But like I said, I'm not calling about that right now. I'm calling to find out if you've heard from Gabriel?"

"You know I can't tell you about other employees, Caleb, and it's not your business to keep track of others, especially if you can't keep track of your own schedule." He wasn't buying the 'attacked in the alley' story.

"He brought a customer his bags last night and never came back. When I called up to the room, there was no answer, and when I went to make sure everything was all right, it was empty. I'm worried that he was taken from the hotel, which is why I was in the alley in the first place."

This caused him to pause for a while; the sound of keystrokes in the background let me know he was looking up something. "I see that you checked in an unknown guest last night, which is impossible since we need a credit card for the room, you know that."

"Yes, sir, and I tried to explain that, but he paid cash and walked away when I tried to call him back. I should never have given him the key, but he had stayed with a group in the past, so I assumed he would provide a credit card when I asked. As I said, I tried to call his room, and he was gone."

"Caleb, I'm not sure what else happened last night, but you left work without telling anyone and are apparently fine after being so viciously attacked you couldn't bother to call in or have someone call in like Gabriel did." My stomach clenched.

"So he's okay? Who called in for him?"

Robert seemed to realize his mistake now that I had jumped all over this new information, so it took him a couple of seconds before he finally replied. "His mother. Now, Caleb, I'm afraid I will have to ask that you not return to the hotel. I cannot trust you if you are going to shirk your responsibilities here. I'm sorry, Caleb, but you're fired."

Admittedly, I wasn't expecting to get fired. I thought a slap on the wrist, maybe a decrease in hours, but losing my job wasn't an option I'd considered. "I really was attacked last night," I began, but he spoke over me.

"Your final check will be in the mail by tomorrow. I'm sorry to have to do this, but I need a team I can trust. Good luck in the future." And with that, he hung up the phone. I tried to process what had just happened, but the fact that someone had called in for Gabriel made me snap back to my senses. I didn't care about the job at the hotel anymore. If the other pack knew where I was working, I wasn't safe there anyway. But at least now I had a lead on finding Gabriel, and I wasn't going to sit around moping. I was going to find him.

Twenty-Five

I used my phone to stalk Gabriel on Insta, and found out that he lived in La Mesa, then I reverse searched his cell number to see if I could find any other numbers associated with his name. I found a number for a potential relative, a woman with the same last name I hoped was his mother. After a few tries, I finally got her to answer.

"He's not here. How did you get this number? Who's calling?"

"I'm a friend from work; he left last night without saying goodbye, and I was checking to see if he was okay." I tried to make my voice sound light, caring, and not like the crazy person I felt like I was in the moment.

"I called the hotel already. He had to come home sick," she replied, sounding suspicious.

"Oh, I know. I was just making sure he was doing okay. Do you know when he might be home? I've tried calling his cell, but it just goes straight to voicemail." I figured if she knew I was trying to reach him directly, it would help my case since he knew me well enough for me to have his number.

Her voice changed and became much less friendly. "No, I don't. I have to go now."

"Wait!" I was in full panic mode. "Can I leave a message to have him call me when he gets back? My name is Caleb, from the hotel."

"Okay, bye." With that, she hung up the phone, but I was, for the first time, beginning to feel a little hope. I searched the phone number I'd just called to see if it was associated with a physical address. My luck was still holding out because an address in La Mesa popped up, but only the first two numbers of the street address were available—probably to stop people like me from tracking it down.

I pulled up the map app on my phone and put in the address with a couple of numbers in the middle. The first two I tried mapped me to nothing, but the third one worked and showed me a house on the outskirts of town. The houses were more spaced out, and there were fewer of them, so going unnoticed might be more of an issue than I'd initially expected.

I had a feeling Adam would know what we needed to do to get Gabriel back without being caught.

My phone vibrated suddenly due to an incoming text, which surprised me. I checked the message from a number I didn't recognize, "Hey, I'm fine. Don't worry about me."

Breathing became nearly impossible as I stared down at my screen. I replied as quickly as my fingers could move, "Gabriel? Where are you?"

A minute later, another message came, "I'm safe." That wasn't good enough; I needed to hear from him directly that he was okay. I called the number, and it went straight to voicemail. There was no personalized message, so I still had no proof it was Gabriel.

I sent another text, hoping he'd respond again, "Gabriel, if this is you, please call me. I need to speak to you!" The silence in the room was so complete that I could hear my heartbeat. When there was a quiet knock on my door, I grabbed my phone, looking at the screen for a new message before realizing the sound I heard was completely different from the one I was hoping for. I went to the door and opened it to find Adam with keys in his hand.

"Ready to go?"

My eyes lit up, and I motioned him into my room, "Yes. I think I may have found out where his mom lives, but I'm not positive. I also got a text from a number I don't know, telling me he was okay. They never claimed to be Gabriel, but they didn't deny it either." I showed him the messages and explained the past several minutes. As I spoke, I paced back and forth and noticed I moved around a little easier than I had before the shower.

"Something about this isn't right, but we won't know what until we find out who's been texting you.

Let's go!" Adam reached for the door and walked out into the hallway.

We moved through the house quietly, so as not to call attention to ourselves as we left. When we got out to his car, another one was driving up the road, and Adam waved at the group, their faces registering in my memory as part of the pack. The first arrivals had already made it. Adam greeted them at their car, all smiles, which was strange considering the situation, but given that there were small children in the back, the smile may have just been part of the show.

After a minute or two, Adam walked back to his car and unlocked the doors; both of us climbed in, and he started the car. He turned toward me as he put the car in reverse, "I told Tyler to let Lorelai know we had gone out to run errands if she asked where we were. That way, she won't worry about our taking off. She'll already know we're doing something stupid."

I looked at him, confused; my brows knit together, "Then why tell her we're gone?"

"Lying to the Alpha isn't possible. You can sneak around behind their backs or omit things, but telling them a direct lie is impossible. So, we avoid the truth until the last minute, so she can't stop us, and we're good to go." There was humor in his eyes, but his dimple was conspicuously absent, so I could tell it was just an act to make me more comfortable. I appreciated that.

"So when I take over, no one will be able to lie to me, or only those in my pack?"

"It only works for those in the pack; you don't control other wolves, so they don't have to do anything for you." Talking about the future helped calm me down, which was precisely what I needed as we drove toward La Mesa, and, hopefully, Gabriel.

"What if they aren't in a pack? Or don't know they're in a pack, like me, before all of this? Can I control them? With my pheromones or whatever?" I was trying to keep my mind off the numbing fear that Gabriel, Carlos, and Rosa were all in trouble.

"Theoretically, if they didn't have a pack and wanted to be part of your pack, then they couldn't lie. But if you just saw them around town, they could. You're not a walking lie detector for all of the Awakened." I could tell he was nervous; I'd asked some pretty ridiculous questions, and he hadn't made fun of me yet. I decided maybe silence was better and just stared out the window as trees and other cars flew past.

After about fifteen minutes of driving, we pulled off the freeway and took a few different surface streets, leading us to the larger plots of land I was expecting. The houses were further apart, and street parking was hard to find. We passed the place I had found online, and Adam kept driving without slowing down until we had gone about four blocks. Then he found a space big enough to pull over to the side and park his car.

"We'll walk from here. That way, no one will hear us coming."

It made sense to me, so I grabbed my cell phone, tried to call the number that texted me one more time, unsuccessfully, and then got out of the car. I stuck close to Adam and stayed in the shadows as much as possible. But since it was the middle of the day, the shadows were few and far between.

We got to the house I found on the computer, but there was a family outside that was definitely not related to Gabriel. We kept walking past another house and another before Adam focused on a small stucco house that looked unremarkable. I smelled the air, which smelled familiar but not especially wolf-like, although I had no idea what I was supposed to smell.

"I think this is the one," Adam said, pulling us off the road into the bushes surrounding it, where we sat down and waited.

My body protested a little when I tried to sit on the ground, but once I was there, I could feel the relief in my legs, which I hadn't realized were sore. I took that as a good sign and tried to keep my eyes on the house. It was completely quiet, with no indication that anyone was even inside, but I wasn't about to give up that easily. "What makes you think that?"

Adam pointed to his nose, "I can smell Gabriel, but it's faint. And there have been a few Awakened in the area recently."

That last part got my attention, and I looked around to see if there were any obvious signs of attack. I didn't notice any apparent damage to the house that I could see from where we were sitting, and I couldn't smell anything, so I just sat there quietly and waited.

After three and a half hours, I had finally had enough of sitting. I decided to stand up, just to do something new. I got into a crouched position to relieve the pressure on my legs. Before I could stand up completely, the sound of a car driving past had me rolling forward onto my face. Adam stifled a laugh next to me, and I threw a stick and some leaves at him. "Shut up, ass."

That made him laugh even harder, which caused me to start laughing until my stomach started to hurt, and I had to take deep breaths to stop. When I finally calmed down, the house's front door opened, and a woman in her forties walked out. She had the same multi-colored hair as Gabriel and the same nose. She had to be his mother. I started to whisper something to Adam, and her eyes looked right at the place we were hiding, so I froze. She glanced away quickly, which made me feel a little better, but the fact that we'd almost been caught scared me more than I wanted to admit.

We watched silently as she got into the car in the driveway and pulled out onto the main street, driving away from where we'd parked. I finally felt comfortable enough to stand up and stretch a little, but I stayed as low as possible. It had now been so long that it was starting to get a little bit darker out.

As the shadows got deeper, I lost hope that we would find Gabriel.

I tried to call and send text messages to the number from earlier with no response. Adam wouldn't let me say that I was outside what I thought was his house in case it wasn't him, so I was stuck with saying things like, "Gabriel, are you there? Where are you? Are you okay? Call me back as soon as you can, please!" I felt like a desperate ex-boyfriend who couldn't let go. If Megan told me a story about a guy who did what I was doing, we would have laughed at how crazy he was, and I would have suggested she recommend psychological help.

Thinking about Megan's lousy track record reminded me of when she called me in a panic from the grocery store. She had been walking down the aisle and spotted a particularly crazy ex-boyfriend in front of her, so she turned and ran in the opposite direction. She hid in the back of the store near the dairy section, her arms filled with milk and orange juice. She thought she'd gotten away, so she started toward the middle of the store and saw him coming toward her. She ran down the first aisle she got to and called me.

She told me she'd been bobbing and weaving through the aisles, trying to avoid talking to him because he'd start crying about the break-up every time they did. And according to her, she didn't have the time or interest in that. I told her she should just set the milk and orange juice down and walk out calmly so no one thought she was trying to steal something, but she told me she couldn't leave without crackers. I laughed at her, thinking she was kidding, but she was determined to get some special crackers, and no ex-boyfriend, crying or otherwise, would keep her from those "little salty treasures." Her words, not mine.

I was still thinking about her adventures in dating when another car drove past our hiding place and pulled into the house's driveway. I snapped back to attention, held my breath, and waited. When the door finally opened, my surprise almost gave us away. I tried to stand up, but Adam held me in place.

"Just wait," he whispered before letting me go. The car backed up and drove off, leaving Gabriel alone in front of the house. "Okay, quietly now."

I stood up and started picking my way through the plants and other debris, but when I looked up, Gabriel was at the door and about to go inside. "Gabriel!" I yelled before I could think about it.

"Aw hell!" Adam yelled behind me.

Gabriel turned around and looked toward me, not moving any closer but not retreating into the house. I figured that was a good sign, and I continued to move forward.

"Gabriel, wait, it's me." I walked out into the street, and now that there were no more shadows to conceal my face, Gabriel looked a little scared and confused.

"Caleb? But I thought you were—I mean, they told me you were—what are you doing here?" He was moving toward me, but didn't seem to realize it because he looked down when his feet touched the grass in his front yard and stopped.

"I came to make sure you were okay. I tried to get in touch with you all day, but you didn't respond." I had reached the edge of his property and stopped, but I continued to look up at him.

"Is it really you? I thought you were dead." He took a step toward me, his eyes wide and his hand slightly extended toward me.

"It's me, and I'm not dead. I'm here to save you." I spoke slowly and took careful steps toward him, reaching my hand out toward his in turn. We needed him to come with us before the others returned. "How did you get away?"

He seemed confused, "They let me go. How did you find me?" He took another step, which put us within touching range. I wrapped my hand around his, and as our fingers connected, the electricity I had expected ran up my arm and down through my leg.

I must have jerked a little because Adam rushed up to stand next to me and grabbed my shoulder. "I hate to rush things along, but we have to go. Gabriel, we'd like you to come with us. We promise we will keep you safe." Adam pulled me back toward the street as he spoke, and since our hands were connected, I pulled Gabriel with us.

"Please come with us. I need to know you're okay, and having you with me is the best way for me to be sure." I looked into Gabriel's eyes, holding his gaze.

"I'll go."

Once we were safe inside Adam's car and headed back toward the house, I felt much better. I reached behind me, found Gabriel's hand, and grabbed it. The electricity felt good, even though it coursed through my body; it let me know he was there with me. After a few seconds, the shock went away, and our hands began warming comfortably together. When we finally got back to Lorelai's house, I was excited to introduce Gabriel to her and the rest of my 'extended family,' as Adam and I had decided we'd be calling the pack.

I jumped out of the car, surprised I could move without any of the pain I had been experiencing throughout the day. I grabbed Gabriel's hand and led him into the house. I could hear everyone talking in the living room, so we walked in that direction. I had just taken a breath to introduce him to everyone when everyone else seemed to notice us simultaneously. Thirty sets of eyes were now staring at us, and I realized I had no idea where to begin.

Twenty-Six

A low growl started around the room, coming from the chests of the adults, while most of the children were being pushed behind their parents. I was frozen in place by the threat from my pack, but I somehow managed to put myself in front of Gabriel. I cleared my throat, "Everyone, this is Gabriel. The same person who came after me also attacked him. Adam and I brought him here so he would be *safe*," I put extra emphasis on that last word. "I know tensions are high, and I know we're all worried about the disappearance of Carlos and Rosa." The growling stopped at the mention of their names, and a soft murmuring began to spread through the room. "But I promise, we're going to figure out what happened."

Once the tension in the room dropped, I continued, "Adam and I are going to put together a group that will try to track them down, and I'd like to have some volunteers to help with that effort. The rest of you will need to stay here and make sure everyone is settled in comfortably." I glanced at Lorelai, who was smiling warmly at me, with a look of pride on her face.

"I completely support my son's decisions, and I expect you will all do as he has requested. His," she seemed to be grasping for the right word, "friend, will be staying with us as long as he and Caleb see fit, and I know no one will disrespect my guest in my home." The pack looked to her before dropping their heads in agreement. They hadn't given me that sign of respect, but I wasn't technically Alpha yet, so I hadn't earned it.

"Good, I'm glad that's settled," Adam spoke up from behind me. "Caleb, Gabriel, I could use your help in the other room." And with that, he turned and walked down the hallway toward the bedrooms. We followed him into the bedroom I had been using, and I closed the door after us. "Now, I think it's time you tell us what exactly happened to you yesterday." Adam looked into Gabriel's eyes and held his gaze.

Gabriel blinked a couple of times, looked from Adam to me, and back again. "I was at work and was asked to bring the guest his bags. I brought them up to the room, and he," Gabriel paused, his eyes locked on mine, "he must have hit me on the head or drugged me or something because I can't remember anything after that."

I looked at Adam, who was still staring at Gabriel; his face was a stony mask, and I had no idea whether he believed what Gabriel had said.

"When I woke up, they told me that you'd been killed and that I should pretend nothing had happened and go on with life as though we'd never met. Then they told me I was going to go home, but before they brought me back, my mom called me and said someone named Caleb had called to check on me. I thought maybe someone was trying to mess with me or make sure I wouldn't say anything I shouldn't. But I couldn't just ignore it, so I sent you that text, telling you I was okay."

I thought back to the short text conversation we'd had this morning and understood now why he'd never said who he was or mentioned anything too detailed.

"When you called, I turned the phone off because I was afraid they'd gotten your phone and were going to use it to trick me. I just wanted to go home and didn't want to do anything to jeopardize that," his eyes darted back and forth between me and Adam, but neither of us said anything. "When I finally got there, you came out of the darkness, and I thought maybe I was seeing things. But now I know they were lying, and you know the rest." His head was down, but he had reached out and grabbed onto my arm, where my sleeve was covering my skin to avoid shocking either one of us.

"Who were these people? Did you know or recognize any of them?" Adam continued with his line of questioning.

"I'm not sure who they were. There were different people around me all morning. Some looked familiar, but most I'd never seen before."

Adam looked like he was going to launch into another set of questions, but before he could do that, I held up my hand to stop him. "I think Gabriel has answered enough for now. I know you're concerned and appreciate that concern, but let's give him a moment to relax here." Adam gave me a look that said he wasn't pleased, but only nodded and left the room.

"Sorry about that," I whispered, "he can be a little intense, but I promise he really is the laid-back guy you met at the mall."

Gabriel sighed and sat down on the bed. "What the hell is going on?"

"I wish I knew, but right now, things seem so crazy that I have no idea what to think. For now, I'd recommend you call your mom and let her know you're okay. I'm going to see if I can find a sleeping bag or extra blankets for tonight so you can stay here." I had turned the handle on the door to open it when Gabriel's words made me pause.

"Thank you, Caleb…for everything." He smiled at me, though it made him look more tired than happy.

"It's nothing, I'm just glad you're safe." I smiled back at him and hoped that I looked more confident and less exhausted than I felt. "I'll be right back."

I closed the door behind me and was on my way to the kitchen when hands shot out and grabbed my arm, pulling me into another bedroom. "He's lying." Adam held me tightly by the arm and wouldn't let go, no matter how hard I pulled away.

"Lying about what?"

"I'm not sure, but he is lying about something. His heart rate increased, and he made a lot of eye contact when talking to us."

I tilted my head and gave him a confused look. "I thought people didn't make eye contact when lying?"

"No. Eye contact means he's making things up, not remembering." I'd never interrogated someone, so I didn't push the issue.

"He did say he couldn't remember much, and you can be kind of intimidating, especially when you put on your 'I'm Scary' face."

"Caleb, I'm being serious. Something isn't right about the events he told us, which means he's either leaving something important out or flat out misleading us. Until we figure out what it is, I don't want you to leave him alone, even for a minute."

"I'm not going to follow him into the bathroom or watch him shower," the idea of that made my cheeks flush, "but I will try to keep him company when he's in public spaces. How's that?"

"Whatever," he grumbled at me. "Just be careful. I mean it."

"Yes, sir," I said, giving him a mock salute. "Now, do me a favor and find something for me to sleep on tonight. He's staying over in my room." I smiled and waved at him before he could protest. "Thanks a bunch!" I walked back to my room and listened carefully to the door before opening it, just in case.

"Yes, ma'am, I'm fine. I'm just staying the night at a friend's house, but I'll be home soon. I'll keep you posted if anything changes." There was a moment of silence, and then he continued. "I love you too. Goodbye." I waited a moment and opened the door as though I'd just gotten back.

"Couldn't find anything, so I asked Adam to see if he could find something for me." I was terrible at small talk, especially with guys I liked. "Did you call your mom?"

"Yeah, I did. Thanks." He smiled at me again, this time looking more happy than tired, and the improvement in his mood seemed to improve mine as well. I refused to focus on what Adam had said. If Gabriel was lying, and I wasn't convinced he was, he probably had a good reason for it. I walked over and sat down next to him on the bed when there was a knock on the door.

"Come in," I called out. Adam opened the door and had an arm full of fabric. He walked over to the chair in the corner and dropped it all.

"Here you go, Caleb. Have a good night." His words were kind, but his voice said something else was happening.

"Thank you," I said as he walked out the door. I went over and looked through the stuff he had dropped off. Most of it was stained, worn down to practically bare threads, or intended for an infant. "Very funny!" I yelled, and I swear I could hear his deep laughter as he continued down the hall. "I guess I'm going to nest in these fabric scraps tonight." I pushed the pile onto the floor and tried to arrange it to maximize the cushion for my body. Thank goodness I had somehow gotten over the rest of the pain that plagued me this morning, or I would have never been able to get onto the ground, let alone fall asleep down there.

" I can't make you sleep on the floor in your room," he said, looking down at me from the bed. I couldn't tell him that it wasn't exactly my room, so I settled for the next best thing.

"I don't mind. I'm sure you need to get some sleep, and the bed will be much more comfortable than anything else available. I don't mind the floor," I lied. "I can fall asleep anywhere." *Except for planes, couches, cars, chairs, and anything else that isn't a bed.*

"Well then, why don't we just share it?"

His question caught me off guard, and I asked him to repeat himself to ensure I didn't hear things due to wishful thinking.

"If you won't let me sleep on the floor, and I won't let you sleep on the floor, it makes the most sense that we share the bed. It's a queen-sized bed; it should be big enough, right?"

"Sure! I mean—right, ye-yes." My voice cracked with excitement, and I felt my cheeks flush, "It should be fine. And you're sure you don't care?" I asked, hoping this wouldn't make him change his mind.

"I don't mind if you don't," he replied, thankfully ignoring my embarrassing display.

I jumped up a little too quickly and crawled back onto the bed. "That's very nice of you, thank you."

"Do you have a shirt I could sleep in? I don't have anything else to wear tomorrow, and this will be all wrinkled if I sleep in it," he held his shirt out away from his body.

"Yeah, no problem." I went into the closet and grabbed two t-shirts I had owned for years. They were worn in, making them soft and perfect for sleeping. "Here you go." I handed him one of the shirts and watched, transfixed, as he pulled his shirt up over his head and folded it carefully before placing it on the chair next to him. He did the same thing with his pants, but I made sure I found something on my shirt to stare at until he was back in bed.

I walked back to my side of the bed and pulled my shirt off, carefully keeping my back to him. My body was slim but not quite as muscular as his, so I wasn't fond of showing it off. I was about to pull my nightshirt over my head when his movement in the bed stopped me. "What's that?" he asked.

I turned around, unsure what he was looking at, "What?"

"Here, it looks like a giant bruise on your back."

I guess I wasn't completely healed. "Oh, nothing. I must have backed into something," I said lamely.

"Does it hurt?" He reached over, and his fingertips barely brushed the skin, causing us to jerk from the shock.

"That did," I said, my voice tight.

"What the…" his voice was quiet, and he touched my back again, this time without pulling away. The shock went away quickly, and the warmth of his hand spread through my back, relaxing the muscles I didn't know were tense. "What the heck?" He continued to touch my back as I tried to maneuver so I could see what was happening.

"What's going on?" I twisted and turned my body to see what he was looking at. "What is it?"

"Your bruise, it's gone."

"What do you mean it's gone? Are you sure there was even a bruise in the first place?" I asked, unsure whether this was some Awakened thing I shouldn't tell him about.

"It was dark purple, and when I touched it, it got lighter. When I left my hand there, it completely went away." I had no idea what to think or say, so I did the only thing I could come up with.

"Lorelai!"

Twenty-Seven

It only took a few seconds before I could hear the running, and Adam burst through my door, followed closely by Lorelai.

"Caleb, what is it?" She looked concerned, eyes darting back and forth from me to Gabriel. I realized then that my shirt was off, and I was in bed with Gabriel, who was still touching my back. We both jumped apart quickly. That didn't look guilty at all.

"I'm not sure; Gabriel touched me, and he said my bruise went away." I watched her expression closely, hoping something like understanding or happiness might show up and that she would be able to help me explain this to him. I saw the confusion on both of their faces, which didn't bode well.

"He what?" she and Adam said at the same time.

Gabriel spoke up at this point, "I noticed a large bruise on Caleb's back, and I barely touched it, and it started to fade. When I left my hand there, it went away completely."

"Show me," she said, pointing to a small bruise on her arm. Gabriel reached out slowly and touched the tip of his finger to her arm. I watched eagerly, hoping to see this fading in action. But after a few seconds, it was clear that nothing was taking place.

"Here," Adam suggested, "maybe it needs to be something larger." He rolled up his sleeve to reveal a massive bruise on his tricep. "Try this one."

Again, Gabriel reached out and touched Adam's bruised skin with his fingertip, but nothing happened. As he was pulling away, I reached over and touched the back of Gabriel's hand. The spark between us felt stronger when I did, and Adam pulled away.

"What the hell was that?" He rubbed his arm a little, but it was clear to the rest of us that something had happened.

"Adam, hold still," I said, grabbing his arm. "Gabriel, try it again." He reached out more confidently this time; the shock was immediate, but soon became the soothing warmth I was used to. Adam's bruise grew less visible as we watched before finally disappearing altogether.

"What in the world?" Lorelai was as confused as the rest of us, but she didn't appear worried. In the grand scheme of things, this seemed like something positive. Healing without changing now seemed less strange than it had this morning.

Then it hit me. "That's what happened." Everyone turned and looked at me as though I were crazy. "Last night when I…" I paused. I realized we hadn't told Gabriel everything that had happened on our end either. "When I was injured, I thought about Gabriel, and I felt better. Maybe there's some sort of connection between us? It helped to heal me, and now it seems like maybe together we can heal other people."

Adam and Lorelai gave me a confused look but said nothing. "Let's not jump to any conclusions here. Something strange is happening, but it's been a very long and stressful day for all of us. Let's get some sleep and talk about this in the morning." She leaned over, careful not to touch Gabriel, and brushed my hair out of my face. "Can you do that?" She seemed to be trying to tell me something with her eyes, but I couldn't understand, so I smiled and nodded. As if to drive her point home, I let out a big yawn, which spread to the others in the room and made us all laugh. We all said our goodnights, and Adam and Lorelai left the room.

Gabriel and I sat quietly in the dark, which was strangely comforting. I usually felt the need to fill the silence, but now I was happy to simply be in the same space as him. He shifted around a little bit, trying to get comfortable again, and I did the same, but found it nearly impossible to relax. I could feel the warmth of his body next to mine, and couldn't stop imagining what it would be like to roll over and hold him in my arms, or have him hold me. I'd never felt this way about anyone, and I wasn't sure how to act around him.

Adam was a forbidden fruit situation, but I always knew after that first couple of days that there was no chance of anything actually happening between us. Gabriel, on the other hand, has always been a legitimate option, and he seemed to like me as much as I liked him. In the few conversations we'd had together, we seemed to have enough in common that a relationship felt like a very real possibility.

I wanted to take the next step with Gabriel and ask him to be my boyfriend, but I was nervous about getting too close and too emotionally attached. Adam's warning still swam in the back of my mind, and no matter what I did to try to chase it away, his words had stuck.

Gabriel had been taken by the pack that killed Karen, but for some reason, they had let him walk away. Something was wrong with his story, but it stayed frustratingly out of focus. I didn't want to ask him about it if it led to questions I couldn't answer, like how I'd found him or why it didn't seem to bother anyone else that my wounds could heal from him touching me.

I was a little surprised he hadn't asked about that and was going to say something when he rolled over and grabbed my hand under the covers. I expected an electric jolt, and I pulled my arm away automatically, but nothing happened, so I reached back out to lace our fingers together. Something about that small comfort put my mind at ease, and my concerns began to slip away into the darkened room. "Thank you again for coming to get me today," his voice was soft but carried easily to my ears.

"It was my pleasure. As I said, I had to make sure you were okay after you disappeared. There was no way I was going to wait around to see if you showed up at work again." The mention of work made me remember that I had lost my job earlier, and I let out a quiet groan.

"What is it?"

"Robert fired me for leaving the front desk last night," I said, laughing.

"He what? That's so unfair! You should have someone explain it to him. I'll say something to him tomorrow if you want." He attempted to keep his voice quiet despite the evident frustration.

I smiled at his concern. "No, it's all right. It's probably for the best anyway. That job had started to be more trouble than it was worth." I didn't go into detail about being followed by a pack of supernatural beings that were trying to kill me. I didn't think he'd believe me or want to stick around if he did.

"Well, if you aren't going to be there, I'll leave too. You were the best part of working there, and I'm sure I can find something else," he said, squeezing my hand softly.

Hearing him say that he would leave his position made me smile. I couldn't consciously worry about it at the time, but the thought of Gabriel being at the hotel where the other pack could find him and did, made me uncomfortable.

"I'm sure you'll have something new in no time," I whispered, trying to keep my voice low. He yawned again, which reminded me just how tired I was. "We should try to get some sleep. Adam and I have a big day tomorrow of trying to find some friends that went missing." I didn't want to say too much and scare him, but I had already mentioned Carlos and Rosa earlier in the evening, so changing the story now would look fishy.

"I'm happy to come with you to look for them if you'd like."

I hated to refuse, but I knew this would probably not be a typical search party. "Thanks for the offer, but I think you should make sure your mom is okay. Plus, you have a job to quit, remember?"

He laughed, "That's right, I do. I never thought I'd quit my first job so quickly, but the idea of it is honestly pretty exciting."

"I imagine it's better than being fired," I said, which caused us both to laugh again. We continued to whisper for the next hour or so, each exchange taking a little bit longer as we fell asleep for a few seconds before responding to the other person. Finally, I decided we should try to go to sleep, so I called it quits just after 1:00 a.m. Gabriel rolled over and faced the outside edge of the bed, and I did the same on my side, but after a couple of seconds, I could hear Gabriel moving around, right before I felt his lips brush against my cheek.

"Goodnight, Caleb." He sounded sleepy as he rolled back over and fluffed his pillow.

I touched my cheek where he had kissed me and smiled, "Goodnight, Gabriel."

I had been asleep for a few hours when I was pulled from my dream about being a wolf and hunting a white rabbit in the woods. Talk about clichés! I was mentally rolling my eyes at the dream when I noticed that my body was automatically reacting to something happening in the room. I couldn't hear anything but Gabriel's snoring, so I slowly opened an eye and tried to see if anyone was on my side of the room. I couldn't see or hear anything unusual and decided I would have to roll over to check the other side. I tried to pretend I was still asleep and adjusting as I rolled over to face Gabriel and that side of the bedroom.

When I finally opened my eyes, nothing was happening along the room's edges, so I tried to listen for something coming from the hallway or outside. After a few minutes of relative silence, I was still at a loss, but the feeling of unease seemed to have passed. I rolled back over and swung my legs over the side of the bed, which helped bring me up into a sitting position, and tried to walk to the bathroom with my eyes still mostly shut. I tripped over a shoe and nearly did a face plant, but I grabbed the dresser before falling over completely.

I opened the door and slipped into the hallway quickly to avoid waking Gabriel. I padded down the hallway to the nearest bathroom that would allow me to flush without waking anyone and opted for a light-off approach. No need to make myself night blind. When I was finished washing my hands, I stumbled back to my bedroom, still trying to stay asleep as long as possible while walking.

When I opened the bedroom door, the smell from the room hit my nostrils, and my senses kicked into overdrive. My eyes shot open; the thought of sleep left my mind, and I crouched low to avoid being attacked easily. The smell of a wolf was overwhelming; it smelled like whoever it was, they were in the room right now. When no one came flying at me, I started to walk toward the bed to check on Gabriel, who was still fast asleep and snoring quietly.

My breath caught in my chest when I looked down at the bed. Running down the middle were five slash marks in the bedding that also ripped into the mattress. When I reached out to check the damage, I realized it fit the size of my hand exactly, and when I looked closer, there were pieces of fabric and thread all over my side of the bed and me.

What the hell happened? I was staring at my now normal-looking hands, afraid of what could have happened if I'd slashed a few more inches away from myself. Something was wrong, but I didn't want to wake Gabriel and have him find out he was nearly attacked in his sleep. Lorelai or Adam might know what to do, but I couldn't risk Gabriel waking up when I was out of the room, so I pulled up a chair, tucked my hands under my legs, and waited for the sun to come up.

Twenty-Eight

Later that morning, I was still sitting in a chair with my hands firmly lodged up under my legs, but my will was beginning to slip. Too much time had passed since I first saw the damage I had done to the bed, and I hadn't gotten enough sleep to keep myself going. I could feel my eyes getting heavier and my head nodding forward or back every once in a while, but I tried to stay awake by any means possible.

Finally, around 6:30, I couldn't sit any longer, so I decided to risk a quick walk out to the kitchen to find something to keep me going. I slipped out of the room, leaving a sleeping Gabriel behind, with a massively damaged mattress and set of sheets. When I got to the kitchen, I was greeted by the smell of freshly brewed coffee, which reminded me of mornings with my parents back home. I was pleasantly surprised to see Lorelai leaning against the counter, drinking from a mug with a picture of a wolf howling at the moon. At least she had a sense of humor about the whole thing.

"Good morning, Caleb. How did you sleep?"

I looked at her and let every ounce of how tired I felt show on my face, "Not well."

"What happened? Was it Gabriel? Did something else happen between you two after we left?" Her interest was nice, and it made me feel like she would understand the things I was going through.

"No, nothing like that. But I woke up in the middle of the night, and there were slashes down the middle of the bed. I'm not positive, but I think I may have attacked it somehow."

She looked at me with her head to one side, seeming to think carefully before replying. "Did you two…you know…last night?"

It took me a second before I understood what she was asking, "Oh! No! No, we didn't do anything like that."

This seemed to confuse her even more, "Were you angry about something that happened, or scared?"

My sleep-deprived brain was chugging along slowly, but I was finally able to respond, "No, Gabriel and I talked until we both fell asleep. I woke up and went to the bathroom, and when I returned to the room, it smelled—" I stopped and realized what my foggy memory had erased.

"Smelled like what?" she asked, taking another sip from her mug.

"It smelled like a wolf, and when I got close to the bed, I noticed slashes down the middle of the bed, and it looked like they were about the same size as my hand."

Her eyes seemed to light up, and her mouth pinched into a thin line. "Has anything like that happened before?"

"Not since the shower incident I told you about a while ago, but I was furious that time. There was nothing to trigger it this time that I can remember."

She nodded but kept her face free of emotion, so I couldn't tell what she was thinking. "Well, try not to think about it too much. It's probably nothing. In the meantime, I'd recommend you cover up the damage so your friend doesn't ask questions."

"I've been awake for hours, afraid of what I might do if I fell asleep again, so can I have some coffee first?"

She poured me a cup, and I added as much cream and sugar as possible. I didn't like the taste of coffee, but the caffeine was a nice boost to my depleted energy. I took a couple of big gulps to get the last of the sleepiness out of my head and then turned back to the bedroom.

"Caleb, before you go, can we talk about what happened before you went to bed last night with the bruises?"

I walked back into the kitchen and decided food sounded good right now, too. "Yeah, I wanted to get your opinion on that. What do you think is happening?" I asked as I rummaged through the pantry and refrigerator.

"I was hoping you could tell me. Adam pulled away as if you had hurt him, but I didn't experience any discomfort. His bruise went away, and mine is still here," she pointed to the small bruise on her arm.

I wasn't sure how to explain it, "Well, sometimes, when Gabriel and I touch, it's like there's this sting of electricity between us. I noticed it when I first met him, but I thought it was a fluke. But now, the more time we spend together, the more it happens."

She nodded, "And does it always heal you?"

"I don't know," I shook my head, which was now buried in the freezer. "I hadn't really noticed it until last night, but my broken nose went away pretty fast, I apparently came back from the dead, and my body felt better after he was around yesterday. I assumed my healing ability was speeding up because I was getting closer to the awakening, but you and Adam both saw what happened when we touched him." I found some frozen waffles and pulled those out.

Lorelai looked down at the counter, seemingly deep in thought, and jumped a little when I put the box of waffles down on the counter near her. "How exactly did you meet this boy, Caleb?" The suspicion in her voice set me on edge.

"He came into my hotel, looking for a job. He ended up getting hired, so we occasionally worked together. Then I ran into him at the mall when I was there with Adam and my friend Megan." I popped a couple of waffles into the toaster and waited.

"Have you seen him with anyone else, inside or outside work?" What was with her and Adam? He had never been anything but friendly to me, and they are all over him like he was the one who killed Karen.

"No, I haven't. He was at the mall alone, and he always showed up at work on his own. But, he's never threatened me, and I haven't told him anything he shouldn't know." My face started to heat.

"I'm not saying he's a bad person, Caleb, but he seemed to get more involved in your life right before you were attacked, and Carlos and Rosa disappeared. It may be a coincidence, but it could also be that something is happening that you aren't aware of yet." Her calm voice had the opposite effect on my emotions, which now, thanks to my lack of sleep, were wildly out of control. The waffles popped up, and I grabbed them without thought, burning my hand, before dropping them back in the toaster.

"I believe him, and I'd appreciate it if you and Adam tried to do the same. Remember, he's a guest here, and you expect everyone to treat him accordingly." It was rude, especially to someone in their own home, but for some reason, the way they were acting toward Gabriel felt like a rejection of me.

"I have been treating him well; I have given you the freedom to make your decisions, but you have to remember that if you are wrong, it doesn't just hurt you, me, or Adam. It can impact everyone here, and I'm cautioning you to keep that in mind."

I hadn't stopped to consider how this might impact the rest of the pack, and I was embarrassed by how I reacted to her question. It seemed I was struggling with this whole Alpha thing more than I realized.

"You're right. I'm sorry. I wasn't thinking about the pack. I was so worried about Gabriel and how everyone would make him feel that I didn't consider how his being around would impact the rest of the pack."

She smiled a little at me, "There's nothing wrong with that, but you also have to learn that when you take over this pack, you will always be responsible for it and the safety of everyone in it."

"I'm not sure I can handle all of that pressure. I'm barely figuring out how to take care of myself, and it's gotten me killed already. Somehow, I doubt others would be lucky enough to walk away from death the way I did."

"I wish I could say otherwise, but you make an excellent point." Her face lost some of the light it had held before. "It certainly didn't happen to—"

She stopped short of saying Karen's name, but the message was clear. I'd already gotten someone in the pack killed, and there was no way to fix that. My stomach tightened, and anger rippled through me. Then I remembered that no one had seen or heard from Carlos or Rosa, and the heat under my skin rose even more. "I won't let that happen again. I'll do whatever it takes to keep anyone else from dying for me."

"Caleb, I want you to know that no one holds you responsible for her death. She was doing what she was supposed to do, exactly what you will have to do once you are awakened. She died to protect not just you but the entire pack as well." She rubbed her hand along my shoulder, trying to comfort me. It did little to help my anger, and I knew what I had to do.

"I have to go talk to Adam. I'll talk to you later. Thanks for your input on everything." I picked up my mug of coffee, grabbed the waffles again, and walked out of the kitchen and back to my room.

Fifteen minutes later, I was dressed and ready to go. I left a note for Gabriel telling him to stay as long as he wanted and that I would be back as soon as possible. Then I threw a blanket over the scratch in the middle of the bed to keep him from finding the damage. It was the only thing I could do with the little time I had to spare. I found Adam sleeping on the couch in the front room with other pack members scattered around the floor and other furniture.

I softly nudged his shoulder to wake him without rousing anyone else and held my finger up to my lips when he finally opened his eyes to stop him from talking. He nodded his head and followed me from the room.

"What's going on?" He asked, rubbing the sleep from his eyes.

"We have to find Rosa and Carlos," I said.

He glanced at his watch, noting the very early hour, and started to protest, "Caleb, I—"

I cut him off before he could start, "I know, you already searched their house and you have people out looking for them, but this is important to me. The longer we wait, the further away they could be, and the less time we have to try to get them back. Plus, if we're walking around before many people are out, we'll attract a lot less attention for sniffing the ground or whatever it is we'll have to do."

He closed his eyes and shook his head. "We don't sniff the ground."

"Well, I don't know! I've never had to try to find someone who was missing." As the words left my mouth, I realized that wasn't true anymore. "Except Gabriel, of course."

"Of course." He took a deep breath and let out a large sigh before continuing, "All right, let me get dressed and wake some of the others. We'll leave in fifteen minutes."

Twenty-Nine

Fifteen minutes later, we were all in the car and racing toward Carlos and Rosa's house. In addition to Adam and me, our group included Brent, who had pretended to kidnap me the first time I'd met him, and Tyler, Will, and Wesley, other adult members of the pack. I'd been forced to fight with Will and Wesley during some of my recent sparring sessions, which had fortunately stopped since my attack.`

Adam had figured out that the last time anyone had seen either Rosa or Carlos had been two days ago, and the last time anyone had spoken to them had been the night Gabriel and I were attacked.

"When we get there, try not to touch anything if possible. I've been through the house already, but I want to take it a bit slower this time. Look for anything that would indicate there was a struggle or pre-planned escape." Adam explained things without emotion, which seemed strange to me since I was still seething.

"You think they might have left town?" Brent asked.

"I don't have any idea what happened. I want everyone to keep an open mind when walking in there." Adam replied, punching the gas pedal down further.

We reached their house in a matter of minutes, thanks to its proximity to Lorelai's house and Adam's total disregard for speed limits. "Everyone, stay close, and keep your eyes out for anything that might be important," Adam said to the group before opening the front door and leading us inside. "Caleb and I will check the bedrooms upstairs, Brent and Tyler, you check the main floor, and Will and Wesley, you two have the house's perimeter. Tell us if you smell anyone who shouldn't have been in the area yesterday. But guys," he paused and looked at me before continuing, "try not to crawl around on the ground if the neighbors are watching." Both men gave him a confused look, but didn't respond. Given the task's severity, it was a surreal moment, but I appreciated that he was trying to keep the mood light.

"I hate you right now," I said before hauling off and punching him in the arm. It hurt my hand again, but it was worth it at the moment. I refused to give him the pleasure of knowing I'd hurt myself, however, so I made sure to keep it at my side.

His smile disappeared from his face, leaving it a blank mask, free of emotion. "Let's go, be thorough, and let me know if you find anything."

We broke into different groups, and I followed Adam up the stairs, lined with photos of Rosa and Carlos standing in front of several landmarks around California, as well as a few from the rest of the country. It reminded me that they weren't just pack members, but also people with long lives behind them.

"Don't worry," I whispered. "We'll find you."

Adam turned and looked at me, then nodded and continued down the hallway to the main bedroom. Inside, the bed was still unmade, just like he'd said it had been when he first found out they were gone. He kept walking into the bathroom, which I assumed was also where the closet was located. I walked to the bed and noticed a couple of pills on the night table and a glass of water.

"Adam, come take a look at this."

He walked back into the room and to the bed. "What is it?"

"I'm not sure; there are some pills here, but I don't know what they are. I thought maybe they were important."

He picked them up and looked closely at each before setting them back down on the table, "Looks like pain killers to me, nothing out of the ordinary."

I let out a breath I'd been holding since he'd picked them up and went back to looking, "Okay, good." The covers were pulled back from the bed, but it was hard to tell if it hadn't been made or if someone else had messed it up. I leaned close to the pillow nearest to me, and I could smell Rosa's perfume. It made me happy for a moment, and I smiled before remembering she was missing.

I moved to the other side of the bed and leaned down to smell the other pillow, expecting to smell Carlos. It smelled like him but had something underneath his usual scent that I couldn't place. I used the edge of my sleeves to flip the pillow over, and the smell became much stronger once I did. I dropped the pillow and stepped back from the bed, trying to get some space between whatever was causing the odor and my nose.

I must have made an unusual noise because Adam came into the room with a look of concern on his face, "What'd you find?"

"It's the pillow—it smells," I struggled to explain it, "I don't know, wrong somehow."

Adam came closer, but when he leaned over, he did not have the same reaction I did. "I don't smell anything unusual," he said, looking at me with concern. "Sorry."

"I swear there is something wrong with the pillow." I stepped closer to the bed and inhaled again. The scent clung to the pillow, making me choke a little. "It smells like the air that has been trapped inside the same space for too long, mixed with copper." Chills ran through my body, and I backed away from the bed again.

He tried again but shook his head, "Sorry, Caleb. I don't smell anything. Why don't you help me look through the bathroom and closet?" He led me from the main part of the bedroom into the en-suite bathroom, which was small but tidy.

"It doesn't look like they took any toiletries with them," I said. Their toothbrushes, toothpaste, hairspray, make-up, and brushes were still arranged on the countertop.

"And their closet still looks like it's full," Adam said as he pointed to the door behind me.

I walked into the small walk-in closet filled with clothes from different decades and outfits for every occasion. "How would you know otherwise? I don't think anything else could fit on these racks, but it'd be impossible to tell if they took the bare minimum."

"True, but their luggage is still here, so if they packed clothes, they didn't take any of their bags."

We finished in the master bedroom and looked through the other two rooms, which were similarly free of anything that suggested something had happened to the couple. We passed the main bedroom on our way downstairs, and the chill from earlier ran from the top of my head down my arms, causing my hair to stand on end. I kept walking and didn't tell Adam about my reaction, worried he would tease me again.

Brent and Tyler were also unlucky on the main floor, finding some strange scuff marks on several walls, but nothing major. "It looks like Rosa kept things pretty clean down here, so there was nothing to find," Brent said to Adam, motioning to the spotless countertops, floors, and shelves. It made me feel like a complete and utter slob since I knew I hadn't cleaned my apartment in over a month, and it was probably to the point where the dust height could be measured.

We all walked back out the front door, where Wesley was waiting for Will to finish his check. "Did you find anything?" Adam asked Wesley, who had walked over to join the rest of us.

"Not so much as a stray leaf in the yard. Will should be done soon; he was just checking the trash cans to be safe." As he finished speaking, Will called out to him from the side of the house. We all walked over to see what he'd found.

"Check it out," he said, opening the trash bin's lid, "there are some rags with a little bit of blood on them, but it smells like someone doused them with bleach." Brent and Adam looked in the bin while the rest of us hung back.

Something about the bleach struck a chord with me, but I couldn't remember why. I wasn't sure I could look at bloody rags just now and took Will at his word. "What does that mean?" I asked, trying to make myself think of something other than blood.

Who knows?" Adam replied. "It could be as simple as blood from meat they'd cooked, but why pour bleach on them to kill the smell?"

Brent spoke up then, "I don't think it's animal blood. It looks too dark to be from anything they would have bought at a store."

My stomach churned at the mention of bloody food, so I added to Brent's thought, "We have to assume it's their blood. Someone cleaned it up and then used the bleach to cover the smell and maybe keep the flies away."

"Caleb's right. We should assume that Carlos and Rosa didn't walk out of the house on their own terms. They were either taken or…" Adam let the rest of the sentence fall away, but the conclusion of his thought was obvious.

The memory clicked into place, and I knew where I'd smelled bleach before. It was in the dumpster behind the hotel the night Gabriel was taken. The presence of blood and bleach in the trash where people I knew were taken was too much of a coincidence to ignore. The other pack had been here, and they were going to pay.

"We have to find them and get revenge." My anger had bubbled to the surface again, and I found it much nicer to be angry than to be scared or sick.

"We can't rush into anything, or we could cause an all-out war between packs. That kind of thing can get everyone killed." Adam spoke to the group but looked only at me. "Though I agree with Caleb, we need to find them and confront the pack about what they've been doing in our territory."

Everyone agreed with Adam, and I finally started to think that maybe this whole thing wouldn't end up that badly. That we might get through it without anyone else getting hurt. But the chill that ran through me as we drove away suggested that I probably wasn't that lucky.

Thirty

When we returned to the house, I went to my room to see if Gabriel was awake. When I opened the door, I noticed the bed was empty, but the blanket I had used to cover the slash marks was still in the same place I'd left it. That was one positive thing in my day; hopefully, it wouldn't be the only good thing. The bathroom door was wide open, and it was empty. I decided to check with Lorelai to see if she had seen Gabriel or if he was in the kitchen with her.

I walked into the living room and kitchen area, but neither Gabriel nor Lorelai was in the room. I got some looks from the kids sitting around the table eating cereal, but they all looked away when I made eye contact. At least someone around here respects me.

"Lorelai?" I called out, but there was no response, so I tried a different approach. "Gabriel?"

"He left," a tiny voice behind me said. I turned around and saw a little girl with bright red hair looking at me nervously.

"He did? Do you know where he went?" Getting information from a child seemed like a bad idea, but her gaze never left mine, so I figured she was an okay source.

"He told Ms. Lorelai that he was going home. He said he needed to see his mom." Long lashes, which were difficult to see because of their light color, framed her brown eyes. She blinked a few times before continuing. "He said that you could call him when you got back."

"Thank you for telling me, sweetie." I smiled down at her, and her mouth spread wide in a smile of her own. And then I remembered that I was responsible for her and the other kids sitting around the table, and I had to leave the room. "Enjoy your breakfast!" I called back to the kids, my voice on the verge of cracking from emotion.

I pulled my cell phone from my pocket and dialed Gabriel's number as I walked back to my bedroom. It rang a few times and then went to his voicemail. "Hey, it's Caleb. I just wanted to make sure everything was okay there. Give me a call back when you can. Talk to you soon." I clicked the 'end' button and shoved the phone back into my pocket.

I had to figure out how to find this other pack, and without any information from Gabriel about where he thought they might have taken him, I was left with an impossibly large area to search. There was no way I could find the pack without something to go on, and current information was pretty hard to come by.

They had to be somewhere in San Diego County because they kept coming back to Downtown, and my gut told me they were staying somewhere close to the city. I was trying to devise a plan, which meant I was staring at the wall, picturing the different ways I would try to kill Dominic, when my phone went off. I checked the text message and was surprised to see it was from Gabriel.

"Got your VM. Can't talk now. Will call U later."

I typed up a quick reply, "Sounds good. Glad you're okay!"

With nothing else left to go on, I left the room to find Lorelai again and get her all caught up on what happened at Carlos and Rosa's house earlier. I knocked softly on her bedroom door, but there was no reply, so I slowly opened it and stuck my head inside. She wasn't in the immediate area, but since I had never been given a tour of her room, I figured a little look around couldn't hurt.

I closed the door and looked around at what she kept in her space. The walls were a pale gray, with a rich dark wood sleigh bed and red accents throughout the room. On one side of the room was a large window that looked out over the backyard, and underneath the window was an oversized leather couch. Some art was on the wall, but the overall aesthetic was simple, clean, and warm.

I was about to move into the bathroom area when I noticed a small, framed picture beside the bed. From where I was standing, I could see a man, a woman, and an infant. My hands started to sweat a little as I moved closer and picked up the picture frame. The woman was Lorelai, but she was younger and happier than she looked now. She had the baby in her arms and was held protectively by the man I assumed was my birth father.

He had dark hair like mine and dark brown eyes that beamed pride and happiness through the picture and out into the world. I could almost feel his stare as if it were a physical thing I was experiencing at that moment. The baby had Lorelai's eyes. My eyes. My mouth dropped open as I realized that the baby was me. I assumed they wouldn't have any photos of me since they'd had me for such a short time and then given me away. Pictures would only remind them of the baby they couldn't keep. But there I was, my cheeks bright red in the sun and my dark hair popping out from a knitted cap.

"You were the most beautiful baby," Lorelai's voice startled me, and I jumped a little before regaining my composure.

"I'm sorry, I didn't mean to snoop," I said, setting the picture back down on the bedside table.

"No, no, it's fine. You aren't snooping. This is your house, too. I'm glad you found the picture. I wanted to show you earlier, but I thought it might seem like I was trying to force a mother/son relationship on you, so I didn't say anything." She walked over to where I was standing and reached across me to pick up the photo before sitting on the edge of the bed. "This was taken right after you were born. We took you to the beach, which was a silly decision. It was the middle of February, and it was still pretty cold, and the wind made us even colder." She smiled at the memory, and I wished that I could have been reliving it with her.

She continued, "We found someone to take our picture, but you started to cry. We had to wait for you to stop crying so we could have a good family photo to send out to the pack. Finally, after about five minutes and long after the would-be photographer left, you calmed down enough that we were able to snap a photo. But it had gotten so cold that most people at the beach had cleared out. We had to go into a store to ask someone to take a photo, and when the woman saw how cute you were, she immediately agreed. You smiled at your father right before we got into position and started giggling. It was the perfect picture on a less-than-perfect day, and my favorite picture of all of us because we were all so happy."

"I can see why it's your favorite." I smiled at her, glad to have a family story with my birth parents in it.

"We were happy, but it's my favorite because, despite the weather and the trouble we had finding someone to take the photo, it made me feel like we could get through anything as long as we were together." She tucked a loose strand of hair behind her ear as she said the last part and looked away from the picture before quickly wiping her eyes.

"That is still true. And now that we're together again, nothing will keep us apart." I hugged her, realizing the years apart didn't matter to me anymore. I still loved my parents; they raised me, provided for me, and kept me safe. Nothing would ever change that. But I was growing closer to Lorelai as we spent time together, because she knew what my future held. And I did feel like we would be able to take on whatever the world threw at us as long as we were together. Suddenly, I realized that I had more love than I had ever had in my life, and I would do anything to protect the people I loved.

She hugged me back and squeezed my hand, smiling again," I am glad you came back to San Diego. I wish I could have kept you safe for longer, but I am happy to have you back."

"I'm glad to be here with you and the pack. There's nowhere else I'd rather be right now." And I realized that it was true. I'd never been in more danger in my life than I was at this moment, but I'd never felt safer.

"Now," she said, clearing her throat and wiping her eyes, "what did you find out from Carlos and Rosa's?"

"Nothing that gives us anything to go on, unfortunately. Will found blood-soaked rags in the garbage, and it seemed like someone poured bleach over everything to cover up the smell." I thought about telling her the similarity to what I smelled in the dumpster but figured it wouldn't matter. We already knew who was behind this. "But other than that, nothing in or around the house indicates they were attacked or abducted." A chill crept down the base of my neck at my memory of the pillow, but I didn't think my weird vibe from the house would be helpful, so I attempted to ignore the feeling.

"What did Adam and the others decide to do?"

"Actually, I decided that we should go after this other pack. They killed Karen, took Gabriel, and did something to Carlos and Rosa, and they need to be punished."

"You aren't ready to fight the other pack. If we attack, they have every right to go after anyone, including you, as part of their self-preservation." Her worry began to spread through my body, but I forced it to stop before it could take over my anger.

"I don't care. I'm not more valuable than the other pack members, especially not right now. We don't know that I could lead even if I did become Alpha, and there's no reason to let someone else's life be payment for my protection." I felt confident in what I was saying, but secretly hoped it would be enough to get me through the actual fighting.

"I am so proud of you. You have come such a long way since that first night we met, and I know you'll be a great leader, as I have already said. Now, it's time for you to believe that as much as you believe you are equal to the other members of the pack."

I was about to respond when a loud bang and even louder voices could be heard from the foyer. We both ran to the door and practically flew down the hallway to the front door, which had been opened with such force that the handle had created a hole in the wall behind it. That accounted for the loud bang, and the voices were easy to figure out since a group of people crowded around something on the floor.

Adam came from somewhere behind me and pushed through the crowd to get to the middle. His look told me something was seriously wrong, and my mind shut down as instinct took over. "Everyone move!" I growled loudly. I was met with shocked, scared, and angry faces, but people quickly backed away, and I could finally see what everyone had crowded around. Lying face down on the floor was Carlos, and from where I was standing, he looked dead.

Thirty-One

"What happened? Where did he come from? Did anyone see what happened?" Questions spilled out of me as I rushed toward Carlos's body, which I could now see was covered in cuts, bruises, and dried blood. No one spoke up to answer my questions, so I looked around the room, making eye contact with as many people as possible, all of whom shook their heads.

"The door flew open, and when I looked over, Carlos was lying where he is now. I didn't see or hear anyone else, and there weren't any cars in the driveway." One of the women in the pack, Sylvia, spoke up. She was Olivia's older sister, and they had the same kind and curious eyes.

"Thank you, Sylvia," I said as I looked down at Carlos. "Will you please find your sister? We need her here, now." She nodded and left the room, taking her son Joshua with her.

I looked up at Adam, whose face was an emotionless mask. "What do you think? Do we risk flipping him over?"

He leaned in close to Carlos's face, placing his ear next to Carlos's mouth, "I can hear faint breathing, so he's alive." A collective sigh spread through the room at Adam's announcement. "But I can't tell if anything is broken, so flipping him over might do more damage than good at this point."

I looked up and saw some familiar faces hanging around, "Wesley, Tyler, will you please do a quick check around the outside of the house. See if you can find anyone else or some explanation for how Carlos made it back, and see if Rosa is out there." They left without saying a word, and some others followed them out, which helped give Olivia more space to work.

She walked into the foyer, already holding her bag of medical supplies, and knelt next to Carlos. I moved back to give her room, but Adam stayed close and refused to budge. She ran her fingers down the middle of Carlos's neck and back and looked up at Adam after a few tense moments. He doesn't appear to have any noticeable spinal damage. It should be safe to flip him, but just in case, we need to take it slow, and try to not twist or bend anything unnecessarily."

Adam moved to the top of his body, Olivia positioned herself at Carlos's feet, and they carefully flipped him over. When they did, it was apparent that the cuts and bruises on his back were nothing compared to what happened to his face and chest. What could only be described as claw marks were all over his body, from his left cheek down to his right thigh. It looked like he had tried to heal deep gashes without any luck. Both eyes were bruised and swollen shut. And his lip was busted open in the middle.

It was hard to look at the damage done to him and even harder to listen when he tried to speak. All that came out was a weak moan. Adam leaned in and whispered in his ear, which caused Carlos to move his head almost imperceptibly up and down, or side to side. After a few questions, Adam spoke to the rest of us.

"The other pack took him and Rosa from their home. He escaped and got himself back here, which means they're closer to us than we thought." Knowing they were close to my pack caused the familiar flush of anger to rise inside me.

"Who did this to them? Was it the same guy who attacked me?"

Adam leaned back down and listened for a few seconds, then replied, "He isn't sure. They didn't see who took them, but he said multiple people attacked them."

My heart started racing as my instincts kicked in, and in this case, I knew they were firmly leaning toward a fight, which was an interesting change. Not long ago, I would have done anything to avoid confrontation, and now I was actively seeking it out. I wasn't sure I liked that new direction, but when it came to protecting my pack, I felt it was the best thing to do.

"Does he know how to get back to them?"

Carlos's head began nodding more adamantly than before, which I took as a good sign and a strong indicator that he was as interested in going after these monsters as I was.

Olivia reached out at that point and put her hand on his head to keep him from doing any damage to himself. "Carlos, have you tried to change so you can heal?" He nodded weakly. "I want you to try to heal parts of yourself for me. I'm going to inject you with something that should help." She pulled a syringe from her back and a small vial of liquid. After drawing some of it into the syringe, she looked down at him again.

"Okay, I'm going to give you some epinephrine, which should make shifting easier. I want you to start by trying to change just your right leg, then your left. Are you ready?" He nodded at her, and she plunged the needle into the exposed skin on his right leg. At first, nothing happened. We all sat there in silence and waited. Finally, the skin around the injection site started to ripple and change. His hair grew longer, and his leg shape began to change. As it did, the wounds closed quickly until they were impossible to see beneath the skin.

"Now, the other leg," Olivia prompted. Again, the skin began to ripple, and the hair grew longer as the skin that had been damaged seemed to rush back together from each side. "Good, good. Now, I want you to try to move the change up through your torso to your arms."

I was accustomed to the sight of the transition from man to animal now, and I watched as wounds that had looked life-threatening moments before became angry, red scars and then wholly melted away into the fur that covered them.

Adam sat next to Carlos, who was now primarily a wolf except for his head. His face was still set and emotionless, but his eyes gave away the fear and relief that battled within him.

"Now, I want you to complete the change if you can, and…" Her voice was cut off by the scream of pain from Carlos's busted lips. Adam was moving now, trying to figure out what was wrong, while Olivia tried to keep Carlos as still as possible. Adam ran his hands along Carlos's sides, feeling for any apparent damage, and when he got down to his hip area, Carlos let out another cry of pain that caused us all to jump.

"Something isn't right. What happened, Olivia?" Adam looked desperate for answers, but Olivia's mouth just opened and closed, and she shook her head, unable to say anything. Carlos began to change back to human form, which caused him to break out in a foul-smelling sweat. "Olivia! Fix this!" Adam was yelling now, which caused her to flinch, but she held her ground, something I wasn't sure I would have been able to do in a similar situation.

"I'm not sure what happened. He should have been fine. You saw it yourself; his wounds were closing…" Then she stopped, and her eyes filled with fear. "He might have closed a wound that wasn't healed, but there's no way to know unless we do a CT scan, which would require a trip to the hospital." The last part of her statement came out quietly because she knew we couldn't take him there.

"Do you think moving him from the floor is safe?" I asked Olivia to focus on what we could do rather than what we couldn't. "I think he might be more comfortable in bed, and then we can reassess his injuries."

"I-I-I think so," she said, her face pale. I had never seen this lack of confidence in her before, and I realized the situation was much worse than I had imagined.

"Okay, good. Adam," I reached over and touched his arm, snapping him out of his stupor. "We need to move Carlos now. Let's take him to my room, and he can lie on my bed." I thought about the damage I had done to it earlier and was glad I covered it up before leaving this morning. "You get his upper body, and Olivia and I will take a side to keep him as stable as possible."

We all got into position and carried him the short distance to my bedroom before laying him gently on the bed. He let out a few small pained noises, but mostly seemed feverish and out of breath. As we stepped back from the bed, Adam looked up at me. "You have to heal him."

My mouth dropped open at his request; I didn't know how to heal him. That was why we had Olivia. "I'm sorry, Adam, but I don't know how it works."

"You and Gabriel made my bruise go away last night. You healed my internal bleeding." His eyes were dilated, and his breathing was uneven.

"But Adam, we did that together. On my own, I don't think I can do anything. And that was a bruise. This," I gestured to Carlos's body, "is much bigger than a bruise. I'm not sure it would work."

"You have to try. Please! For me." He gave me an intense look that told me there was more going on inside his head than he was willing to share at the moment, so I did the only thing I could think of, I texted Gabriel.

I reached out and touched Carlos's arm to see if I could somehow make his wounds heal. "Adam, will you please get a cool, wet cloth for Carlos's forehead?" I kept my hand on Carlos, but I didn't know what to do to heal him, so I thought about my energy flowing into him and taking the damage away. My hand heated up, and he started to move around a little, but then he cried out in pain, and I pulled my hand away.

"What did you do?" Adam asked, stepping back into the room.

"I just thought about healing him and tried to force energy into his body. But I don't think this will work without Gabriel."

As I said it, my phone's screen lit up with a response. Gabriel wrote back, "Sorry, I can't right now. Will call when I can." It wasn't the text I'd hoped to receive, so I didn't tell Adam what he'd said. Finally, I heard the front door close, and soon after that, Tyler and Wesley walked into the bedroom, which distracted him.

"Did you find anything?" I asked, hoping they had more luck outside than we seemed to have inside.

"No," Wesley replied, "I looked around the whole property and even went down the road, trying to see if I could find anything or anyone that shouldn't have been there. Some of the others took their cars and are driving around to see if they can find anything, but we've got nothing right now." The mood in the room got worse, and I realized we'd been so caught up in Carlos's pain that we had momentarily forgotten he wasn't the only one missing.

"Where's Rosa?" I asked the room, unsure if Carlos was still coherent enough to respond.

Adam leaned down and whispered to Carlos, who began to moan again as tears, tinged pink with blood, streamed down his face. Adam looked up at me, his eyes glowing with rage, "She didn't make it."

I could feel my senses snap to attention as everything became clearer and more sensitive, and my anger rolled through my body. That was the final straw. They'd killed and abducted too many members of my pack, and now they would face the consequences of their actions. If Carlos had escaped and made his way back on foot, we should be able to find our way back to where they were hiding, but I wasn't going to waste another minute.

"Everyone who is willing to fight, get ready. We have to leave. Now!"

Thirty-Two

"Someone needs to stay and look after Carlos," Adam said to the room. Olivia volunteered to do what she could, and the rest of us left them there and tried to find more people to come with us to find the other pack. Adam had been able to get some information on the pack's location from Carlos and created directions based on what he'd said.

"We need to be careful, this pack will not hesitate to kill any of us, and I refuse to lose anyone else!" I tried to make my voice sound authoritative as I spoke to the group of people that had gathered. "My goal is to get them to leave, but I will fight if I have to." A chorus of agreement rang out through the crowd, which wasn't exactly what I wanted, but I figured if it came down to it, having people willing to fight would be better for us.

Adam and Brent took off in the lead while the rest of us split up between a few other cars. I rode with Lorelai, Sylvia, and Sylvia's husband, Jon.

"Um, Lorelai, can I ask you a question about Adam and Carlos?"

She turned her head to acknowledge me, "You want to know why Adam is so upset about what happened to him?"

"Yes, it feels like he's lost a parent or something. They aren't related, are they?"

"No, they're not related, but when Adam was first awakened, Carlos was the one who taught him everything he knew. He was his mentor and friend, but their relationship was as close as father and son. Adam grew up in the pack, as you know, but his mother died during childbirth, and his father chose to leave the pack afterward."

"He was abandoned?" Things began to click together in my mind and made more sense as she explained Adam's history.

"Exactly. Carlos and Rosa took him in, as we all did, and raised him as a pack member. But those two were practically inseparable, and when you moved back to San Diego, they both worked to keep you safe. Carlos ensured you were always being watched, and Adam was usually the one to do it. He has become Carlos's second in command, so to speak, which shows just how much respect they share for each other."

Hearing about the relationship and history between the two struck a nerve, and I was even more determined to do whatever it took to heal him and get the other pack to move on or pay for what they'd done. Letting Carlos and me go was a mistake they should never have made. Now we knew who they were and where they had been hiding. And our time of suffering was about to come to an end.

We sped down the winding, narrow roads that led to the part of the city Carlos said he'd come from. He described the houses he had passed and the street names whenever he could recall. We drove in a long line of vehicles until we finally found the place. The house was a ranch-style home that looked surprisingly normal. I'm not sure what I was expecting, maybe something old and run down, or something unwelcoming, with barbed wire all over. This sage green one-story made me reconsider who I thought this group was.

As planned, we drove past the house and kept going, looking for somewhere easy to hide, and then most of us jumped out of the car while one person from each vehicle took off, so we wouldn't have to hide all of them.

The property spanned almost six acres, so we could get relatively close to the house without being seen. As Carlos had described, there was a large barn structure that looked like it had horse stalls in it, but according to Carlos, they were outfitted for a very different purpose. Once we found a suitable area, we all spread out and waited for nightfall.

After a few hours of waiting, the sun began to dip below the horizon, and the brilliant gold and oranges gave way to rich pinks and deep purples, slowly becoming dark navy and finally total blackness. Bright spots of light from distant stars helped make finding our way toward the house just a little bit easier.

Looking around at some of the others, I could see their eyes reflecting the dim light, and I realized that I was probably the only one struggling to see my way toward the house. This was even easier to tell when you listened to the noises everyone was making, or in actuality, the noises they weren't, whereas I seemed to find every dried leaf to crunch and rock to kick along the way.

I started to feel claustrophobic in the darkness, even though it was a wide-open space; it felt like the night was closing in on me. The nightmare I continued to have almost every night came to mind as the familiar panic began to spread through me. I was about to start yelling and clawing at the darkness when a hand came out of nowhere and grabbed onto me. It helped anchor me to reality, where the dark was beautiful and not something to fear.

I squeezed the hand, unsure whose it was, and then released it, feeling more comfortable knowing that I was not out here alone. The pack had just crossed into a covered arena, with bleachers on one end and low walls surrounding the outside edge, when the night was suddenly ablaze with white light.

I could hear the others cry out in pain, and judging by the amount of pain my eyes were experiencing at the sudden onslaught of light, I could only imagine what the others were going through.

A voice that was amplified by speakers that surrounded us welcomed the group. "We were beginning to think you would not come. You had been sitting in the trees for so long that we thought we might have to come to you. But this works out so much better." The voice was familiar, but I couldn't place it without a face to go along with it. I tried to open my eyes, and though it was a little blurry and still pretty painful, my vision was returning, and I could see that about 20 people now surrounded us.

Still covering his eyes, Adam called out to the voice, "What are you doing here? Why are you attacking us unprovoked?"

The voice laughed before replying, "Tsk tsk, you're talking out of turn, aren't you? We are only interested in speaking to your Alpha."

My stomach dropped, but I tried not to let it show. I threw my shoulders back and tried to match Adam's volume and confidence, "I'm the Alpha. Answer me! Why are you in our territory, attacking our pack?"

The man laughed again, his voice bouncing around the arena. "Little alpha, you misunderstood. We don't want to speak to a pup. You can't even change and, therefore, cannot rule. Though admittedly, I'm surprised to see you here since I thought I'd killed you." There was some rumbling among the people outside the arena, which I assumed meant they were discussing how I was still alive. Their voices seemed to disappear as soon as his words sank in. Dominic was here, and he seemed to be in charge. There was no way I could face him again; he'd already killed me once, and it had been magic or a miracle that brought me back. Somehow, I didn't think I would be lucky enough to come back to life a second time.

"Silence!" The voice called out angrily, and everyone stopped talking immediately. "As I said, we are only interested in speaking with the Alpha."

Lorelai stepped forward and wore an expression of confidence and boredom, which I thought was a bold choice. "I'm here. What do you have to say?"

"We want your territory. We will give you a chance to be part of our pack and continue to live here, but we will rule. If you accept, the killing will stop. If you refuse, we will do what is necessary." As he said it, a gunshot exploded from somewhere behind us, and Jon fell forward. The bullet had blown out his knee. "You can see we are serious and willing to follow through with this threat."

Lorelai looked carefully down the row of people on each side of her, and I watched as each person in the row shook their head, "It looks like we're refusing your offer, but before you start with the threats, hear me. You can leave our territory now, and we will not hunt you down and kill you all."

Laughter filled the arena again, but this time it was not amplified as it had been, and one of the men from the perimeter stepped inside the illuminated area. After blinking a few times, I recognized Dominic, and chills ran down my spine. "I hardly think you are in any position to argue. You saw what we could do, which was merely a warning shot."

Lorelai smiled, "But you assume these are the only people we have in the area. If you saw us coming, then you surely saw many of us leave. Are you confident you know exactly where they are?" I wasn't sure whether she was bluffing or telling the truth, but I hoped other members of our pack were out there waiting to help us. And I hoped they were already on their way.

Dominic's smile faltered, and he turned around to look behind him long enough that Lorelai was able to close the distance between the two of them before anyone else could react. What happened next was difficult to follow, but it ended in a blur of action and an explosion of sound. Lorelai reached out and broke his neck, which caused him to fall to the ground where he was. In the meantime, the rest of the pack, myself included, scrambled to get out of the center of the arena and away from the bullets flying through the air.

The sounds of fighting, gunshots, and what I hoped was fabric ripping filled the air as I continued to run. I was just about to cross to the outside of the arena and the relative safety of the darkness beyond when I ran straight into one of the members of the other pack. We fell away from each other, and my head smacked against the ground. After I gathered my thoughts, I realized that where our skin touched, I felt a spark. I scrambled to my hands and knees and looked up, then realized I was face-to-face with an equally shocked Gabriel.

Thirty-Three

"Caleb? What're you doing here?" He jumped to his feet, pulling me up with him.

I pulled my arm out of his grasp and backed away carefully, "I could ask you the same thing. I thought you were busy?" My confusion didn't allow me to see the obvious answer at first. And then the realization of the situation clicked into place. "You're one of them, aren't you? You were never abducted from the hotel; you left voluntarily with him. And you've been lying to me ever since."

"They told me they'd kill you if I didn't. And that they would kill my mother if I said anything to you. But then they said you were dead, so when I told you I thought your calls were a trick, that was the truth. I just assumed your pack was trying to trick me."

"You've known who I was this whole time?" I felt sick and betrayed, unsure if I could continue looking at him.

"I only knew you were someone the pack wanted to be watched. That's why I got the job at the hotel. They wanted someone to keep an eye on you without giving away the pack."

I didn't know how to react. He had violated my privacy and knowingly lied to me about things since I'd met him. I should have listened to Adam and Lorelai when they told me something was off with him. I should have listened to my body! Touching someone was not supposed to hurt all the time, and he smelled like a wolf. It should have been incredibly obvious to me. I'd blocked it out and refused to see what was staring me in the face the whole time.

But then, a tiny voice in my head objected to my anger. *He healed you more than once. Thinking about him could have saved your life, and someone who isn't supposed to be in your life could never have done that.* I wasn't sure what to do, so I sat there, dumbfounded.

"Caleb, we have to go!" Gabriel said, pulling me further away from the fighting. I could hear the sounds of what was happening behind me, and I knew I shouldn't turn my back on my family, but it was so easy to be pulled away by Gabriel. Before we went too far away, I dug my feet in and refused to take another step.

"I have to help them!" I pulled away from his grasp. "They're my responsibility. I can't just walk away." I turned around and saw that, for the most part, no one on either side looked significantly injured except for Dominic. His body was still lying in the middle of the illuminated area, and the fighting continued around him.

Then slowly, starting on one end of the arena and moving across toward where Gabriel and I stood, hidden in the shadows, the fighting stopped, and each pack backed away from the other. I moved into the light to figure out what had happened and saw him.

Carlos was walking in from the opposite side, and he looked better than he had when we left the house earlier in the day. His face was no longer swollen and bruised, and he moved as though he were free of pain.

"She did it," I said, knowing that Olivia had somehow worked her medical magic on Carlos and gotten him back on his feet. I noticed my pack was all smiling and coming together in a group, so I started walking toward them before realizing Gabriel wasn't coming with me. I turned and looked at him, but he seemed unsure of what to do and finally decided to join the other pack. I could see the woman I had assumed to be his mother there waiting. It wasn't ideal, but at least he had someone looking out for him.

I still wasn't sure why the fighting had stopped, but when Carlos quit moving toward our pack as he reached the middle of the two groups, I saw that I wasn't the only one confused by his actions. I assumed they had stopped fighting because they knew they were outnumbered as more of our pack joined in the battle, but no one else entered the arena after Carlos, so our numbers remained pretty even.

"Lorelai," I whispered, "what's happening?" She never took her eyes off of Carlos but gave me a subtle shake of her head to let me know she wasn't sure.

"Lorelai," Carlos's voice surprised me with its strength and volume. He seemed to want everyone to hear what he was about to say. "You have come here, the mate of a fallen Alpha and mother to the next Alpha of your pack. You can no longer rule on your own, and though I have been loyal to your pack for all these years, you never once considered making me the rightful leader, hoping instead that I would train your son to take on the role that should have been mine!"

His words were angry, their meaning was surprising, and confusion seemed to spread like fire through our pack. The same could not be said of the other pack, which didn't look at all surprised by this turn of events.

"When you refused to name me Alpha, I knew I only had to bide my time until a challenger would come for Caleb, and then I would be able to make my move." As he said it, he turned to look at the other pack, currently behind him, who quickly bowed their heads in submission. "The Alpha of this pack was the challenger I'd been waiting for, and when she made her intentions known by entering our territory, I knew my time had come."

Knowledge spread across Lorelai's face, but I was still confused by what he was saying. Adam looked like he'd been slapped across the face.

"And what of the Alpha in question? Where is she now?" Lorelai's voice matched Carlos's volume, but not his anger; hers sounded more confident than cocky.

"I'm the Alpha now, and I challenge you for your pack." The blood drained from my face as I realized what had happened. Carlos had killed the other pack's Alpha to gain the right to challenge me for control. He was supposed to be my teacher, and there was no way for him to challenge me from within our pack, so he found another and took over.

Thinking back on the past couple of weeks of fight training, he had never stopped, no matter how injured I'd become, and he made Adam leave me vulnerable the night I was attacked, pretending that he would send someone else to watch me. If I had died that night, there would have been no one else in the pack to take over for Lorelai, and he would have won. I wasn't going to let that happen, and right before I stepped forward to say so, Adam spoke up and cut off my chance.

"I challenge you, Alpha, for your pack." Adam stepped forward into the middle of our two groups and faced Carlos. His face was locked in its expressionless mask, but I knew that this must have been killing him on the inside. He would have to kill

Carlos, the man who was basically his father, to keep him from attacking Lorelai.

"Challenge accepted." Carlos's eyes began to glow in the bright light, his smile became all teeth as his mouth stretched into a snout, and his body changed into a large gray wolf. Adam's change was almost as swift, becoming a massive sandy-colored wolf. Once they had both shifted, the attack was nearly instantaneous, as Carlos ripped the fur from Adam's body in an attempt to clamp down on his throat. Adam countered, tore a chunk of flesh from Carlos's shoulder, then backed quickly away.

He then reared back, getting his neck out of biting range, before landing heavily on top of Carlos and trying to force him into submission. As a wolf, Adam was massive compared to Carlos, but Carlos's body was densely packed with muscle, and he was not giving up easily. I could see that Carlos's shoulder seemed to be shimmering, and then the wound Adam inflicted started to heal.

Carlos was quickly able to shake Adam off. While Adam tried to turn around to attack again, Carlos darted in, biting the skin above the knee joint on Adam's hind leg, ripping it open. Blood spilled onto the dirt as Adam's cry filled the night air. He quickly spun around, the hair on his neck and back raised, making him look even larger and more imposing than he had moments earlier. Adam tried to get in a similar attack, but Carlos must have expected that. He spun in the opposite direction and tried to overpower Adam that way.

Adam took advantage of Carlos's head being down and lunged for his neck. He bit down hard, and Carlos let out a deep growl, which turned into a high-pitched howl. The two broke apart, and on their next bout of attacks, they kicked up so much dust that it was hard to see exactly what was happening.

When they pulled apart again, Adam's ear had been torn in half and was now adding to the puddle of blood beneath the two wolves. The pain of the attacks seemed to be getting to him, and he kept shaking his head like he was trying to dry off. Carlos took advantage of this distraction at every possible moment and got in a few more strong attacks that left Adam limping. In his last, particularly vicious attack, Carlos grabbed Adam's tail and pulled on it, causing him to flip over onto his back. Once there, Carlos bit his stomach, chest, and throat, opening even more wounds, which he would have to change to heal.

Adam had difficulty fighting against Carlos, even though they should have been evenly matched. His refusal to heal himself spoke louder than his attacks, and finally, Adam relented. Carlos picked him up by the throat, something I would have thought impossible, and threw him a few feet away. Adam lay there, crumpled and broken, a soft whine escaping his lips as blood poured out of him.

At this point, Carlos turned on Lorelai, and I knew I had to do something, or I was at risk of losing the only blood relative I had left. I stepped in front of her and looked Carlos in the eyes, "Carlos, I challenge you for control of your pack!"

As the words left my mouth, it felt like my senses were giving out on me. The noises around me seemed to get muffled and then completely disappear as the light in the arena dimmed. The last thing I saw before my vision failed me was Gabriel forcing his way through his pack and running to my side. As our hands gripped onto one another, the familiar shock was noticeably absent, but in its place was a warmth that spread from my hand, up my arm to my head, and then down the rest of my body to the tips of my toes.

It encompassed me as the darkness closed in around me, and even though I knew I could move, it was impossible to escape. I realized my nightmare had become a reality, and if I didn't get my vision back soon, I would be dead before I even had a chance to fight. As my mind tried to process the lack of senses, it failed to notice the one thing still registering in my brain, my sense of touch. I felt as though I was being engulfed in flames, and my skin was peeling off my body.

I tried to scream, but nothing came out of my mouth that now felt like I was wearing a mask. I could still feel Gabriel's hand in my own, and based on the pressure it was exerting, it seemed like he was perhaps equally afflicted. My legs buckled under me, and I curled into a ball as my stomach muscles went into spasm, contracting harder than any crunch I'd ever done. I squeezed my eyes tight and hoped it would be over quickly, and almost as if my body was responding to my mind, the pain went away, and I could see and hear again without any issue.

The lack of sight or sound seemed to make those senses especially sensitive, and I could hear the heartbeat of everyone in the arena and the distant sounds of freeway traffic. I realized I could see in much more detail, but the color clarity seemed to have changed, giving the world a tint I'd never seen before.

As my muscles relaxed, I tried to stand up but noticed I was already standing on all four of my legs. I looked down and did a double-take, then a triple-take, trying to wrap my brain around it.

I'd actually changed! Somehow, even before turning 18, I'd awakened and changed into a wolf. My heart was racing at this realization, and I had so many questions flood my mind at the same time, but I knew I didn't have time to worry about that now.

I glanced to where Gabriel should have been and saw another confused-looking wolf staring back at me. His fur was bluish-black, reflecting the arena's lights, making his coat seem to glisten. I looked down at my fur, which was the same color as Gabriel's, and if I could have smiled in this form, I would have. As it was, I think my tongue flopped out of the side of my mouth.

Then I realized I must have looked foolish because I challenged Carlos for his pack, and now I was standing here like an idiot, with my tongue out.

But as I looked around at the others, no one seemed to have noticed my lengthy delay, and I hoped that maybe everything happened a lot faster in reality than it did in my mind. As I made eye contact with my pack, they bowed their heads and sometimes even went to their knees, so they were down at my height. I looked across to the other pack and realized they were doing the same, but they seemed to focus more on Gabriel than on me. I realized then that I could smell something coming off each of us. It smelled like power, and I liked it.

Thirty-Four

I looked at Carlos and was hopeful that he had come to his senses, especially now that his new pack's loyalty had shifted. But he was still staring me down, his brown eyes filled with a very human level of hatred. He walked to one of his pack members and got in her face, growling low. She didn't respond, so he bit down on her shoulder until she screamed and cowered away from him. Almost immediately, I could smell the blood as it poured from her wound. A woman next to the girl pulled her away from Carlos and tried to calm her down as Carlos continued to stalk around the arena.

Gabriel growled beside me, and I somehow knew what he was thinking. She was not old enough to turn yet, so she didn't stand a chance against Carlos.

When I let out a growl, he was getting ready to attack another person kneeling on the ground. *Fight me, you coward!* He turned toward me as though he had heard my thought. I continued; *I'm the one you want. Leave them alone unless you don't think you can handle someone as young as me.* I admit that taunting a werewolf would have been on my list of things never to do, but being faced with the option of fighting or letting others get hurt, I would have to choose to fight.

Let's do this. Again, I couldn't hear anything or even read his mind, but I could tell from how Carlos had positioned his body and raised his hackles at me that he was ready for the challenge. I took a deep breath and let it out as a bark, which surprised me, but I figured it was as good a way of saying, "Bring it on," as any.

Carlos lunged at me, and I backed away, running into Gabriel, who was still standing beside me. I mentally asked Gabriel to move away from the fight and was happy to feel him pad away quickly. I turned back to face Carlos and realized that we were evenly matched height-wise. He was a lot thicker and more muscular than me, whereas I was leaner and built for speed. That was the only thing I had going for me as I ran around the arena, avoiding Carlos the best way I could.

I tried to remember the moves Adam and the others had taught me during my training, but almost none of it applied now that I had paws and jaws. I kept thinking about dodging and staying out of the way of Carlos when he lunged, but after he grabbed my fur a few times, I realized I was thinking about what I would do before I moved, which probably meant he knew what I was planning. I couldn't avoid him forever, so I thought hard about dodging and then lunged forward with my mouth open and bit down the second I felt my teeth connect.

I whipped my head back and forth before feeling his jaws clamp down on the back of my neck; then, I bit down even harder and yanked as I backed up. I had grabbed his front left leg and opened up a few holes, but he didn't respond like it bothered him. While I watched, I could see his fur starting to thin as his skin rippled and the wounds I'd just inflicted disappeared. I realized I didn't know how to shift back and would have no way to heal like Carlos. The way he looked at me suggested that he knew what I had realized, and if wolves could smile, I'd swear he was doing it.

He took my distraction as an opportunity and lunged at me again, biting down on the side of my neck. He shook his muzzle back and forth, piercing the skin and opening the wounds even more. I yelped out a high-pitched noise and backed away quickly, trying to get away. However, Carlos refused to let me go and clamped down harder, which ripped open the wounds, causing blood to start running through my fur and into the dirt.

I could hear Gabriel whining behind me and saw him darting in repeatedly, biting Carlos's withers, back, and hind leg. He tore open small wounds all over Carlos's body and ran away fast enough to avoid injury himself. Carlos was forced to release me to chase after Gabriel, who had circled behind us and was now on my other side. He brushed against my side and briefly leaned into me, which helped heal some of the deeper wounds Carlos had caused. I guess I had a way to recover after all; I shook my head in relief as some of the pain abated.

Carlos faced both of us down, his lips curling back, exposing canines covered in blood and fur. I could hear Gabriel return the threat and decided to join in, which made Carlos take a tiny step backward. We advanced on him together, and then I made the mistake of turning my attention to Gabriel, who looked back at me before he was attacked. Carlos leaped into the air and landed on top of Gabriel, forcing him to the ground, where he bit into his underbelly.

I ran forward, trying to pull Carlos off by the skin of his withers, but couldn't get him to release his hold. I repeatedly tried to bite down on what I assumed would be sensitive areas, but nothing seemed to work, and I could smell the blood coming from Gabriel's body. I mentally tried to tell Gabriel everything would be okay if he just held on, and I tried to clear my mind. The movement in front of me began to slow, and I could see details I hadn't noticed before. Carlos's jaw gripped him tightly, but he kept moving it slightly, allowing me to get to him while he was readjusting. I waited for his next move and then launched into his side, which spun him away from Gabriel and into the middle of the arena.

I made sure Gabriel was okay before squaring off against him again. When I looked back, Carlos was running toward me, but moving so slowly that I could figure out his attack before he executed it. I sank my teeth into his thigh as he ran past me. He turned around to attack again, and I saw Gabriel walk around behind Carlos, realizing what we would have to do to survive. We would have to work together as a team. I flicked my eyes for a split second to Gabriel. *Now!* I ran full speed toward Carlos, who was preparing for my frontal attack, just as Gabriel was biting his back, right above his tail.

Carlos whipped his head around to fight off Gabriel, and I took the opening I had. I grabbed him under the neck and bit down hard, thinking about cutting off his air supply, but he was able to get out of my hold by rolling his head quickly to one side. Once he was out from under me, he spun around and pinned Gabriel to the ground again, this time by his throat. Then, I got a distinct mental picture of Carlos doing something similar to Rosa. He looked down at her, but something was off, and I realized her face was buried beneath his pillow. It felt as though I was reliving the memory with him, and my nonexistent fingers ached from holding the pillow tight.

The strange smell I had noticed in their bedroom had been death, or what I assumed was her dying breath. He intended to do the same thing to Gabriel, and I refused to let that happen! My conscious mind shut off, and instinct took over. I launched into the air and onto Carlos's back. I bit down hard on the back of his neck and then repositioned myself, feeling my upper and lower canines pierce his skin. Carlos yelped under me and let go of Gabriel, who ducked his snout under Carlos's lower jaw and bit down on his windpipe.

I could feel Carlos trying desperately to shake Gabriel and me off or loosen our hold on him, but neither of us let up. After a few seconds of this, I could feel him begin to sway under me, and finally, he fell to the ground. I let go hesitantly, and when he didn't move again, I nudged him with my nose. He started to move around a little, and I let out a low growl, raising my hackles and baring my teeth. He kept moving little by little, but then Gabriel's head and neck popped up from the other side of him, and I realized he was the one moving Carlos's body as he tried to get out from beneath it.

When he got free, Gabriel nudged Carlos, then looked up at me, wondering what we should do. I could hear faint breathing coming from him, so we hadn't killed him, but I wasn't sure what the challenge rules were. Adam had warned me that I might have to fight to the death, but didn't say it was strictly necessary. I didn't want to kill Carlos when it came down to it. He may have been power-hungry and led the other pack in their recent attacks on us, but I refused to be the kind of Alpha he was. I shook my head at Gabriel; he walked around the body and joined me, our noses touching. As they did, heat rushed through my body, and when I looked down, I was my human self again. Gabriel's hand reached out and touched mine, and I looked up and smiled at him.

We'd made it together, and I couldn't have been happier. I looked over at Lorelai, who smiled at me with a look of pride clear in her gaze. She brought Gabriel and me each a large tarp that she must have found somewhere, and it was then that I realized my clothing didn't survive my first shift.

I thanked her for the fabric, and then I looked over at Adam, still in wolf form, as he oozed blood slowly onto the ground. Gabriel and I rushed over to him and reached toward him without saying a word to each other, and then linked our hands. I pictured Adam's wounds healing from our combined touch. I willed his skin to knit itself back together without him changing, and I sent my new power into him.

Warmth spread down my arm and into Adam's body beneath my hand. As it did, I could feel the muscles and bones shifting, and when I looked down again, Adam was himself and free of any damage. He looked up at me and smiled.

"Thanks for the help." I smiled back and was about to respond when his expression changed, and he pushed me out of the way. I turned around to see Carlos running at me, and then an explosion of sound ripped through the night again.

Carlos's body was thrown sideways with the force of the bullet. Two more gunshots rang out, and it was clear that there was no recovering from the damage. The woman who held the gun dropped it before kneeling next to the girl Carlos had attacked earlier. She held her tightly while Gabriel and I ran to their side and closed the bite wound on the girl's neck. She smiled weakly up at Gabriel, and she and the woman both bowed their heads at me before the rest of the pack did the same. Gabriel looked at me then, and his smile was contagious. Before long, we were both grinning like fools, and the people around us visibly relaxed. There would be no more bloodshed, at least not tonight.

I looked back at Adam, whose face was a war of emotions. He was upset to see his friend and mentor shot dead in front of him, but there was also a hint of acceptance or satisfaction. I left Gabriel with his family and walked back to be by Adam's side.

"I know this is a stupid question, but are you okay?"

Adam laughed and shook his head, "Not even remotely. But I will be."

"I'm sorry about Carlos. I know how much he meant to you."

He wiped his hand down his face, "I'll remember him the way he was before he tried to take over the pack. This wasn't the Carlos I knew and loved, and I won't mourn the death of this monster." His words were harsh, but the building amount of unshed tears in his eyes made it clear that he would miss Carlos. I didn't want to make him feel like he needed to maintain a brave front for me, so I gripped his arm, nodded at him, and then left him to grieve.

I made my way back to Lorelai, who was next to Carlos's ruined body, tears spilling down her face. "I'm so sorry, I'm sorry…" Her voice was soft as she repeated her apologies to him. When I approached, she wiped away her tears and stood to face me.

"I'm sorry he had to die," I said, looking at him again. "I didn't want him to, but I guess I wasn't the only one in the equation tonight." She wrapped her arms around me and held me close to her.

"Don't apologize, Caleb. You did exactly what you should have done. You beat him but didn't punish him unnecessarily. That is the kind of Alpha I hoped you would become. Unfortunately, beating your opponent doesn't always mean they'll give up. The most important thing is that you're okay."

I smiled at her despite the situation and hoped that my survival would continue. Especially now that I'd awakened early. Unfortunately, I wasn't so sure that was a guarantee anyone could make. I realized then that it hadn't just been me who had awakened early, and I looked over at Gabriel, who was across the arena being held in a similar position by his mother. Our eyes met, and I smiled at him, glad that we were in this together and that, through our collective actions, our separate packs had the chance to become one. Hopefully, whatever awaited us would be made easier by our expanded group of friends and family.

"So, what happened to you after you challenged Carlos?" Lorelai asked, holding me at arm's length from her body so she could see my face.

I looked back at her, confused, "What do you mean?"

"Well," she began, "you just stood there for about five minutes with your tongue hanging out."

Apparently, time had only moved slowly for me, and I did look like an idiot to everyone else. Typical.

Acknowledgments:

I want to thank several people for their help during this process. To my friends, you have been a place of inspiration for most of my stories, from high school on, and I love that even though I've told you I'm going to write about you one day, you keep telling me your stories. Thank you all for your guidance and distraction when I needed it! Thanks to Casey, Kelly, Karin, Kathryn, Andrew, and Brenna for lending parts of yourselves to my characters. You've made them real, and I appreciate that.

Thank you to my family, who have asked questions about my books and stories over the years and allowed me to share drafts, ideas, and run questions by them. Your support means everything to me!

About the Author

Kenneth Creech is an award-winning author known for his LGBTQ+ young adult fiction. His work includes With What I Now Know, a short story featured in the 2022 anthology Queer for the New Year, and his young adult novels, including the Awakened series and Fate, Coincidence, and Other Curse Words. A lifelong reader, Kenneth was inspired by stories of LGBTQ+ characters coming out, but wanted to write about characters already comfortable in their skin.

Since starting his writing journey, Kenneth has continued to craft stories where being LGBTQ+ is part of the character's life, but not their main struggle. In his professional life, he's worn many hats: teaching Sociology, advising Gay-Straight Alliances, helping students get into college, and planning weddings. He lives outside Houston, TX with his husband and their dorkie (daschund/yorkie).

www.kennethcreech.com

www.ingramcontent.com/pod-product-compliance
Lightning Source LLC
Chambersburg PA
CBHW021225310726
48971CB00006B/1697